Autograph Page

DECEPTION
LIES
and
Truth

Dwayne Vernon

NORCARJO Publishing
P.O. Box 47446
District Heights, MD 20753
www.norcarjo.com

Manufactured in the United States of American.

ISBN:978-0-69200279-7

Editors: Trent Johnson (wtrentjohnson@yahoo.com)
          Jamilah Munir (jamilahmunir@aol.com)
          Theresa Tellock (ttellock@gmail.com)
          Phyllis Owens (Owens8767@yahoo.com)

Book cover: Life Changing Books
Photographer: Paul Graves www.photosrusstudio.com

Acknowledgements

Thank you, God, for blessing me with the talent to write.

Thank you, Alyson and Dad (Leroy Herron), for always pushing me to do my best.

Thanks to all my family, particularly Nora Reis-Herron, Carlton Reis-Herron, Joseph Reis-Herron , and Jarrett Herron.

Thank you Angelo F. Hart, for pushing me to continue to write. Friends to the end.

Thanks to my Aunts, Zelma, Yvonne, Mae Mae, Helen and Cousin Cheryl Herron, Carmon Mbroh, Vera Cherry, Roy Carter, Jr and Dorshell Clark for your guidance and acceptance.

Thank you to My Boyz – Larry Maddox, Robert Beatty (Blue), Michael Rogers, Curtis Cross, B. Henderson, Darryl M. Smith, Keith Warren, Amandeus (Man) Watkins and Hector Cruz guys have always been supportive and had my back.

Thanks to Sharwyn Fryer, LaPhena Westray, Toni Ricks, Angie Davis, Ledra Dildy, Marcus Roberson, Lakesha Morake, Donna Sheats, Steven Robinson, Shelia Owens, Debra Atkinson-Hyman and Anthony Echols critics and true friends. Thanks for keeping it real and encouraging me at the same time.

Thanks to Mia Harley, Ramona (Mona) Crowder and Ronnie Patterson for just being you genuine, thoughtful and sharing people.

I definitely can't forget my "Brag Crew," who are truly like family.

A real special group of friends. Terry Stroman, Lisa Robinson, Charles Joyner, Carlene Hardie, Marie Achy, Nathan Hubbard (Bud), Annette Bell, Ricardo Magloire, James Medlay, Calvin Warren and Fenton George. See you guys on Friday.

A special thank you to Larry Maddox, Patti Achy and Sonya Carr who I've known for over twenty years. You guys have always been the cornerstone of my life.

Thank you Mrs. Ruth Taylor, Business Partner and Friend you have truly been a blessing and I can always count on you. Thank you for just being you.

Ms. Lisa Cox. What can I say. You have truly been an inspiration through the process. You have been candid and honest. Boy you had me doing rewrite after rewrite. Thank you for that. Truly that helped to make this a better story and for that I thank you and your friendship is a true blessing.

Again, I'd like to personally thank my editor's for being so patience. Jamilah Munir, Phyllis Owens, Theresa Tellock and Trent Johnson. Thanks to Tini Anderson for all your help.

Dwayne Vernon

Character Index

* Mia and Daunte are engaged. She is standing by her man's side while he is incarcerated.
* Curtis and Carlton, the two bad boys in prison.
* Reese trying to fulfill his dream of being a NFL player.
* Mike is Reese's lover and trying to be supportive of his man.
* Antonio is standing by his friend Reese's side. He is dealing with the fact that he is about to become a father.
* Larry stalks his ex-girl friend, refusing to let her go.
* Barbara and Tonya are two ghetto hoochies. They hang out at clubs where the big ballers hang. Having sex with the players and poking holes in the condoms, trying to trap them into marriage.
* Keith is a friend of Antonio and Reese. He sets out to expose Barbara and Tonya.
* Jay & Ricky are enjoying each other. Wil, who dated Jay, wants to destroy their relationship.
* Chuck's singing career is going well and his Tour is ending , so he and Tyrell will be coming home with their secret which threatens to destroy their relationship with the boys.

In Memory of...

This book is in memory of some very special people who have impacted my life and made me a better person.

To you, my Mother (Shirley Herron), I love and miss you. Thank you for watching over me and protecting me.

Cornell Smith, (Corn), I miss you man.

Annie Crupi, It was great working with you and you are truly missed.

Wendell Huffin, You were the best.

Mathia Belle Manning (Macy),
I'm really going to miss you. Love you.

Chapter 1
The Gang

The guys were at Tyrell's house, the night before, happily toasting in the New Year with champagne. The past year had been filled with sorrow and happiness. Everyone was glad to see it go. Chuck woke with the taste of alcohol in his mouth, as if he had been up drinking all night. Beep! Beep! Beep! The sound of the horn blowing outside wouldn't allow him to go back to sleep.

'I should have eaten something before drinking,' he thought. He moaned all the way to the bathroom, his head spinning as he bent to turn the knob for the shower. 'My God, this water feels good. I could stay in here all day,' he thought. Finally, stepping out of the shower, he quickly grabbed for the bottle of aspirin that sat on the counter. The scent of Tyrell's bacon crept into the bathroom. Lazily, Chuck brushed his teeth then walked back into the bedroom.

Chuck looked around the bedroom and thought how glad he was that he finally moved out of the halfway house and in with Tyrell. No bathroom to share with a bunch of guys. No worries about the noises from the other guys that lived in the adjoining rooms. Chuck finally made his way downstairs.

"Happy New Year, baby," Tyrell said, as he saw Chuck's crooked smile.

"Happy New Year to you, too," Chuck managed to get out.

"Are you feeling okay?" Tyrell asked.

"Slightly hung over but I'll live. I should have eaten something."

"Was it not I who told you to eat something?" Tyrell asked.

"Yeah, baby, you did and I should have listened," Chuck

said as he sat slowly.

"Let me fix you a cup of coffee," Tyrell offered.

"Oh baby, thank you, thank you and I'll have a few slices of that bacon," Chuck said holding his head. "How did you sleep last night?"

"Slept like a baby," Tyrell said, as he walked over and sat a plate of bacon and cup of coffee in front of Chuck."

Tyrell Smiled. "So what did you want to do today?"

"How 'bout we catch a movie," Chuck suggested, as he sipped his coffee.

"Do you feel well enough to catch a movie?"

"I'll be fine. I took a couple of aspirin upstairs and the shower helped."

"What is there to see?" Tyrell asked, as he sat down across from Chuck.

"We can check the paper," Chuck said, as he got up and headed to the front door.

Tyrell watched Chuck walk away and thought to himself, 'My baby looks good in the sweats I bought him for Christmas.'

Chuck opened the door and was greeted by the cold wind. He grabbed the newspaper and quickly closed the door.

"It's chilly out there, ain't it?" Tyrell yelled from the kitchen.

Chuck headed toward the kitchen and immediately stopped in his tracks. A puzzled look crossed his face when he noticed the only part of the paper delivered was the obituary section. 'What the fuck?' Chuck thought.

Tyrell called out to Chuck, but got no answer. Entering the living room, Tyrell noticed Chuck had plopped down on the sofa.

"What's up man? Chuck, do you hear me talking to you?" Tyrell asked, as he sat next to Chuck on the sofa. Chuck tried to hide the newspaper from Tyrell.

"What's in the paper that got you so quiet all of a sudden?" Tyrell asked, as he grabbed for it. "Baby, these are the obituaries, what did you do with the rest of it?"

The look on Chuck's face told him all he needed to know. Tyrell tried not to show his fear. The last thing he needed was for

Chuck to do something stupid.

"This shit has got to stop," Chuck said, as he jumped up.

"Do you want some more coffee?" Tyrell headed back to the kitchen with Chuck right on his heels.

"Don't try to distract me, Tyrell. That shit ain't going to work this time. We need to find out who the hell is doing this," Chuck said, shaking the paper in his hand.

Tyrell looked down at the floor, deep in thought. Then he looked at Chuck. Tyrell snapped his finger.

"Baby, I have an idea!"

"A'ight what's up?" Chuck asked impatiently.

"Give me one second," Tyrell replied. Tyrell walked over to the telephone and dialed Reese and Mike's number. The phone rang, eventually going to voice mail.

"Hey guys, it's me, Tyrell. I'd hoped to catch you at home. I wanted to know if I could borrow your camcorder. Give me a call on my cell. Chuck and I might be out."

"What you need a camcorder for?" Chuck asked. "You want to tell me what's going on in that head of yours?"

"I can get Reese's and Mike's camcorder. We can set it up somewhere in the front of the house and maybe catch whoever is doing this on film."

"Damn baby!" Chuck spit out, "Don't let me find out a brutha going CSI on me and shit!"

Tyrell laughed. "I just know I need to take care of this quick, before you lose your mind and hurt somebody!"

"Man, I will go straight hood on anybody that tries to hurt my niggah. The police better get this mutha fucker before I do!" Chuck said, as he stormed out of the room.

Tyrell watched him leave and thought, "Lord, let the police get this person before he does."

Chuck and Tyrell were making the bed when the phone rang.

Tyrell answered, "Hello." The look on Tyrell's face told Chuck who it was.

Tyrell, now past irritated, hissed, "I know who you are and if its games you want to play, it games that you're going to get!"

Tyrell slammed the phone on the cradle without turning. Feeling Chuck's eyes on his back, he gathered his composure and turned around to face Chuck.

"So you know who it is?" Chuck joked.

Tyrell could only laugh. "Naw, but the caller doesn't know that." Tyrell was glad that Chuck had calmed down a little even though he knew Chuck did it to help him relax.

"Baby, let me ask you…" Chuck paused in mid thought. "We know that whoever is calling you has your work and home number and that they know where you live."

"Right, so what are you getting at?" Tyrell asked, as he leaned up against the wall.

Chuck, now in detective mode asked, "When you changed your home number, you only got the calls at work. Now they have started back up here at the house. So who do you remember giving your number to?"

Tyrell stared through Chuck, as he made a mental list. "I gave it to all the guys of course and to Ms. Reed my next door neighbor."

"Well," Chuck replied, "we know it ain't none of the guys."

Tyrell chuckled, "Well, we know it can't be Ms. Reed."

"And why can't it be?" Chuck asked, tilting his head.

"Come on, baby, why would that little old lady do that. Plus I've known her for years."

"Yeah, but do you really ever know your neighbors?" As far as I'm concerned, she's at the top of the list. Who else did you give your number too?"

"Co-workers and that's it."

"Ty, the camcorder idea is a good one, but we don't know when we might hear back from Reese and Mike. So why don't we stop by that electronic shop across town and pick up a spy cam. We can wrap it in the wreath on the door. Plus, I think that would be easier to hide."

"That's a good idea man," Tyrell said with assurance.

* * *

Early the next morning, Mike and Reese lay in the bed

watching the Lifetime network. Mike lay on his side with Reese spooned up behind him. Reese looked over at the answering machine and saw the blinking light.

"Did you hear the phone ring this morning, baby boy?" Reese asked.

"No, I didn't, but check the message. It may be important," Mike suggested.

Reese got out of the bed and walked toward the answering machine, scratching the top of his curly head. As he pushed the play button, he let out a yawn and stretched. The message on the machine was from Tyrell, from the day before. Mike turned over in the bed and looked over at Reese.

"Why does Tyrell need the camcorder?"

"Maybe he and Chuck want to make movies," Reese replied in a loud laugh.

Reese ran over and jumped in the bed on top of Mike, kissing him playfully. "Maybe we can make a movie of our own one day to look back on."

"Hmm. How 'bout we do a dry run right now and then if you ever try to leave me, I can use that against you," Mike laughed, amused with himself.

"On second thought, maybe we better skip the camera." They both broke out in laughter. Reese reached over and started to tickle Mike.

"You're going to do what? You're going to do what?"

"Stop baby! Stop baby!" Mike managed to get out between laughs. "I was joking, I was joking."

"Who's your daddy? Tell me, who's your daddy?" Reese asked.

"You baby! You baby! Stop tickling me!"

Reese stopped and looked Mike in the eyes. "Baby, I really love you and I don't know where I would be without you."

Mike rubbed his fingers through Reese's curly hair. "I love you too man and you need a hair cut." Mike kissed him softly and playfully bit Reese's lip. "Now get your heavy butt off me," Mike said.

"I'm not that heavy," Reese said, as he rolled over, "but

you're right, I do need a haircut. I need to get up, and take a shower, go to the barber shop and hit the gym. I'll grab the camcorder and drop it off to Tyrell on the way."

"It's New Year's Day, don't they give you a day off?" Mike asked.

"Nope. The NFL never rests, but the season is almost over."

"Well, I'll be right here in bed waiting for you when you get back," Mike said.

"You promise?" Reese asked, as he threw Mike a seductive wink.

"I promise."

Reese finally dressed. "Baby, I'm going to run downstairs and fix something quick to eat. Are you hungry?"

"A little. Whatever you make for yourself make for me too."

Reese came back up stairs with a sandwich for Mike. "Here you go."

"Thanks, what is it?" Mike asked.

"It's your favorite."

"My favorite?" Mike asked.

"It's a bacon sandwich," Reese said taking a bite, "Well, Baby I got to run." Reese gobbled down his sandwich.

"Okay, see you later and don't forget to get the camcorder out the other room," Mike reminded him.

"I won't."

Reese grabbed his coat from the closet, went to get the camcorder and headed to his car. Sitting in the car, he rubbed his hands together to keep them warm.

Turning the knob on the radio he thought, 'Why does my baby keep changing my CD's?' Reese decided to drive over to Tyrell's house before going to the gym. He didn't want to take the chance of leaving the camcorder in the car while he was working out.

After a 15 minute drive, Reese pulled up to Tyrell's house and saw the cars in the driveway. He grabbed his cell phone, dialed Tyrell, but it went straight to voice mail.

Reese headed for the door to ring the bell. He noticed some movement on Tyrell's porch as he got closer. It was someone he didn't recognize.

"Hey man, you need some help?" Reese shouted. Turning at the sound of Reese's voice, the stranger dropped a can of paint, spilling it all over the porch.

"What are you doing with that paint, man?" Reese asked.

The stranger came at Reese. Reese dropped the camcorder then quickly grabbed the stranger's arm. The stranger swung. Reese pushed the small framed guy to the ground. He jumped up and swung again at Reese. Reese ducked and punched him in the face.

One of the neighbors saw the scuffle and called the police. Minutes later, a squad car pulled up. The stranger tried to run but Reese caught him by the leg. Two officers jumped out the car. The officer from the passenger side pulled his weapon.

"Freeze or I'll shoot!" He ordered.

Reese let go of the stranger and raised his hands. The stranger followed suit. The other officer handcuffed them both. He immediately put the stranger into the squad car. The officer had called for another car for Reese.

The officers walked into the precinct with Reese and the stranger in handcuffs. "You guys have a seat and behave."

Reese sat across from the stranger. Reese looked at him, shaking his head.

"What the fuck is your problem brutha?!" Reese spat out.

"You the one with the problem, man!"

"Both you guys need to shut your mouths, before I lock you both up!"

Reese looked at the officer, "Can I make my phone call please?"

"You'll get your phone call, man. Don't worry."

Mike was worried. He looked at his watch again. It was late in the evening and he hadn't heard from Reese. He walked over to the phone and called Reese's cell but got no answer. He must be over at Tyrell's house and I bet they are in the basement, where you can't get any service. Mike hung up the phone and dialed Tyrell's home number.

"Hello?" Tyrell said, half sleep.

"'Sup Ty, sounds like you sleep."

"Chuck and I took it easy today, watched some movies and chilled. What's up with you?" Tyrell asked.

"Have you seen Reese today? He was supposed to come over and drop the camcorder over to you."

"Oh damn, man, I forgot I called you guys about that, but no, I haven't seen Reese nor have I heard from him. Chuck and I were upstairs in the bedroom, so he could have come by without us hearing him ring the doorbell or knock."

"Okay, but I'm a little worried. It's not like Reese not to call. Hold on for a second. My phone is beeping"

"Hello," Mike said."

"Hey baby, it's me."

"You had me worried. Where are you?" Mike said, feeling relieved.

"I've been arrested."

"Arrested! What you mean?"

"I went to drop the camcorder over at Tyrell's house and some guy was on his porch, shredding his paper and dumping some paint on the porch. I got out to see what was going on and this guy started a fight. I guess someone called the police. Now they've arrested me, 'cause the guy said that I attacked him for no reason."

"Baby, I got Tyrell on the line and we are on our way. I love you."

"I love you too, man. Hurry and get me out of here please. Oh yeah, let Tyrell know the camcorder is in his yard. After all the confusion, I forgot about it."

Mike disconnected the call. "Hey, Tyrell. That was Reese."

"Good. Is he okay?"

"No, he's in jail."

"In jail! What you mean?"

"He told me the camcorder is in your yard. He came by to drop it off. He saw some guy on your porch and he said something about a shredded paper on your porch."

Tyrell walked toward the front door, opened it, and saw the shredded newspaper and the paint on the porch. A few feet away, he saw the camcorder lying on its side in the grass.

"Mike, I see the camcorder and newspaper. Chuck and I will meet you at the station." As Mike and Tyrell ended the call, Mike ran upstairs, grabbed his coat and check book. While Mike looked for his checkbook, his cell phone rang again.

"Hello," Mike said, frazzled.

"Hey, Mike this is Jay. What's up?"

"I can't talk right, now."

"What's wrong?" Jay detected the concern in Mike's voice.

"I'll have to fill you in later." Jay, insisted that Mike tell him now.

"Jay, I can't talk, Reese has been arrested and I'm on my way to the station.

"I'll meet you there," Jay said. "Are Chuck and Tyrell going to be there?"

"They're going to meet me there," Mike explained.

"So will I," Jay added.

"Okay. I'll see you there."

Jay pulled into the parking lot of the police station. He dashed inside the jail to find out what was going on with his boy. Frantically, he walked up to the desk. He saw Reese sitting on a bench, handcuffed. Jay made a u-turn to where Reese sat.

"Reese, what happened?"

The police officer stepped in, "Excuse me sir, but you will have to wait. This defendant has to be questioned."

"Questioned for what?" Jay asked. Jay's protective mode kicked in. "Who's in charge here? I need to talk to someone in charge." Seconds, later Mike walked in and saw Reese handcuffed and Jay at the front desk.

Mike walked toward Reese. "Excuse me," the police officer said, "but you can't talk to him right now. We have to finish processing him." A few feet away, Reese noticed a distinguished gentleman with glasses hanging halfway off his nose. The gentleman watched the scene with curious attention.

"Excuse me sir," the gentleman said to Reese, "You're Reese Rogers, you play for the Houston Bullets?" Reese shook his head.

"My name is Dirk Parks and I work with the Houston Chronicle."

"Shit," Reese thought. Meanwhile Mike and Jay were off in a corner getting cleared on the details.

Jay was furious, "So who is this niggah that fucked with my boy?"

Chuck and Tyrell walked in the door with Tariff and Demetrious.

"Where's Reese?" Tariff asked.

"They have him handcuffed over there like a common criminal."

Mike looked at Demetrious. "Can you calm Jay down, while I try to figure this nightmare out?"

"Sure, man. I got it," Demetrious responded. Demetrious immediately walked over and tapped Jay. "Let's go get these guys a soda or something," Demetrious said, that being the first thing to come to his mind.

Jay, with his keen intuition, immediately yelled, "You guys trying to get rid of me?"

"Naw, man they got this," Tariff said. Jay hesitated for a second then went willingly.

"Hey guys, we will be back, I mean right back." Jay said firmly.

Chuck and Tyrell started to explain to the officer the problems that Tyrell had been having. Mike listened. The police officer finally spoke, "I understand what you're saying sir, but right now it's your buddy's word against his. We don't know who to believe."

"Officer, can we at least talk to Reese before you take him back?" Mike asked.

Chuck, Tyrell, Mike and Tariff listened to Reese as he filled them in.

"Guys, you got to get me out of here. If the press gets a hold of this I could be ruined."

Chuck looked at the guys, "Listen. I got a hunch. I got to

run out, but I will be right back." Tyrell looked at Reese and shrugged his shoulders.

The officer brought the stranger out to finish his processing. Reese nodded toward him to clue the guys in. Demetrious and Jay walked back into the area where the guys were. Demetrious and Jay noticed that all the guys were looking at the stranger.

"What's going on?" Jay asked.

"That's the guy Reese got into a fight with," Mike said. Jay started to walk toward the guy and Demetrious grabbed Jay's arm.

"Chill out, man. Chill out. We don't need to be trying to get you out of here too," Demetrious said.

Mike looked at Tyrell. "Do you know that guy?"

Tyrell shrugged his shoulders, "He doesn't mean anything to me."

"Do you think Chuck might know him?" Tariff asked.

Tyrell responded, "I don't know."

Tariff noticed Mr. Parks glance toward their direction as he sat writing feverishly in a note pad. After twenty minutes or so Chuck walked in. He looked at Tyrell then walked over to the officer. He handed the officer the spy cam that he and Tyrell had stuck inside the wreath.

"Officer, I think if you look at this, it will clear all this mess up," Chuck explained.

Tyrell motioned for Chuck.

"Hey baby," Tyrell whispered in his ear, "that's the guy that was ripping up my paper. Does he look familiar to you?"

Chuck took a look. He didn't recognize him either.

Tyrell turned to hear a familiar voice calling his name. As Tyrell turned he saw Ms. Reed.

"Ms. Reed," Tyrell addressed her, "what are you doing here?"

"My grandson has got into some trouble and called me."

"Your grandson?" Tyrell responded.

"I'm on a fixed income and he has been staying with me to help me out with bills, but I couldn't tell anyone 'cause if the state found out, they would cut my check."

Tyrell and Chuck looked at each other in amazement. "Ms. Reed," Tyrell asked as he pointed, "is that your grandson over there?"

Ms. Reed turned to look, "That's him. That's him right there."

"Ms Reed, your grandson was arrested for fighting my best friend here."

"There's got to be some mistake. Why would my grandson be fighting him?"

By this time the officer came over and un-cuffed Reese.

"Sir, you're free to go, sorry about all the confusion."

"What about my grandson?" Ms. Reed asked with much concern.

The police officer lifted up the microchip.

"This film shows your grandson shredding this man's paper and throwing paint. It also shows him initiating a fight with this gentleman, as well," the officer said, as he pointed to Reese.

The other police officer grabbed the defendant and took him to the back.

Ms. Reed looked at her grandson, "Why would you do this to this man?"

"Grandma, they're gay, they're all a bunch of FAGGOTS. I saw them through the window kissing."

Jay stepped up, "So what the hell does that have to do with you?"

"You guys are sick, you're all sick. You disgust me," the grandson said through clinched teeth.

Tyrell looked down and then looked at him. "How did you get my phone numbers?"

The grandson looked at the guys with anger, "I got it off the piece of paper on my grandmother's refrigerator."

"Take him back," the officer said, "Take this piece of trash back and book him."

With downcast eyes, Ms. Reed apologized to everyone. "I am so sorry for the trouble he has caused." She looked at her grandson, shook her head, and walked out.

Reese stood up, massaging his wrist to ease the discomfort

he felt from the handcuffs and watched Mr. Park as he rushed out of the police station. Mike looked at Reese. "Let's go home and put this all behind us."

Reese stared in the direction of the door and shook his head. "Baby boy, this is not over. It's just beginning."

Chapter 2
Barbara, Tonya, Antonio & Keith

Barbara sat in IHOP with her cell phone glued to the side of her face. She was engaged in verbal warfare with her angry landlord.

'Tonya, where are you?' Barbara thought, as the sound of Ms. Hardie's voice boomed over the phone. She looked toward the restaurant entrance for Tonya and noticed that not only was the place completely full, but there was also a crowd of hungry looking people waiting to be seated.

"Barbara!" Ms. Hardie yelled through the phone. "Dammit! I want my money or your ass is out!"

Barbara returned her attention to the menacing crow of Ms. Hardie and just as the tone of her threats began to pinch her nerves, she caught the hostess eyeing her in a disdain fashion. "Bitch please!" Barbara hissed from a set of clinched teeth, "You want something to shake your head at, Bitch, shake this!" Barbara said, as she gave her the finger and rolled her eyes. In an effort to ignore Ms. Hardie's ranting and raving, she let her focus float across the restaurant. She was immediately offended by the other customers gawking at her. So in a mannerism that reflected an I don't give a damn attitude, she pierced back with an ugly stare and dared them to say something. Barbara wanted to scream and tell everyone to mind their business, but how could she when her lengthy, obnoxious telephone conversation with Ms. Hardie had exposed to everyone that she was late with her rent.

Barbara was considered by her own stretch of imagination, a hoochie mama. You know the type, loud fluorescent colored lipstick and sporting large bamboo hoop style earrings, and last but not least she took particular care in her perfectly arched eye brows that were designed with patience to compliment her beautiful oval shape eye's.

Barbara began to absent mindedly finger her bamboo earrings when her friend Tonya walked through the restaurant entry.

Tonya stood about five feet eight inches tall and it was undisputedly agreed upon by the big money ballers that Tonya was PHAT. Flawless complexion, full C cup size breasts flattering her small petite waist and perfectly shaped ass. Tonya was all around pretty, but it was the born and bred ghetto mentality that cast a cloud over the potential that she possessed.

Tonya let her gaze lay a visual blanket across the crowded restaurant patrons.

'Girl, I know you're in here,' Tonya thought, as her head swiveled slowly from side to side as she navigated through the maze of human statues. No sooner than the thought was finished, Barbara's high pitch voice grabbed Tonya's attention.

"Okay. There you are," Tonya replied to the sound of Barbara's tone. She then made a couple of polite gestures opening up a path leading to where her friend was seated.

"Hey Hookah!" Tonya said, as she took a seat opposite of Barbara, "How you doing?" she smiled lightly.

"Ms. Hardie, I'll be by your office later this week to pay you your damn money!" Barbara slammed her cell phone closed and looked across the table with concern at Tonya. "Tonya you look like shit! Are you feeling okay?" Barbara asked, as she slid her glass of water to the side. The waitress placed a plate of stacked pancakes in front of her. "About damn time," Barbara let slip, as she was already in a foul mood.

The waitress shot her a look as to say, "whatever."

"Thanks for the compliment," Tonya replied sarcastically and exhausted. "Then again, shit is exactly how I am feeling right now. I think I'm pregnant," Tonya blurted out.

"Well, that's good news," Barbara said, as she smiled and continued to stuff her mouth with pancakes.

"Yeah, right!" Tonya stated rhetorically. "Good news."

"Tonya, hold up girl!" Barbara dropped her silverware with so much force that the plate chipped.

"What the hell is that suppose to mean?" Barbara asked.

"Barbara, I don't know who the father is!"

"What!" Barbara snapped, "You don't know who the damn daddy is? How could that be when Antonio is the only one you been screwing."

"Kind of like the only one."

"Bitch, stop with the games a'ight, because I am not feeling this shit right here, so say exactly what the hell you mean!"

"Well, you see, what had happened was…" Tonya paused for a second hoping to see some form of pity on Barbara's face. Not seeing any, Tonya continued with reservations. "You remember my ex Larry right?"

"Yeah. What about his broke ass?" Barbara asked, as she leaned back and folded her arms.

"Well, he came over my house a couple of times and we …you know."

"No, I don't know!"

"We got busy girl, damn!" Tonya spit out.

"Oh my God, No this hookah didn't just say what I thought she said." Barbara was talking to herself while looking up at Tonya. "Girl, you mean to tell me you slept with that tired ass brutha and didn't even use any protection?" Barbara banged her fist on the table in frustration sending the fork flying across the restaurant, not even looking to see where it may have landed.

"Girl, when we were hooking up I thought he had his own condoms, but all the time, ole boy was plucking them out of my stash from my drawer."

"Why?" Barbara hunched her shoulders, "And how would he know where you kept your rubbers?"

"We dated for three years." Tonya flagged the waitress and ordered a glass of orange juice

"Tonya, help me out here cause, I'm still not getting it!"

"Barbara, come on now!" Tonya sighed and sucked some air between her teeth then she continued, "The sex was like old times B, and just before we would get down, the natural inclination of habit took over. I was lost in the moment and didn't realize that he was taking the tampered condoms out of my drawer. Anyway, the first thing I got to do is find out if I'm pregnant for sure." Tonya reached in her purse and pulled out a pregnancy kit. "The first test I took came up positive; I want to be sure so I picked up another kit."

"Tonya, I just don't know why you would sleep with Larry after all the shit he put you through. The physical abuse alone should have taught you something. That fool is crazy! With all that on the back burner, have you thought about what-chu gonna do? Have you even forgotten our plans?"

"No, Barbara, I haven't."

"I think you have, Tonya! Let me remind you so that we both are clear. You were supposed to use the condoms only when you slept with the big ballers with cash. We poked holes through the condoms so one of us could get pregnant and paid, but how in the hell do you expect our plan to work when you let some dumb ass, broke niggah like Larry come along and possibly get you pregnant? Damn, girl, how, why did you let this happen?"

"I don't know." Tonya replied.

"Damn girl!" Barbara pushed the plate of pancakes to the center of the table. "You had to go and fuck around with a three strike kinda guy like Larry!"

"Three what!?" Tonya looked genuinely confused.

"Three strikes Tonya, as in he's an ex-con, he's crazy and the monkey ass fool ain't got no money! You get it?"

"Yeah, girl, I got it. All ten and a half inches of it, you hear me? That brother can lay some pipe!"

"Bitch, listen at you! Your ass talking just like a crack head!" Barbara paused for a second before she continued, "You suppose to be the smart one, but all because of some dick, you might have cost us some money."

"We'll think of something." Tonya stood up.

"Where are you going?" Barbara balled up a napkin and tossed it on top of her left over food.

"I'm feeling sick. I'll be right back."

"Well, hurry up Tonya, cause we have got to come up with a plan."

Barbara pinned her eyes to Tonya's back as her friend

walked away in the direction of the restrooms. 'Dumb Bitch!' Barbara thought absently, as she silently signaled the waitress for the check.

* * *

Antonio grabbed for his cell phone just as he and his buddy Keith walked into the gym. "Sup girl!" Antonio had peeped his cell phone's caller ID. "I'm at the gym right now, but I'll hit you soon as I 'm bout to bounce."

"Who was that? One of your ladies?" Keith eyed Antonio with anticipation.

"Yeah, man that was Tonya," Antonio said hesitantly. He wanted to avoid Keith and his unsolicited advice.

"Damn Antonio! Dawg, you still boning that ghetto hoochie you met at the club months back!"

"What's wrong with that?" Antonio's demeanor turned defensive.

"Antonio, man that chick is just after you for the money," Keith said. "You remember her friend Barbara?"

"Yeah, I remember her, nice li'l hood rat."

"Well, I dropped that li'l hoodrat cause she had gold digger written straight across her forehead and you know what they say about birds of a feather…"

"They flock together," Antonio finished the sentence as he eyed Keith. "Is that how it goes?"

"Yeah, Antonio, that's exactly how it goes."

"Keith, come on man. Let's just get our workout on cause you is straight up paranoid."

"Well, my paranoia protected me all these years. I'm just trying to help you. I got a bad feeling about those two girls."

"You got a bad feeling about all women you meet Keith."

"Do you remember where we met them at?" Keith paused briefly. Before Antonio could respond, he continued. "The club. And you know as well as I do that gold diggers nest up in that joint. Man, all you was supposed to do was fuck her, not fall in love."

"Who said anything about being in love? I know Tonya is a little ruff around the edges, but shorty ain't all that bad. She's pretty cool."

"You don't have to say anything about love Antonio. I know you bru," Keith responded sarcastically. "Instead of working your muscles out here at the gym, you need to exercise that brain of yours."

"Watch your mouth, Dawg!" Antonio squared his shoulders at his friend. "I'm six two, two hundred twenty solid pounds and I'll pimp your skinny ass like a whore and slap you like you's my bitch!"

"Look, man, I'm your boy and I don't mean no disrespect, I got your best interest at heart," Keith said, as he pushed Antonio, jokingly.

"I know, man." Antonio gave Keith a high five and then he apologized for losing his temper. Deep down he knew Keith was looking out for him in his own way.

"So did you tell Tonya you were a pro football player?"

"Naw, I haven't told her yet."

"Well, you just said she's pretty cool. Why don't you just tell her?" Keith asked.

"I just want her to see me and not my bank account."

"So how are you going to explain all your traveling? You just said she's pretty cool so help me to understand why you haven't told her?"

"I just want to be sure about her, Keith."

"So again, how do you explain all the traveling?"

"Well, right now she thinks my traveling is due to my work in pharmaceutical sales."

"Aw, hell naw!" Keith smiled behind a throaty laugh. "That's a dumb ass hookah if she bought that shit!"

Antonio ignored Keith's comment. "She seemed a little suspicious, but before I tell her the truth, I need to be sure she ain't trying to hook a brutha for his paper."

"Well, at least you still got some lights on upstairs."

Chapter 3
Curtis, Daunte, Mia, Carlton

Curtis thought the rec room was unusually noisy, as he watched the angry antics of two convicts arguing over a domino game. 'How did my ass get caught up in this shit right here? Almost four years in this joint.' Curtis continued to half mumble to himself eyeing a group of inmates dressed in pumpkin orange jumpers, glued to a 19 inch television, watching the Lakers/Pistons game.

"What up dawg?" Carlton's voice snapped Curtis out of his revelry.

"Sup dude. Where you been?" Curtis looked Carlton up, then down for a sign of the answer to come. Curtis was about 6 feet tall, an inch or two taller than Carlton. Carlton was also a tad bit muscular and sported the ball head where as Curtis kept his hair cut real short. Curtis was always told he looked like a young version of Denzel Washington.

"I've been checking out the load of new prisoners that came in today." Carlton looked just past Curtis' right shoulder and into the eyes of one particular new arrival who appeared to be real nervous. "Yeah man," Carlton continued, "I need some new recruits to help me move these tits." Carlton rolled his fist so that it opened palm up and flashed a hand full of tiny, colorful balloons stuffed with cocaine.

"So how did it go?" Curtis asked, as he continued to eye the surroundings of the cell block.

"I got a couple of prospects already trapped in the crosshairs of potential, my brother." Carlton licked his lips with the appetite of a hungry predator and then with an eye to eye stare, he asked, "Curtis bro! Sup with that dude who stays stuck up under you like some kind of bitch!"

"You mean my man, Daunte?" Curtis asked with concern in his voice.

"I didn't ask you what that joker's name was," Carlton expressed himself with raw sarcasm, "I asked you what's the 411 on dude!"

"Carlton man, don't even go there! My dude Daunte ain't cut from the same cloth as us. Plus all he's got is a six month bid."

"Curtis, fuck that shit you poppin! Haven't you got it through your head yet?" Carlton asked, with his index finger to the side of Curtis' head. "Man, we need as many mules as possible to move this shit! As a matter of fact, here comes your boy now. I think he just might want to volunteer."

"Sup Curtis! What-chu up to?" Daunte walked up but his presence didn't interrupt Carlton's intentions.

"Daunte! My man, What's going on?" Curtis said, as he embraced his friend in an act of respect and protection. "Carlton, this is Daunte and Daunte this my boy Carlton."

"Hey." Daunte said, as he stretched his hand out, but the expression on Carlton's face caused Daunte to eye his own palm as if it had been mysteriously filled with a pile of shit.

"You creep ass mutha fucker!" Carlton looked evil and with his sight pinned on a space between Daunte's feet, Carlton spat a glob of phlegm at the spot and then walked away. "I don't know your punk ass!" Carlton mumbled, as he walked away.

Daunte balled his fist, but then remembered any type of trouble he got in could cause him to be in this place longer then he wanted to be. He stood there and watched Carlton walk away and then turned to look at Curtis.

"Damn Curtis, what's up with your boy?" Daunte said, as he took a seat on the plastic stool that was mounted to a picnic style table.

"Daunte, listen to me good!" Curtis eased into the seat directly across from his friend. "Carlton is my boy but dude got mad issues so stay away from him as far as possible. He's bad news, A'ight!"

"Okay, man. No problem."

"One more thing, Daunte," Curtis leaned forward making sure no one else could hear their conversation, "If Carlton approaches you for any reason, I want you to just walk away then find me and let me know."

"Cool. Whatever you say, but just out of curiosity Curtis, what's the deal?"

"Daunte, kill it with the questions and just do like I ask you okay? You do that and stay clear of Carlton, you'll be out of here at the end of your six month stint."

"Thanks Curtis. Good looking out."

"Daunte man, you really don't belong here." Curtis pulled his hand from Daunte's grip and then stood up. "Now come on," he said in an effort to lighten the mood, "Let's go to your cell, so I can whip yo ass in a game of chess."

Curtis and Daunte walked in the direction of the iron staircase that led to the cell blocks top tier where Daunte's room was. No matter how hard Curtis tried to relax, his spirit still remained disturbed as the energy of Carlton's anger whispered to him like a wicked lover. 'I know just how dangerous ole boy can be,' Curtis thought, as he took one last glance in Carlton's direction.

* * *

The next day, Daunte walked toward his cell and the bounce in his steps made him appear to be walking on air. 'I couldn't think or sleep at all last night,' Daunte thought, as he waved his hand and called out to the correction officer inside the security bubble. "After seeing my baby today, I'm on top of the world, just me and my girl," he sang in a sing-song voice.

Once Daunte got back to his cell, the door slid open and soon as there was room enough to squeeze through, he rushed into the tiny space of his living quarters. Daunte was inexperienced at doing jail time but it didn't take him long to learn how powerful a sheet of paper and a good pencil were.

He snatched his small communication package which consisted of one yellow legal pad, two pencils and three stamped envelopes from a makeshift shelf and slipped his feet under a steel desk. He had just touched a pencil tip to his tongue when the shadow of a man filled the doorway.

"Daunte, my man what's up?" Curtis stepped inside Daunte's cell.

"Sup C," Daunte put his pencil down on the desk top.

"Ain't shit," Curtis replied. "How your visit go?"

"Man words can't even explain what I'm feeling right now, bro." Daunte's emotions radiated from deep down, causing his face to glow like a moon on a starless night.

"Curtis man, I can't wait to get out of here and back with my lady."

"Hey Daunte," Curtis commented, shifting the conversation's direction, "exactly what did you do to end up in this shit hole?"

"Man its crazy" Daunte's mind drifted and it was just like he was reliving the day he got arrested.

"What happened?"

"I thought Mia was cheating on me with this guy named Demetrious and before I could learn the truth, shit got out of control. I got in a fight, Dude got hurt and the next thing you know I'm in here."

"So the way it sounds, you lost your temper."

"Curtis, my actions nearly killed a man. I was irresponsible, and it wasn't really called for."

"What makes you say that?" Curtis shuffled his feet with his body angled next to Daunte's bunk as he sat down.

"Well C, it turns out that the dude I accused Mia of having a fling with is a gay friend of hers." Daunte paused briefly. "The dude and Mia are more like girlfriends, I guess you could say."

"Damn, man." Curtis shook his head as his own situation settled on his mind. "Yeah bro, you fucked up for sure."

"What about you C?" Daunte asked, as he noticed the blank far away look plastered on Curtis' face.

"What brought you to the royal accommodations of the joint?"

"I accidently killed a guy."

"How do you accidently kill someone? Was it self defense?" Daunte asked, before Curtis could respond.

"Oh naw. Not hardly!" Curtis mentally kicked himself in the ass for the one millionth time. "One day, me, Carlton and this dude named Chuck was hanging out at this local car wash when we spotted this gay dude with a nice ass car. One thing led to another and for no other reason than the guy being a homo, me and my boys decided to carjack him. So while the robbery was going down, ole boy made some funny movements and like I said, his death was an accident."

"Naw Curtis, what happened does not come under the category of accidents and if you ask me, what you just described was a premeditated act!"

"I guess you're right Daunte. I say that because when I'm lying in my bunk late at night, I don't have any problem with eyeing my guilt face to face."

"Is that the application of self psychotherapy that I'm hearing Curtis?"

"Not exactly, Daunte, as a matter of fact, because of my hateful misconception of perfectly innocent people, I immersed myself into a professional counseling group." Curtis inhaled and then exhaled a deep breath of satisfaction regarding his achievements at understanding homosexual men.

"My psychologist helped me to not only see gay people as individuals, she has also assisted me in accepting my Three!"

"My Three?" Daunte's face twisted into a frown of curiosity. "What the heck is the Three?"

"My three, Daunte, are really simple. The hate that I thought was justifiable and directed at gay men was in reality my own inner fear and not knowing how to comprehend those fears, I made homosexuals the object of my prejudice. That means, I had my own FAV three! Hate, fear and prejudice. When I began to put my emotions in proper perspective, I was able to see gays as human beings who are no different than you or me."

"Curtis man, it sounds like somewhere behind your veil of bad judgment you've gotten in touch with some form of remorse."

"Daunte, I think the only way you could see it as I see it,

you would have to wear my shoes bro. I mean that, literally. But in the reality of it all D, I know something now that I didn't know back when I committed the crime."

"What's that Curtis?"

"That no man should be judged because of the characteristics that give him his own individuality."

"I agree with you on that bro." Daunte's focus was now drawn to the limited space of his living quarters. "How much time did they give you, Curtis?"

"I got life!" Curtis eyed the limitations of his existence. "It's right here within the belly of this tomb that my life will play out."

"I'm sorry to hear that," Daunte said. "How does it make you feel when you think about the man's life you took?"

Curtis sat quietly on the edge of Daunte's bunk as the echo of quietness resonated on the back of Daunte's question. I'm going to my cell, Daunte, it's almost count time." Slowly, he stood up and before Daunte could prod him any further, Curtis was gone.

"We'll finish this up tomorrow." The statement drifted from Curtis' mouth in the hushed tones of a mumble.

Chapter 4
Barbara, Tonya, Antonio & Larry

"Damn!" Tonya snatched the phone receiver from its rocker as she looked at the caller ID.

"Hello!" Tonya barked.

"Hey baby," the smooth rumble of a deep voice said. "How you doing?"

"I'm fine!" Tonya was unable to control her attitude. "What you want?"

"Damn, baby, did I catch you at a bad time?"

"Well, for one thing, I'm tired and trying to take me a nap." 'But then again,' Tonya thought, 'whenever you call it's a bad time.'

"Tonya, sup with you and all this sleeping you been doing lately?"

"Look, there ain't no need for you to worry yourself about me."

"You sure? All this sleeping and the mood swings and taking time off from work! Sup with that?"

"Check this out real quick, man," Tonya paused then her voice went flat, "What can a sister do for you?"

"I'm trying to holler back at chu again boo, so when you think I can come over?"

"Larry, honey, let me school you real quick. Right now I'm a what-chu would call involved with someone."

"Whoa! Wait a minute.! Tonya, what are you trying to say?" Larry was now irritated.

"What I'm saying is that that there is no room for you and me except as friends!"

"Friends! Bitch, you got some nerve to think you can dictate some shit like that to me! I don't know when the last time you checked but I'm not that mutha fucker you can just pick up and put down whenever you feel like it! As a matter of fact, I'll be by your house tomorrow!"

"Why, Larry? I don't want you no more. Why would you come over here?"

"Why? Because when you got involved with me there was a written cardinal rule that you seem to have forgotten."

"What kind of fuckin' rule are you talking about?"

"The one that says if I can't have you then nobody else will either."

"Is that supposed to be a threat Larry? This is what you can do with your rule." Tonya slammed the phone on its cradle. "It's over dammit!" she screamed in the direction of the phone as it fell to the floor.

Larry sat there yelling into the phone. "Hello! Hello!" He looked at the phone in his hand. 'We'll see about that!' Larry became angry by his thought.

*   *   *

Tonya sat glued to the comfort of her couch as the irritating weight of Larry's comments brought her back to the severity of the situation. 'Larry your ass is fucking with the wrong bitch,' Tonya was thinking, as she looked at the knife that sat on the dining room table. Her heart jumped in her chest as the phone started to ring. "Son of a bitch!" she mumbled. Tonya hesitantly reached for the receiver while the phone rang twice more. Slowly, she wrapped her fingers around the phone's neck and no sooner than the feeling of the black plastic settled into her grip, Tonya experienced a outer body illusion that gave her the satisfaction of choking the shit out of Larry.

"Hello!" Tonya accidentally banged herself up side the head with the receiver.

"Hey, Baby Girl, its Antonio, sounds like somebody done pissed you off."

"Hey baby. What's good with my man?" Tonya's demeanor shifted to a delightful mood. "Did they work you hard today?"

"Yeah, it was kind of busy but we can talk about my day later. How was your day?" Antonio asked.

"I'm feeling okay and I'll probably be doing a lot better soon as I fill this prescription I got from the doctor." Tonya let a playful hint of a smile dance on the corners of her mouth.

"A prescription?" Antonio asked openly expressing his curiosity. "What kind of script? Are you okay?"

"Well, it says right here that I get a hundred milligrams of Antonio with as many refills as I want." Tonya and Antonio both burst into laughter.

"So what time are these medicines suppose to be taken?" Antonio felt himself become aroused.

"Let me s-e-e." Tonya pretended to be reading her words from a medicine bottle. "According to the doctor's instructions, at midnight I should take enough until I'm completely satisfied and then at six a.m. I can have another long and lengthy dose."

"Sounds like we need to start the application of these meds right away." Antonio's said, as he started to massage his dick.

"I agree." Tonya walked into her bedroom and lay across her bed. "So does that mean I'll be seeing you tonight, handsome?" Tonya fingered her nipple lightly.

"That's what the doctor ordered, right? I'm on my way."

"I'll be here waiting for you. I need to talk to you, too."

"About what? Is everything okay?" Tonya's statement sent his erection from hard to soft. 'Damn, she done fucked up the mood,' Antonio thought. "So is everything okay?"

"Naw. I mean, yeah! Honey everything is cool. We'll talk when you get here."

As Antonio sat there on the bed, he tried to figure out what she wanted to talk about. His dick had now gone from super hard to super soft. 'Should I even go over there? Do I want to hear what she has to tell me?' Questions, one after another, popped up in his head.

Tonya sat flickering through the channels on the television until she was abruptly startled by the phone. Picking up the phone, she started to chastise herself when she saw that the call was marked private. She knew it had to be Larry. Who else would call and block their number.

"Hello! Who is this?" Tonya barked into the phone.

"Girl, what's your problem?" Barbara asked, as she looked toward the sound of the running water coming from the bathroom.

"Barbara, please don't start, okay! You call my house and block your number! Where your ass calling from?"

"Tonya, I didn't block this number and what the hell is your problem? Never mind. We will talk about that later. Anyway, listen, I'm using this guy's phone that I met at the bar and I called your house hoping his number would show up on your caller ID."

"Why didn't you just call your house?" Tonya asked.

"They turned off my house phone and cell phone. That's what I get for having both services under the same company, but they both should be back on in a couple of days when I get paid."

"Well, the number is marked private girl. Who is he? For you to be at his house, he has got to be a baller." Tonya said.

"I'm not sure." Barbara clamped the tip of her manicured nail between her teeth. "Looking at the size of this house and the price tag on the car we rode in, I'd have to say this man is well off."

"Well, where is he right now?" Tonya asked.

"Right now he's taking a shower."

"So, why don't you take a peep inside the wallet?"

"Now you know that was the first thing to cross my mind, but this niggah undressed in the bathroom," Barbara said, as she looked in the direction of the bathroom and listened to see if he was still in the shower.

"So what does he look like?"

"Girl, my man is fine as hell and whoever said light skin brothers were played out obviously hasn't met this brutha. He has this sparkle in his eyes that captured a girl's attention." Barbara looked toward the bathroom once more as she looked inside the drawers on the night stand. "He has these dimples that make my panties wet just thinking about them."

Tonya broke out in a laugh. "Girl, you are crazy and you

calling him your man already."

"Hey, Tonya, I got to go."

"Why, what's wrong?"

"Nothing, but I just heard him turn off the water in the shower."

"Okay, girl. Call me tomorrow."

"I will. Got to go."

Chapter 5
Tonya, Antonio & Larry

Tonya stepped from under the soothing, steady beat of the hot shower and for about five minutes she let her body drip dry while she lustfully admired the curves of her anatomy in a full length mirror. She pampered herself for a couple more minutes with splashes of some Baby Phat Goddess fragrance and then she picked out a deep purple Victoria's Secret ensemble for the evening.

Tonya was pulling the thin ruffled silk straps over her shoulder when the doorbell echoed a melody throughout the house. She took another quick second to splash a little more fragrance behind each ear and then headed down the staircase as if it were her own personal runway.

"Larry! M-a-n, what the hell are you doing here?" Tonya spoke with a low pitch disdain as she looked out the peephole.

"What?" Larry inconspicuously tried to open the door. "Girl stop playing. I came by to see you."

"Larry, I have a long day tomorrow and I'm trying to get some sleep, plus I don't feel that great and for real, now is not a good time." Tonya yelled this through the door trying to get rid of him before Antonio showed up.

"Come on Tonya," Larry pleaded, "Baby, just give me a minute. I promise I won't be long, plus you know I'm not going to leave until you let me in."

Tonya knew he meant what he said. Against her better judgment, slowly and very reluctantly, she unlocked the door. She never saw Larry's mischievous looks as he leaned his ear against the door in a sneaky fashion listening to see if he heard her unlocking the door.

"Ahh, thank you, baby," Larry responded surprisingly when the door swung open. "I just wanted to see how you were doing," he said, as he walked right pass her and took a seat on the sofa. "Come on over here and have a seat next to daddy," he said, as he patted the empty space next to him.

Tonya stood next to the open front door and watched Larry as he sat there on the sofa. 'I can't believe this fool,' she thought as she watched him patting the empty space on the sofa. 'This mutha fucka must think I'm his pet.'

Tonya pushed the front door closed with her foot and crossed the living room. She angled herself so that a glass coffee table separated the distance between them.

"Larry, you need to leave and I mean like now!" Tonya said, as she crossed her arms over her body in a protective mode.

"You think getting rid of me is that easy? And why are you all dolled up? Cause I know you don't have some other niggah coming by here." Larry stood up and maneuvered his body to block any escape for Tonya. "You just made a big mistake!"

"Don't make me call the police on you, Larry!" Tonya tried to sound fearless but looking up into the towering eyes of Larry's five foot, ten inches, one eighty five pound frame caused a rainfall of doubt to drown out her rush of hope.

"You want to try it!" Larry stepped to the side and with his vision he drew a line between Tonya and the telephone. "Go ahead and let's see how far you get!"

Tonya flinched. She faked a move in one direction and then darted desperately in the opposite way. She made a dashing grab swooping the phone up from the pocket of its station. Tonya was only a breath away from punching the last digit that would bring the police to her rescue when the vice like grip of a wild animal ripped the receiver from her clutch.

"I don't believe it!" Larry threw his head skyward and in a deep roar, he filled the room with laughter. "You were actually going to call them boys on me, huh?" He pushed Tonya knocking her to the floor.

Larry stepped to where a fragile Tonya lay at his mercy. He reached down and literally ripped the cloth to shreds exposing her perky breast.

"Larry please just leave," she said, as tears ran down her face.

"Shut up!" Larry hissed between grinding teeth and then he leaned and pinched one of her nipples.

"Stop it please! Stop it!"

"Bitch!" Larry drew his large fist in the line of Tonya's vision, "say another mutha fucking word and I'll hit you so hard you'll die with your eyes wide open."

Tonya retreated inside of her own fear. There were none of the earlier signs of bravado left. There were only the silent tears and occasional sniffles.

"Why you have to make me act ugly, baby?" Larry stroked Tonya's exposed flesh with what he intended to be a display of affection.

"Larry, please go." Tonya managed to speak between sniffles. "Just leave me alone."

"I'm going to leave." Larry paused and from behind a mask of genuine affection, he continued, "Tonya girl, I love you, but when you don't show me no respect then this is what happens. You're the cause of this."

"Okay, Larry, I'm sorry, but baby I'm tired." Tonya's words came in snatches between the sniffles. "Just let me get some rest."

Larry methodically formed the features of his face into a sinister mask and through the eyes of evil he reached out to Tonya. He raked his fingers across the crown of Tonya's head, smoothing her hair the way a mother would, sooth a newborn.

"I told you earlier that tomorrow would be a good day for me to come by, but you had to go and get Manish, so I thought it would be best to bring you the understanding of what I mean today." Larry let the tips of his fingers make a trail down the side of Tonya's jaw line.

"Now listen closely," he said, "because I don't want any more misunderstandings. Do you hear me?"

"Yes Larry." Tonya spoke just above a whisper.

"Repeat after me, I, Tonya, will always be ready for Larry."

"I, Tonya, will always be ready for Larry," she repeated.

"ANYTIME THAT HE COMES OVER!" Larry screamed the demands with such anger that Tonya's face was drenched in spit. "Now say it you little BITCH!"

"I, Tonya, will always be ready, for Larry, anytime he comes over." Tonya's body shuddered in response to her submission to the dehumanizing demands of Larry.

Larry gently let the palm of his big hand softly brush against the tender flesh of Tonya's breast as he stood up. He walked toward the front door and the fleeting thought of Tonya calling the police crossed his mind. 'Fuck it,' he decided. Larry pulled the front door open and without turning in Tonya's direction, he kissed the center of his hand and blew the kiss into the air.

"Tonya, remember what I said. If I can't have you, there ain't another living soul that I'll surrender you to." The door swung shut.

"Just get out," Tonya said softly. She barely heard it herself.

Tonya gathered up enough energy to begin the task of erasing the mental and physical stench of Larry's presence. She turned away from the door and proceeded to take one pain-staking step at a time. She climbed the steps with the sexy night gown falling down around her ankles.

Tonya took another quick shower and then changed into a different outfit. It consisted of nothing more than a pair of blood red panties and an oversized white T shirt. She aimlessly moved about from the bathroom to the bedroom and then the act was repeated until Tonya found herself staring in the bathroom mirror at a mentally battered woman.

She snatched a bottle of eye drops from the medicine cabinet, after dripping two puddles of the liquid in each eye to remove the redness, she started to apply globs of make up to the puffy areas of her face. She'd just finished masking her physical signs of trama when someone rang the doorbell.

Tonya's heart fluttered in her chest with hopeful anticipation that the person ringing the doorbell was Antonio, but at the same time she was filled with a fearful apprehension that Larry had returned.

"Who is it?" Tonya's voice was so timid that the man standing outside didn't even hear her.

"Bing, Bong, Bing, Bong, B-i-n-g...B-o-n-g." Antonio leaned persistently on the ringer.

"Who is it?" Tonya's voice was a high pitch shrill.

"Antonio, baby! Open the door!"

"Yes!" Tonya pumped her fist and a mili-second later she flung open the front door, practically knocking Antonio down when she jumped into his arms.

"Okay." Antonio smiled. "I can definitely get used to greetings like this."

"Baby, I'm so glad to see you!" Tonya smothered Antonio with kisses.

"If that's the case pumpkin then why are you trembling?" Antonio gripped Tonya by the shoulders and held her at arms length. "What's wrong?" He asked.

"Nothing baby," Tonya lied. "I was feeling kind of lonely so when you knocked, I got kind of spooked."

"You sure?" Antonio asked, as he cocked his head sideways. "Don't lie to me."

"Come on in, Baby, the neighbors are starting to stare," Tonya said, as she looked up and down the block with the pretense of seeing which of her neighbors was watching. In actuality, she was keeping an eye out for Larry.

"Tonya, why do I get the feeling that you're not telling me the whole truth?" Antonio let himself be pulled obediently into the house.

"I'm okay." Tonya walked towards the mini bar while Antonio locked the front door. "Honey, would you like a drink?" She asked.

"Just give me a beer, sweetheart. I got a feeling I'm-ah need it."

"What makes you say that?" Tonya pranced around making the drinks, as she poured it on real thick to stall for the moment to come.

She took her time and casually walked back to the center of

her living room. There, she met Antonio who had already taken a seat on the couch. She put the drinks down and then slid into the space right next to him.

"So what is it we need to talk about?" Antonio's face was etched into a soft expression of puzzlement, as he looked through the window of Tonya's soul for the truth.

"Antonio, I went to see the doctor." Tonya anxiously exhaled a very long excited breath and, before Antonio could react she blurted out her hidden secret. "The doctor says I'm pregnant!"

Antonio's mind blew a fuse and he sat there staring momentarily into a really dark canyon of mixed emotions.

"Tonya, I don't understand." Antonio shook his head from side to side in cold disbelief. "Baby, we always used protection. Besides, I'm not ready to be a father."

"Antonio, sweetheart, you're the only person I've slept with." Tonya went back to rule number one for ghetto fabulous women. Lie without any remorse and never bat an eye in the process. "Also, Antonio," she continued, "you remember I had to pull condoms out of me a couple of times, because they slipped off inside of me."

"S-o-o-o how are we going to handle this?" Antonio only meant to stand up but unconsciously he began shuffling back and forth.

"I know you're not asking me if I am going to have an abortion," Tonya said, as she crossed her arms over her chest.

Antonio stopped pacing. Sitting back down next to Tonya, he tried to ease the rise of tension with a compassionate gesture of slipping Tonya's hand into his own.

"Take it easy, Baby," Antonio said, looking deeply into Tonya's eyes, "you just caught me off guard."

"Believe me, baby, I understand." Tonya kissed the back of Antonio's hands. "I was totally speechless."

"Did you find out exactly how far along you are?"

"According to the doctor, I'm almost ten weeks."

"Tonya, baby, I heard what you said about being monogamous with me, but I need you to think about it for a minute. Is there the slightest possibility that I might not be the father?"

"What!" Tonya snapped, "I can't believe that you just asked me that. You think I am some kind of tramp?" Tonya angrily yanked her hands from Antonio's gentle grip. Getting up from her seat, she walked over to the bay window that overlooked the front lawn. She stood with her back to Antonio and diversifying the moment with another rule from the gold digger's manuscript, she began to silently count to herself the number of seconds that it took Antonio to respond guiltily to her ploy by asking for forgiveness.

"I'm sorry, baby girl." Antonio walked up behind Tonya and wrapped his arms around her waist. "We'll get through this together," he said, as he kissed Tonya on her neck.

Chapter 6
Mike, Reese & Antonio

It's been a few of months since the incident at Tyrell's house when Reese got arrested. Reese's bulging arms cradled Mike as they lay together watching the Sunday morning news. Mike rested his head on Reese's rock hard chest.

"Have you heard from any of the guys?" Reese turned his attention away from the television as the Sunday news anchor went to a commercial break.

"As a matter of fact, Tyrell called me from Los Angeles earlier this week. He mentioned how well Chuck's tour was going and he said as soon as they wrap things up in Cali, their next stop would be Denver."

"That's great." Reese intertwined his legs with Mikes as they both lay comfortably. "Chuck's career has really taken off."

"How 'bout you, me, Ricky and Jay meet up with Tyrell and those guys in Denver. I miss them."

"Sounds good to me. As a matter of fact, I'll call Tyrell later today right after I talk with Jay."

"Good. The draft is coming up, mini-camp and before we know it, spring training. When that happens, I won't have any time to do anything. You know how crazy my schedule gets then."

"Don't remind me."

"Yeah, Baby Boy." Reese smiled. "With my new long-term contract your man has it made."

Reese reached over to hug Mike but was interrupted by the ringing of his cell phone. A quick glance at the caller ID and Reese hit the speaker on his cell. "What's up Antonio?"

"Reese, man, I need to see you! In person."

Reese hunched his shoulders in response to the silent question written on Mike's face.

"Antonio, what's up bro? What's wrong?"

"Reese, its important man, we need to talk! You know where the café is near the stadium?"

"Yeah."

"A'ight, meet me there ASAP."

Mike looked at the phone and then at Reese reading the puzzled expression on hiss face. "What was that all about?"

"I don't know, Baby Boy. But it sounds important."

"Are you a'ight with me going to see what the problem is?"

"Sure, man. Go ahead. I hope everything is okay."

Reese squeezed Mike tightly and quietly thanked God for the safety and security of their love. Mike watched Reese slip from under the covers and marveled over how his Calvin Klein's caressed his body.

"I won't be long," Reese said, as he headed towards the bathroom.

"It's okay," Mike said, pulling at the Ralph Lauren covers until they were tucked under his neck. "I'll be right here keeping things nice and warm until you get back."

Reese took a minute-man's bird bath to freshen up and chose an oversize white t-shirt and a gray cotton sweat suit. Sitting on the bed, he pushed his feet into a pair of Air Force One's. Looking over at Mike, he smiled when he saw Mike had fallen back to sleep so quickly.

Reese snatched the hat with his Teams logo from a hook in the closet. He strolled over to the bedside, bent and kissed Mike softly on the lips.

"See you when I get back."

Reese headed down the stairs and out the front door. The sun was shining brightly, but it wasn't too hot and the perfect breeze carried a very welcome coolness.

"Good afternoon, Ms. Waters," Reese said to his neighbor. She had a strong appetite for younger men. Reese hopped in his car and, twenty minutes after backing out of the driveway of his home, he pulled up to the café where he and Antonio agreed to meet. As Reese walked through the double glass doors, his attention was immediately drawn to the nervous energy of a lone individual sitting in a corner booth away from the crowd. Antonio was so distracted by the emails on his Blackberry that he didn't see Reese step up to the table.

"This situation of yours that got me out of my warm bed had better be important," Reese said sarcastically, as he slid in the booth across from Antonio.

"Believe me bru, this thing is so important I don't even know where to begin."

Reese became concerned. "Sounds like it, Antonio, man. What's up?"

Antonio raised his gaze from the email messages and for the first time Reese could see just how uncomfortable his friend actually was.

"Whatever it is, I can see that it's really bothering you. Spit it out man."

"Reese, I want you to know something before we start this convo. You are my boy and nothing else matters." Antonio looked around to make sure that no one had drifted into the privacy of their conversation.

"This is more serious than I thought."

"It is, man. Dawg, I have this friend and, in exchange for me getting them locker room interviews with the team, they keep me informed about the coming articles to be printed concerning our team or any of our teammates."

"Okay." Reese had locked Antonio into the bull's eye of his curiosity. Reese's gaze never faltered. "Go ahead, Antonio, go ahead and finish."

"Well, anyway," Antonio paused as the waitress approached.

"Hello, gentleman." The waitress smiled with some recognition. "Would you guys like to order now?" Her pen hovered just above the order book.

"I'll have a cup of coffee," Antonio replied

"Make that two," Reese responded quickly. "So what's going on?" He asked Antonio, as the waitress disappeared behind the counter.

"Reese, I don't mean any disrespect, bru and I don't know any other way to ask you this, Reese, are you gay?"

Reese looked like a deer trapped in the spotlight of a hunter. His throat felt constricted from the lack of moisture and for a couple of awkward minutes, he just sat there staring into space.

"Why," he swallowed once in hidden desperation, "Why would you ask me a question like that Antonio?"

"Like I said Reese, my friend who works for this magazine spoke to one of their reporter buddies and just in the manner of column gossip, he told my contact about an incident that took place at a police station involving you a few months back. One thing led to another and soon the rumors started to take on a life of their own."

Reese leaned back in his seat without responding to Antonio. His mind was inundated by one thought after another and soon with nothing but the idea of his career being on the line, small beads of sweat started to form on his brow.

"So it's true." Antonio reacted to Reese's silence. "Why didn't you tell me man?"

Reese remained quiet, as he was trapped between the thought of trusting his friend and the right of every human being to have their privacy and individuality.

"Reese, look man, whatever you do in the privacy of your own home is your business and I'm not here to judge you. I'm your boy no matter what. I'm not one of those brothers who trips when he finds out one of his boys are gay. I'm very secure in my manhood. If you ask me the ones that do trip aren't secure with who they are."

"Antonio, thanks, man. I know you really mean what you say."

"Reese, did I ever tell you about what happened right around the time I graduated from college?" Antonio offered a secret of his own to validate his honesty.

"Reese, man, I came home from college and after all those years of growing up, I find out that my mom is a lesbian. But what could I say? This was the same woman who had raised me and supported the household by working two jobs when my pops wasn't there! It did take me a minute to adjust." Antonio paused and then asked Reese the million dollar question.

"Reese, are you one of those brothers categorized as a down low brother?"

"No, Antonio, that's not me. I'm not one of them guys who go around sleeping with women to hide who they are."

"So how are you going to handle this when it comes out?"

"I really don't know." Reese sat shaking his head from side to side and then chuckled to himself. He couldn't believe he was having this conversation with Antonio.

"Well, let me know if there is anyway I can help."

"Antonio, man you're helping me right now more than you can imagine. Thanks for being a good friend."

"Reese, you've always been there for me, bru. I can remember the times I was just ready to give up and just quit, but you pushed me and encouraged me to keep going. And for that, I will always be grateful. You stood by me, man, and in my book that means a lot. Hell, I'm proud to be your friend. So whatever you need just let me know."

Antonio and Reese sat talking for another hour or so trying to decide how to handle all the madness that was about to surface. Finally, they both decided it was time to go. Each one stood up, embraced their friendship and then started to walk through the restaurant's foyer. Antonio watched Reese as they exited the restaurant. He could see the fingers of anxiety gripping his friend.

"Reese, I can't even image how you feel right now or what you might be thinking, but if you need me just hit me up." Antonio embraced his friend once again when they reached their cars. He wanted to let Reese know that no matter what lifestyle he lived, they would always be boys. "I'm here for you Reese."

"Thanks again, Ant."

Reese climbed clumsily into his ride and pulling the door closed, he gave Antonio one last glance before pulling off. Arriving home, Reese parked in the driveway and slowly walked up the stairs, slipped the key in the door and went inside. He could faintly hear the TV on upstairs. 'Mike must have stayed in bed the whole time I was gone,' Reese thought, just as he crossed the kitchen threshold.

"Oh shit!" Reese was startled by Mike's presence in the kitchen. "I heard the TV and thought you were still in bed."

"All that waiting made me hungry." Mike sensed something was wrong. "What's the matter Reese? How did your meeting go with Antonio? Is he okay? He swung his body off the stool and walked up behind Reese where he stood looking out the kitchen window. "You seem a little tense." Mike snaked his arms around his lover's waist and Reese damn near melted to his touch.

Reese turned around and looked Mike in his eyes. "You know I love you so much, Baby Boy."

"I love you too, man."

Reese grabbed Mikes arm. "It's been a long morning and I just want to go back to bed and fall asleep in your arms."

Mike flashed his Colgate smile. "Well, go ahead upstairs and get in bed and I'll fix us some lunch." Mike watched Reese head upstairs. Deep down he knew something was wrong. 'He'll tell me when he's ready,' Mike thought, before he finished.

Chapter 7
Barbara & Tonya

"Hey girl!" Tonya's voice was full of smiles. "So how was your date the other night?" Tonya asked, as she adjusted the phone between her ear and shoulder.

"Girl, he was off the hook." Barbara exclaimed with excitement. "Plus, he took me to dinner last night!"

"Did you get the 411 on him yet?" Tonya asked.

"Girl, I'm working on it, but in the mean time what's up with you and Antonio?"

"Oh, we cool. I just got to figure out what I'm going to do about Larry's crazy ass."

"Larry!" Barbara snapped in surprise. "Why, what happened?"

"That damn fool called the other day and I told his ass that seeing him was a mistake."

"Girl, I know he acted like an idiot."

"Yes he did and the next thing I knew, he showed up acting like a crazy fool. I was about to call the police."

"Tonya, I still don't understand how you went back after all the abuse."

"B, we all make mistakes."

"Tonya, you my girl and all, but you knew that asshole was crazy. That's more than a mistake."

"I know girl. He told me if he couldn't have me then no one else would either. Girl, he busted in my place, he threw me to the floor and ripped my gown damn near off my body. I ain't gonna lie, I was a scared bitch, girl."

"Did you tell Antonio about what happened?"

"Not yet." Tonya sighed heavily. "Actually I really don't

know what to do."

"Does he even know about Larry and what about the pregnancy? Did you tell Antonio?"

"No, he doesn't know about him, but we did discuss the pregnancy."

"Tonya, all I can say is just don't go on The Maury Show." Barbara and Tonya both laughed.

Tonya got quiet. The irony of her situation made her no different than the women on his show.

"I wouldn't worry, girl. Antonio's probably the baby daddy anyway." Barbara tried to encourage her friend.

"I'm not." Tonya's confidence turned shallow.

"Well, you know I got your back either way."

"I know you do, Barbara," Tonya said as she yawned. "I'll talk to you later, I'm going to lay here and take a nap."

Tonya hung up her phone and just before laying across the bed, she casually looked out her bedroom window onto the street. Panic and fear snatched Tonya's breath when she spotted Larry sitting in his car outside the house staring right at her.

Larry blew a kiss in Tonya's direction. The gesture pushed her backwards and the curtains swung closed as the material slipped from her hand. Tonya sat down on the edge of her bed, but overwhelming fear pulled her back to the window.

She peered through the small slit in the curtain only to find that Larry was gone. A blanket of relief covered Tonya's body.

Chapter 8
Daunte, Mia & Carlton

Daunte was in his cell relaxing, lying across his rack, when Officer Stroman stopped briefly in front of his cell and tossed a letter in the room. Daunte swung his feet to the floor scooping up the letter, as he thought, 'This is what keeps a brutha from going crazy.'

Daunte pressed the envelope to his nose and took a deep breath with the expectations of inhaling the sweet familiar fragrance of Mia. It had been a couple of weeks since he had received a letter and the lack of communication was killing him. When he didn't receive the anticipated scent he longed for, Daunte began to open the letter with desperation that only Mia's sweet words could relieve. His expectations were quickly diminished.

Dear Daunte:

I know it's been a while since we've had any form of communication with each other, so I thought that I would be the first to break the ice. First, let me say that I'm sorry that things came to a head the way that they did. You wouldn't be where you are now if it hadn't been for all the deceit and lies that you were told just to keep a secret from you. I should've told you from the very beginning of our friendship that I was gay. It wasn't fair to you or the friendship that we shared. Before you say it, yes, we are still friends. I miss hanging with you as a workout partner and shooting the shit. As for the rest of the guys, they have long since forgiven you, as well, for what happened with Demetrious. It was just my hard headedness that kept me from reaching out to you.

Ricky and I are going strong. Demetrious, Tariff, Tyrell and Chuck are all on tour. Since the guys are on tour, Demetrious asked me to check up on you and Mia to make sure things are going okay. He really feels bad about everything that has happened. I have gotten to know Mia and she is an exceptional woman. I can see why you fell in love with her. You're lucky to have her. Well, I don't want to talk your ear off. I hope they're treating you right in there and as soon as I can I will be up to visit. Take care.

Love, Jay

Daunte folded the letter and thought about what happened that day to get him locked up. It felt like it happened yesterday. *Daunte was sitting in the barber's chair and when he saw the picture of Mia and Jay's friend, Demetrious, he immediately lost his temper. Wihout even finding out what the picture was all about, he got into a fight with Demetrious. Demetrious got seriously hurt and almost died. He felt like a fool when he found out Demetrious was gay and he only had the picture taped to barber's mirror to throw off the other barbers so they wouldn't find out about him being gay. He should have trusted Mia and talked to her first before losing his temper, he realized this all to late. Not only did he end up in prison, but he almost lost his best friend, as well. He really didn't fault Jay for not telling him about being gay himself.*

Daunte snapped out his thoughts when he heard Officer Stroman call his name.

"You got a visitor," Officer Stroman said, as he pulled out his handcuffs.

"A visitor." Daunte hopped up off his bunk. "Who is it – you know?"

"No, I don't son. I'm just an escort. Now if you want your full time, you better get a move on."

"I'm ready." Daunte walked over to the officer and turned around putting his hands behind his back waiting to be handcuffed.

"Let's go, son."

"Aw man." As he walked, he noticed that he left the letter from Jay lying on his bunk. "Officer Stroman you think I could put my mail away?"

"I have other prisoners to get. We got to go, son. Besides

no ones going to take your mail." The guard nudged Daunte in the direction of the visitor's hall. Just as they left the area, Carlton walked up to Daunte's cell. Carlton peeped through the doorway and when he saw that the guard and Daunte were gone, he walked over to the cot and picked up the letter.

'That Mutha Fucka,' Carlton thought. "I knew it was something funny about dude. He a goddam faggot lover.' He balled the letter up and tossed it back on the bed.

"I think this homo lover needs to learn a lesson," Carlton mumbled, as he made a bee line straight to a couple of guys he was sure would join him in teaching Daunte a lesson.

"Hey fellas, I need your help."

The two men followed Carlton up to one of the guards. The taller of the two inmates whispered something in the guard's ear and then he pressed a wad of bills in the CO's hand. The guard looked around before taking the money, slid it in his pocket and then walked away.

*   *   *

"Hey baby," Mia said. She was all smiles as Daunte approached. "You look surprised."

Mia touched the plastic that separated the two with her left hand and grabbed the phone they used to talk with each other.

"I didn't know you were coming today," Daunte said, as he touched the plastic with his hand to match hers.

"I woke up this morning with a funny feeling today and I felt I needed to see you. Are you okay?"

"I'm fine baby, just counting down the days until I get to hold you in my arms again. A few more months of this and it's a wrap." Daunted sounded relieved.

"Well, don't worry. It will be over before you know it and we can continue on with our plans to get married," Mia said, as she played with her engagement ring.

"Mia, baby, are you okay? You look a little tired."

"I'm good. I don't know what it was, but I had to see you today and make sure you were okay."

"I like that." Daunte smiled affectionately. "My baby worrying about me!"

"Daunte, I'll always worry about you. All this is my fault. My bad judgment is what got you here."

"Don't talk like that. What's done is done and when my time is up we'll get through this. Now guess who I got a letter from today."

"I don't know, who?"

"Jay. I got a letter from Jay."

"He told me he was going to write you."

"He did?" Now Daunte was confused.

"Yes baby. Jay and Ricky called me a few weeks ago to see how I was doing. All three of us had dinner a couple of times and in the midst of putting all this madness behind us, Jay mentioned that he was going to write you and he also mentioned a possible visit. He asked me not to tell you. He wanted it to be a surprise."

"That's my boy a'ight. If Jay says something, you can best believe he'll stick to it 100 percent."

"Well, Jay and Ricky are doing great, so hopefully, when you get out of here, we can all get together for an outing."

"Jay spoke about Ricky in his letter, so I guess if he and I are going to be friends, then getting to know Ricky and accepting them for who they are is a must."

"I love you, baby."

"But I love you more," Daunte replied, "and one day I will make this up to you."

Mia watched the Security Officer walk up behind Daunte tapping him on the shoulder.

"Your time is up," the CO said.

"Okay, man."

"I love you, Daunte. I'll be back in a few days to see you."

"I hate it when you have to leave," Daunte said.

"Me too, but it won't be long," Mia said, as she watched Daunte being escorted away. "Be careful. I love you and see you soon," Mia whispered, as she turned toward the exit.

Chapter 9
Daunte, Curtis & Carlton

Daunte and the guard reached his cell. Daunte turned his back toward the guard so he could remove the handcuffs and massaged his wrist as he walked back into his cell. Daunte felt a haunting chill as he picked up the crinkled letter that he received from Jay. He stuck the letter inside the envelope and looked around. 'Someone has been in my cell,' he thought. Putting the letter inside his drawer, he walked out of the cell and headed to the gym area to workout.

Daunte found Curtis at the gym. The two worked out for an hour.

"Man, that workout felt good." Curtis flexed his huge biceps.

"Yeah, it did, man," Daunte replied, as he wiped the pouring sweat from his face. "It helped me a lot with my frustration over not being able to be with Mia everyday."

"I saw you being escorted out earlier. Was that Mia visiting you?"

"Yep, that was her. Man, I love that girl so much," Daunte said.

"I had a love like that once."

"You, Curtis?" Daunte snapped surprisingly. "What happened to her?"

"It's a long story, but one of these day's I'll tell you about it."

"I'm going to hold you to it."

"Daunte, did the prison personnel ever tell you why they locked you up with offenders like me? Normally, they keep you guys separate from us."

"From what I understand there was a mix-up in my paper-work when I got here. They're supposed to be looking into it, but no one has addressed it yet."

"Man, those assholes work so slow." Curtis replied.

"Curtis, where's your boy Carlton?"

"He's around," Curtis replied, considering Carlton's behavior. "I don't know about that brutha. He's getting out of control."

"What do you mean?"

"I mean he's changed since we've been in prison."

"Well, one thing I can tell you is that it doesn't take a rocket scientist to figure out that he is bad news and the brutha don't like me."

"Daunte, right now Carlton doesn't like anybody, including himself. But just remember what I told you. Stay away from him and, if he gives you any trouble just bring the problem to me."

"Don't worry, Curtis, man, I heard the first warning you gave me. I intend to stay clear of all trouble."

"You'll be okay, Daunte and when you do get out don't ever look back." Curtis looked around the crowded workout room and was sincerely bewildered at the ratio of men who were repeat offenders. 'I wish I had the same chance,' Curtis thought. 'I would do things differently.'

"Daunte, I'm not proud of what happened, but this is my life and as much as I hate having to become a product of my environment, it's the only way I can survive. Man, I can't show any signs of weakness or I would subject myself to becoming a victim."

"Curtis, man, can I ask you a personal question about your situation?"

"Sure, Daunte, go ahead."

"Do you regret killing that guy?"

"At first I didn't, but now I can honestly say yes...yes I regret killing dude and I also regret a lot of other things that have happened in my life. But would I admit the same thing to someone else in here? No! No, I wouldn't, Daunte, but you're different than most of these guys up in here. You're easy to talk to."

"I'm glad you feel that way Curtis and anytime you need

somebody to listen, I'm here for you."

"Thanks, Daunte." Curtis wrapped a dry gym towel around his neck. "I'm going to go by the canteen before they close and then hit the shower. Do you need anything?"

"I'm straight. Thanks anyway. I'm just going to go and hit the showers. I'll meet you back on the block."

Daunte was feeling really good. His visit with Mia was sweet, the letter from Jay and the extra strenuous work out had helped him to relax a bit. He made a quick stop at his cell and after grabbing his toiletries he headed to the showers.

Daunte had grown accustomed to observing his surroundings in the short time he'd been in prison. He casually noted that there were only a couple of inmates in what the prisoners called the watering hole. He began to undress and a funny feeling shot up his spine. As he pulled his white tee off, he took a furtive glance at the other inmates whose presence made him feel uneasy.

Daunte turned his attention to the place where a correctional officer was supposed to be posted at all times. 'I wonder where the CO is?' Daunte thought, as the small group of cons all conveniently finished their showers at the same time and left.

Daunte ignored his internal alarms that sounded a warning. He stepped under the splash of water, wishing the soothing warmth could wash away all the mistakes of his life.

"Well, well, well," said a familiar voice.

Daunte's thoughts were interrupted by the familiar voice. He turned around to find Carlton standing in the shower's doorway. Daunte nodded at Carlton in a familiar gesture and continued to lather his body. Daunte felt uncomfortable with the man's presence, so he finished his shower not noticing the wicked smile that crept across Carlton's face.

Daunte had just finished rinsing his body free of soap when, with his hand poised to turn off the water, he felt somebody grab him from behind.

"What the fuck?!" Daunte said, as he tried to break free.

"Don't worry," he heard a husky voice say. The man held him in a vice like grip and promised, "It won't hurt."

Daunte was slammed to the floor and for the first time he

could see the two men who were slinging him around like a rag doll. The two cons flipped Daunte, over and pinned him down. Daunte looked up into the eyes of Carlton, who was bending down before him.

"So you like hanging with faggots, huh? Well, I'm going to show you what we do to homo lover's like you. Your ass is probably one of those Down Low jokers."

In mock seduction Carlton unzipped his prison issued jumper. As he licked his lips, he flipped his thick manhood through the slit in his boxers. He stroked himself and with each pass of his hand, Carlton's dick grew harder and harder until the fleshy piece of meat was completely rigid.

Carlton gave his two associates a nod and, before Daunte could resist, they had turned him onto his stomach. Carlton eyed Daunte's ass while he reached down and scooped up Daunte's lotion. Carlton filled his palm with a large mound of gooey lotion and then used it to lubricate his dick.

"E-z accessssssssss." Carlton laughed. "You want this don't you, li'l punk?"

Carlton dropped down to his knees and immediately Daunte started to struggle against the weight of Carlton on the back of his legs.

"Carlton, man, please!" Daunte pleaded, as he continued to resist. "Don't do this, man!"

Carlton pinned Daunte's legs down to the floor and with determination Carlton pushed deep inside him. 'Damn!' Carlton thought. "This boy's ass is nice and tight," he said through clinch teeth.

Carlton humped Daunte's ass with a new purpose when he realized that he was busting a virgin. He slammed every inch of his manhood inside of Daunte. Carlton palmed his hands on each of Daunte's hips then he pulled his ass toward his tool and fucked Daunte like he was fucking a woman.

Wham! Wham! Wham! Carlton felt the oncoming eruption. Knowing he was about to explode, Carlton dug into Daunte and tightened his grip on Daunte's hips.

"Awhhhhhh shit!" Carlton yelled, still pumping frantically.

"Awhhh shit!" Carlton threw his head back and spurted thick hot semen inside of Daunte.

Carlton fell limp onto Daunte's back and while he breathed heavily in the humiliated man's ear, he whispered. "You're my bitch now."

"Man, y'all should try some of this ass!" Carlton said, as he looked at his two conspirators and smacked Daunte on his naked ass.

"Yeah, you know I want to hit it," the more muscular of the two cons said, as the print of his dick got bigger in his pants.

The muscle man traded places with Carlton. 'You're going to love me boy,' he thought as he spreaded Daunte's legs and read-ied himself to enter. All three guys were so engrossed in violating Daunte, that not one of them saw Curtis come into the area. Curtis was about to walk out when he saw what was happening, then he noticed it was Daunte that the guys had pinned to the floor.

"Mother fuckers!" Curtis hissed. He took two leaping steps and kicked the convict who was about to enter Daunte. Cur-tis turned and kneed the other guy who fell and hit his head on the marble floor and laid there lifeless.

"Carlton, man what the fuck you doing?" he asked, as he stood in front of Daunte.

"What the fuck do it look like man?" Carlton asked, as he stood up. "Your boy a faggot lover Curtis." Carlton smiled. "So I gave him what he wanted."

Curtis couldn't believe how stupid Carlton sounded. He looked down at Daunte then back at Carlton.

"Niggah, I'm goin to kill your ass," Curtis said, as he started toward Carlton.

Curtis jumped on Carlton fast and with intense furry. As the two men tussled angrily around the shower stall, Daunte lay motionless with drops of blood on his buttocks.

Daunte eventually managed to drag himself up off the floor. He got up and in a staggering motion, he moved under the flow of shower water in the pretense of washing away the filthy memory of what had just happened. Daunte hugged himself protectively and with tears streaming down his face, he cried out with the breath of a newborn baby who'd been painfully delivered from the safety of his mother's womb.

Curtis continued to unleash his anger upon Carlton through stiff lefts and rights. Curtis punched Carlton on the side of his face sending him stumbling into a wall. Carlton's energy had been zapped and not wanting to endure the punishment of Curtis anymore, he used the last of his strength to run away.

Curtis looked to Carlton's conspirators. One followed and ran along with Carlton while the third lay sprawled out on the floor with blood leaking from a whole in his head.

Curtis rushed over to Daunte and grabbed him by the shoulder to help him but the events of being raped left Daunte in shock.

"No! No!" Daunte screamed

"Daunte! Daunte! It's me Curtis!" Curtis said, as he grabbed him, once more. "Come on man! We got to get out of here before the guard shows up."

Curtis draped a white towel around Daunte while simultaneously grabbing his friend's toiletries. The two walked out stepping over the con that lay on the floor. Making it down the tier outside of the showers, they headed to Daunte's cell. 'Thank God for the Piston and Laker game," Curtis thought, as they went unnoticed by the guys in the recreation room. Their focus was on the television.

"Come on, man." Curtis spoke in a hush tone. "Just a few more steps." He ushered Daunte through the cell entry and then eased his friend onto his bunk.

"I can't believe this shit," Daunte said, as his tears turned to anger. "Tell me I'm dreaming. I got be dreaming."

"Relax, Daunte," Curtis said, as he grabbed a t-shirt and underwear out of Daunte's drawer.

"Why man?" Daunte exploded with anger. "What the fuck did I do to deserve this?"

"Daunte, you're a strong man. You'll get through this. I promise."

Curtis gently helped his friend to get in bed, but no matter how gentle a hand he used, the excruciating pain between the darkness of Daunte's buttocks still won.

"Here man," Curtis said. "Try lying on your side. Then maybe you can get some sleep." Curtis pulled the wool institution issued blanket up around Daunte's shoulders.

"Curtis, thanks man, for helping me." Daunte looked sincerely at Curtis. "I don't even know how to begin to repay you."

"Daunte, you don't owe me for being a friend. Just do me a favor and try to get some sleep."

"I don't know if I'll ever sleep again," Daunte said solemnly.

"Don't worry, Daunte. I'll stay here until lock down. Nobody else is going to hurt you anymore. I promise you that."

All the activities of the day came crashing down on Daunte and he drifted off to sleep. Curtis watched Daunte, as the evident expression of humiliation was replaced with the milestone of acceptance. Curtis began to reminisce about what had happened to him on his very first day in prison. He was so ashamed of what he went through that day so much so, that he had never told another soul that he had been raped, not even his buddy Carlton who'd just committed the very same act. At that very moment Curtis vowed that Carlton was now his worst enemy.

Chapter 10
Jay, Wil & Ricky

Jay sat behind his desk, in the comfort of a leather high back chair, preparing to bring the day to an end. He'd just tapped the final key on the keypad that would shut his computer down when he decided to call Ricky.

He grabbed his cell phone from his desk and by the time he had dialed the digits to Ricky's phone, he was standing up holding the sleek frame of his phone firmly between his cheek and shoulder. Jay slipped his suit coat on as he waited for Ricky to answer but instead of it ringing, he was surprised by the sudden sound of a familiar voice coming from the other end. Jay's blood began to boil when he realized who the person was. 'Damn not again,' Jay thought.

"Did you not hear me the night we talked outside of Tariff's house?"

"Yes, Jay! I heard what you said. As a matter of fact, I heard you loud and clear. But I just can't understand why you won't give me another chance or at least let us be friends."

"Wil, No! What's best for the both of us is that we just cut all ties. Wil, you need to get some help before you hurt somebody. Your temper is out of control"

"Jay, are those feelings in your heart?" Silence was the reply and the echo of quiet left Wil's curiosity suspended in the air. "I take that as a yes," he said. "Well, I won't bother you again."

"I would appreciate that, Wil. All this is your fault. Remember you cheated on me, I didn't cheat on you, and you put your hands on me," Jay said, and hung up without giving Wil a chance to say another word.

Jay plopped down in his chair, as he let out a long frustrated sigh. Just as he began to relax, the unexpected vibration of his cell pissed him off.

"Hey man, I was just about to call you," Jay said, looking at the caller ID realizing it was Ricky.

"I guess I must have ESP. I could feel you." Ricky laughed lightly.

"Yeah, you must." Jay laughed a little, still distracted with the previous conversation.

"Jay, you okay? You sound distracted."

"I'm good. I just finished dealing with a phone call that left me a little irritated. I nipped it in the bud. It won't come up again," Jay hoped.

"Oh, okay I'm going to go hit the gym, so I'll see you at dinner tonight, a'ight?"

"Sounds like a plan to me." Jay was already walking out of his office. "Have a good workout."

Thirty minutes later Ricky walked into the gym's locker room. He was feeling pumped up. He noticed how crowded the gym was this evening. Ricky was just about to give up on finding an empty locker when he spotted one all the way at the end of the room.

"Excuse me. You mind if I squeeze in here and use this locker next to yours?"

"Sure man, no problem."

"Thanks a lot." Ricky said, as he started to slip off his tie.

"This time of day gets really crowded in here. I just started working out here about a month ago. I've never seen you in here."

"Well, my hours changed at work and this is the only time I can get in here." Ricky responded.

The gentleman extended his hand to Ricky. "My name is William, but my friends call me Wil."

"Nice to meet you, Wil. My name is Ricky and my friends call me Ricky." They both broke out in laughter.

"So Ricky, are you from the area?"

"Naw, man, moved here a few months back. I'm from North Carolina."

"Do you have a workout partner?"

"I did, but they opened a new gym across from his office so he's there now. So a brother's solo now." Ricky said.

"Well, man if you looking for a workout partner, I'm definitely looking for one too. Wil smiled to himself and thought, 'Jay would be pissed if he knew I was trying to get his new man.'

"So Ricky, what brought you here?"

"I'm an attorney and I got a new job with a law firm here."

"Do you have family here? Have you gotten a chance to see the city and meet new friends?" Wil started shooting out questions.

'Damn bru,' Ricky thought. 'You need to pump your breaks with all these questions.' "Naw, Wil, no family. I do have some cool friends I met since I've been here. They've become like family to me."

Wil started to think about how close he was with the guys when he was with Jay. When he and Jay broke up he didn't talk to the guys at all, so he knew exactly what Ricky was saying about meeting good friends. Now those guys where his friends.

"What about you, Wil, are you from the area?"

"I was born and raised right here in Houston," Wil boasted.

With that said, Wil and Ricky closed their lockers and headed into the workout area. Walking into the cardio area, Ricky extended his hand. "Nice to meet you, Wil. I'm about to jump on this treadmill."

"A'ight, Ricky. I'm going over and hit the bike. Man, let me go holler at this girl over here first. Maybe we can workout together after the cardio?"

"That's cool, man," Ricky said, as he watched Wil walk away and chat with this sister by the water fountain. Ricky dismissed his uncomfortable feeling about Wil and took it as him just being hospitable.

Chapter 11
Mia, Ricky, Jay, Reese & Antonio

"Hello," Mia said, as she leaned over the visitor's log and signed her name and the person she was there to visit.

"Good morning, ma'am," the guard responded. He remembered Mia from last week and he already knew that he was going to have to turn her away. "Miss, your friend Daunte Rollins won't be receiving visitors today."

"What!? What do you mean? Is he okay? He's expecting me." Mia spit out question after question.

"Slow down, ma'am." The guard held up one palm. "Normally, when an inmate declines a visit an email's sent and we attach it to the log. Unfortunately, there's nothing here, so you're going to have to wait until he calls you."

"Is there anyone I can speak with?" Mia asked politely. "I need to know what's going on with my fiancé."

"I'm sorry ma'am, right now there isn't anyone you can speak with, but you can get in contact with his case worker. She'll be in tomorrow. I wish I could do more for you, but all I have is that he's not accepting visitors."

"Thank you, sir," Mia said, as she slowly gathered her sunglasses and purse and walked away. Mia headed out and got into her car and sat for a few minutes. 'Why would Daunte not want to see me? Something has to be wrong.' Mia reached in the glove compartment and grabbed her cell phone. Mia scrolled her contacts list and called Ricky.

"Hey Mia!" Ricky quickly answered. He was on the way home from the gym.

"Ricky, I need your help!"

"Sure, Mia. Calm down. What's wrong?"

"I don't know. Maybe I'm over reacting." Mia took a breath. "I just tried to visit Daunte today and they turned me away. They said he didn't want to see me."

"Did they give you any kind of explanation, Mia?"

"No, they just told me he refused my visit. That's not like Daunte. Ricky, something is wrong. Something is wrong."

"Look Mia, let me make a couple of phone calls and see what I can find out and I will call you back as soon as I find something out."

"Thanks, Ricky. Thank you so much."

Finally arriving home, Ricky pulled up in the driveway and grabbed his cell phone and made the calls he promised Mia. His first attempt with administration came up an empty effort. No one could really give him any information on Daunte's situation. All he knew was that Daunte wasn't in the infirmary hurt. Ricky was just about to give Mia a call when Jay walked up and tapped on the glass.

"Hey baby, how you doing?" Jay asked, as he looked affectionately at Ricky.

"I'm cool, how bout you?" Ricky asked, as he stepped out of the car and gave Jay a peck as they headed in the house.

"I actually had a pretty good day. Who were you about to call?"

"I was about to call Mia back." Ricky flipped his phone closed. "She went to see Daunte earlier and was turned away without an explanation, now she's all upset."

"Oh wow!" Jay said, "Sounds to me like she has a good reason to be worried. The way Daunte worships Mia, there has to be something wrong if he's refusing her visit.

"It appears everything is okay. I was about to call her back."

"What are you going to tell her?"

"That everything appears to be fine."

"I hear you Ricky, but I don't think it is. When you talk to her, tell her I'll go to the prison and talk with him," Jay said, as he affectionately rubbed Ricky's arm.

"Okay, I'll call the jail tomorrow and pull some strings with a couple of my contacts and get you on the visitors list."

*   *   *

Reese spent most of his days trying to stay in shape so he would be ready for Spring Training. He walked into the locker room and sat down on the bench in front of his locker with sweat pouring down his face. By the look of it you might have thought he had just run a 10K marathon.

Reese reached up and opened his locker and the first thing he noticed was a piece of paper. Not able to quite read the paper, he stood up. The note read, "Yeah, I know your story, so here is something you can use after you get dicked down, you punk ass faggot."

Reese noticed immediately that the note was attached to a box of tampons. He slammed his locker shut and then started to pace around the locker room to see if anyone was lurking in the shadows. A few seconds later Antonio appeared from the shower.

"Sup Antonio, anybody else back there in the showers?" Reese asked, as he looked over Antonio's shoulder.

"Naw Reese, just me, man. Why you asking?" Reese remained silent for awhile. He knew Antonio could be trusted, it was just that he didn't know exactly how to put his feelings into words.

"Reese, what's wrong man?" Antonio's voice broke Reese's concentration, "Man, you really look pissed."

Reese walked over to his locker and swung the door open. "Take a look!"

Antonio stepped up beside Reese and following the intensity of his friend's gaze, he reached inside the locker and pulled the note from the shelf.

Antonio read the words on the paper, not once but twice. He grabbed the tampon box with as much anger as Reese was feeling and after ripping both objects into shreds, he slammed the remains in the trash can.

"Man, I have something to ask you." Reese gave Antonio a look that totally confused Antonio.

"Sure man," Antonio calmly replied while he unconsciously shuffled idea after idea as to where Reese was going, "Go
ahead, man. Speak your mind."

"That personal conversation you and I had about my sexuality," Reese took a deep breath, "Did you share that conversation
with anyone else?" Reese pierced Antonio with an intense stare
looking for the truth and in return Antonio gazed wide eyed at
Reese in complete shock.

"Reese, m-a-n. Aw naw dawg…how could?" Antonio
placed his hand on Reese's shoulder. "Man, you don't have to ask
me about that, I already promised I wouldn't! Reese, I gave you
my word."

"Antonio, I'm sorry." Reese immediately felt that he had
betrayed their friendship. "I don't know how I ever thought that it
came from you, but at least now I know that what we discussed is
not a secret. Someone else around here knows." Reese grabbed
his toiletries and headed for the shower leaving Antonio standing
in front of the open locker. "What am I going to do?" he mumbled.

Antonio went to his own locker and began to get dressed.
'Who could be cruel enough to do some backward ass shit like
this?' He thought.

Chapter 12
Cutis & Daunte

Curtis walked down the cell block's top tier in the direction of Daunte's cell. 'I bet my man is having a good time on his visit.' Curtis thought.

Curtis had decided to kill some time in the T.V. room while he waited for Daunte to come back off his visit. He was just passing by Daunte's room when he instinctively glanced in.

"Daunte!" Curtis mouth dropped in total surprise. "Man-what's up? I thought you were still on your visit with Mia."

"She came." Daunte lay on his bunk curled into a fetal position.

"Did you go see her?" Curtis took a couple of steps until he was standing only a few feet from Daunte's bunk.

"I just can't see her right now." Daunte winced at his pain and curled up tighter. "I just can't do it."

"Daunte, man, Mia loves you and what you need now more than anything is the love and support of those who care about you, especially Mia!"

"Curtis, your boy destroyed me! He raped me of my dignity, literally."

"No, Daunte, don't give up and for God sake man, don't ever let what you cannot control have that kind of power over you. And don't you worry about Carlton, I'll take care of him."

"Well, when you ready to take care of him, let me know."

"I got this Daunte," Curtis said.

"What are you going to do?"

"The less you know the better off you'll be."

"Curtis, why? You don't owe me anything. Why put yourself in jeopardy for me?"

"Daunte, I consider you my friend and it's been a long time since I've had one of those. Curtis looked at the man he'd just called his friend and at that moment he felt it was time to tell the truth. Curtis pondered doing so as he sat next to Daunte.

"Daunte you want to hear something that I've never spoken to another living soul."

"What?" What could be worst than a man being viciously raped?"

"Exactly," Curtis said.

"What?" Daunte was confused at first and then it dawned on him what Curtis was saying. "Naw, man. No way. Not you!"

"Yes, Daunte."

Curtis unrolled the red carpet of honesty and with no room for turning back, he walked the runway of trust. "The same thing that happened to you is the very thing that I had to endure when I first got here and, until this very second, I haven't shared that information with anyone."

"Man, Curtis you got to be kidding. Carlton did the same thing to you?"

"No, it wasn't Carlton. It was a couple other inmates," Curtis said.

"Come on Curtis, you have got to be joking."

"Do you feel like what happened to you is a joke?"

"No, Curtis, I didn't mean it like that. It's definitely not a laughing matter. So, how long did it take you to get over it?"

"For real, bru, I deal with that shit everyday of my life! But!" Curtis snapped with confidence, "I had to show them dudes that I was a soldier and I had to get their respect, I couldn't let them jokers think they had gained some type of power over me."

"So what happened to those guys? Where are they now?"

"It doesn't matter Daunte," Curtis said.

Daunte sat quiet as he mentally thought about this philosophical approach to an otherwise crushing obstacle to a man's existence.

"Daunte, come back man," Curtis could literally see the wheels turning in his friends head, as he searched for some kind of understanding. "Daunte, why did Carlton call you a faggot lover?"

"I've thought about that for a while and the only thing I can think of is that he went into my cell while I was on my visit with Mia and read a letter I left laying on my bunk. It was from a friend of mine who was gay. I guess Carlton must have come to the conclusion that I was gay too."

"Man!" Curtis said, as he shook his head. "Carlton does have a habit of getting into other people's business, but hey, it's a new day. So how about you give Mia a call and let her know how much you miss her."

"That sounds good, but Mia knows me like the back of her hand and the minute she talks to me, she'll figure out something is wrong."

"Have you thought about just telling her straight up what went down?"

"Shit man! I haven't even come to grips with this shit myself, so I know I ain't about to drop something as heavy as this on my baby."

"Just give me a couple more days. I'll call her."

"Well, I don't think you give Mia enough credit, but it's your decision. Remember Daunte, this wasn't your fault. I'm going to go and hit the weights," Curtis said, "You coming?"

"Naw, man. I'm just going to chill out in here for a while."

"A'ight D, that's on you – but whatever you do man, don't let them monkeys see fear."

"I hear you. But right now, I need some time to clear my head. I'm sure you can understand that."

"Yeah I do." Curtis had no problem identifying with the stuff Daunte was going through. "Do what you need to do to work through this," he said, "but remember man, you don't want to look like you're hiding out. Curtis gave Daunte some dap and then he left his friend alone to think. As Curtis started to walk away, his mind was consumed with thoughts of Daunte and he became aroused. Curtis couldn't understand what was happening to him. Shaking the thoughts, he continued on his way.

Chapter 13
Keith, Antonio & Reese

Keith, Antonio and Reese hit the Jacuzzi after a vigorous two hour work out. The propeller on the water jets instantly went to work relaxing them with a watery massage.

"Aw m-a-n, this is almost as good as sex," Keith said, "It's just what the doctor ordered cause these workouts are killing me."

"Boy, oh boy," Antonio eased himself into a comfortable position. "I can't believe how much punishment we put our bodies through."

"Reese…" Keith nodded his head at Antonio, as he eyed Reese.

"A-yo Reese, man your ass is in a whole other world…What you thinking about?"

"Umm. My bad. I just got some pretty heavy stuff on my mind." Reese pressed his lower back directly up against one of the power jets.

"Talk to your boys," Keith smiled playfully. "Let your boys help you out." His smile continued to grow, as he completed his thoughts, "especially if it's female problems, cause you know women are my specialty."

"Naw man, I'm good…I pretty much got everything under control, but thanks." Reese shot Keith a cosmetic smile that was a fake through and through.

"Well, since we're on the subject of women," Keith said, as he looked straight at Antonio and directed his comment to Reese, "You know your boy Antonio is in love with that chick he met at the club the night we all hung out."

"Yeah, he told me," Reese said, as he nodded his head. "I hope things work out for him."

"Oh it's working out!" Antonio watched the Jacuzzi water

as it rose and fell in small miniature waves. "Man, the way shit is going, I just might marry this girl."

"Marry!!!" Keith and Reese replied at the same time.

"Yeah." Antonio rocked his head like a man completely baffled. "Turns out baby girl is pregnant."

"Pregnant! How in the hell did you let some bullshit like that happen?" Keith asked but before Antonio could respond, Keith continued. "Man, all we were supposed to do that night was get our dicks wet. Now you telling your boys that you been banging that chick without a raincoat."

"Keith, give Ant a chance to finish. Let's hear the whole story."

Antonio became defensive. "We used condoms every time, but you know they ain't a hundred percent guaranteed."

"Get a paternity test ASAP, man. You know them tricks be using that baby daddy stuff to get paid."

"Does she know that you're a profootball player?" Reese asked.

Keith said, without giving Antonio a chance to respond. "Our boy, Ant here, told her he was a pharmaceutical sales rep."

Reese shook his head, as he remembered what happened when lies came to surface. But he also knew Antonio was his boy and could see that Ant was uncomfortable talking about this right now. "Whatever you need man, I'm there. I will say if you like this girl you definitely don't want to continue your relationship based on lies."

"Bru, let me school you right quick." Keith looked directly at Antonio ignoring Reese's comment. "A woman with a plan cannot be stopped."

"Whatever, man!" Antonio was irritated. "Keith you wrong about this one. Plus she told me that I'm the only guy she's been sleeping with."

"Man, please! Antonio, women can be just as slick as us, but the only difference between the two species is men always got to run their mouth to the fellas." Keith looked at the clock on the wall, speaking to no one in particular. "I got to bounce, man. I gotta hit the showers."

Chapter 14
Barbara, Tonya & Larry

Barbara walked up to Tonya's front door. She pushed the door bell with the ball of her knuckle to protect her freshly painted finger nails. Barbara had just pulled her hand away from the buzzer when the door flung open. She ran into the house and headed straight to the front window.

"Girl, what are you doing?" Tonya asked, curiously looking at Barbara, "And why the hell are you peeping out the window like that?"

"Tonya, I ain't trying to scare you, but isn't that Larry's ass parked across the street?"

"Damn!" Tonya peeped through a crack in the curtain without moving it. "Hell yeah. That's his tired ass."

"Girl, call the police!" Barbara handed Tonya her cell phone without taking her eyes off of Larry.

"I can't do that," Tonya said, as she peeped out the curtain once more.

"Why not?"

"Because that ain't going to do shit but piss him off and then his ass will really come after me."

"Who gives a shit about his ass being pissed?"

"Well, right now, I do." Tonya turned her eyes away from the window. "Should he ever decide to really act crazy, then I'll call the police."

"Go pack a bag!" Barbara snapped.

"Pack a bag?" Tonya asked completely confused. "For what? Where am I going?"

"With, me!" Barbara turned and started towards Tonya's bedroom. "I'm not letting you stay here by yourself with that fool camped out in front of this house."

"Barbara!" Tonya shouted. "If that fool see me leave with you, all he going to do is follow us and you don't want him to know where you live."

"Tonya, this is me you're talking to. Just go pack a bag like I said. I got this."

"Oh yeah, I almost forgot," Tonya let out a hardy laugh. "Ms. Barbara, The Great, always has a plan."

"You got that right. This is how this is going to go down." Barbara's hands moved animatedly as she talked. "You're going to leave out the back door and I'm going to leave out the front. So he will think I'm leaving you here alone. Anyway, while he's thinking the obvious, you just shoot through the alley and I'll meet you around the corner."

"But Barbara what if he follows you?"

"Why the hell would he follow me? You're the one he wants. Even if he decides to follow me, I'll just call you on your cell phone."

"Okay, I'm going to pack." Tonya quickly headed up stairs. She hurriedly stuffed a cream colored Coach traveling bag with a couple days worth of casual wear she could relax in, some cosmetics and most importantly her vitamins and her feminine hygiene kit. Tonya headed downstairs. "Is he still out there?"

"Yeah, his dumb ass is still sitting out there. Dumb Mutha fucker. You got everything you need?"

"Yeah," Tonya said as she grabbed her bag.

"Good. Go ahead out the back door and I'll lock it behind you. Tonya headed down the steps to the back porch.

Barbara locked the door behind her and walked through the house to the front door. Casually, Barbara walked out the house and in the pretense of talking to someone, she said, "Okay, girl. Call me later." Barbara didn't even look in Larry's direction. She hopped in her car and rolled out. Driving off she looked in her rearview mirror making sure Larry wasn't following her. Two minutes later, she pulled up around the corner and drove up to where Tonya stood.

"I told you it would work. Now slump down in your seat

while, I drive past your place."

"Why?" Tonya snapped

"Just do it," Barbara snapped back, as she slowly turned her car onto the street were Tonya lived.

"Girl, you won't believe this shit!"

"What? Tonya asked anxiously.

"That dumb ass is standing on the front porch of your house banging on the door."

"Barbara, come on," Tonya popped her head up for a quick look. "Let's just get the hell out of here."

"Tonya, I don't care what you say about pissing him off, first thing tomorrow, you need to get a restraining order on his crazy ass."

"You right girl. Thanks for having my back," Tonya said, as she slid up in her seat and watched Larry standing on her porch.

Chapter 15
Curtis, Carlton

Curtis left his cell and headed to the institution's Tag Shop where some of the inmates worked to remove the stickers off old license plates. He was coming down the narrow walk that led to the shop when he caught sight of Carlton. This was the first time Curtis had seen Carlton since the rape had taken place. Curtis and Carlton locked gazes and then Carlton angled his body so that he was directly in Curtis' path.

"So how's my bitch doing?" Carlton asked, as he grabbed his crotch. "Is that whore of yours looking for some more dick?"

"Carlton, you really crossed the line this time."

"Why you feel like that, Curtis?" Carlton asked, as he slowly stroked his semi hard penis. "You just mad cause you ain't tap that virgin ass first? Or is it that you're upset cause you wanted all this dick for yourself?"

"Niggah, you must don't know, I will kill your monkey ass…"

"Kill this bitch!" Carlton clamped his hand down hard and yanked his penis at Curtis. "And while you at it mutha-fucker, tell your boy Daunte that he got some real good pussy for a boy."

"Now who's the faggot?" Curtis spit out.

"You know something Curtis?" Carlton gritted his teeth as he spoke "You shouldn't have stepped in the middle of this, dude. I thought we were boys."

"Carlton, you right, we were boys, past tense, but you're out of control."

"Niggah you changed. When the old Curtis comes back, you know where to find me."

Curtis walked up close to Carlton and leaned in to whisper

in his ear. Curtis started to speak, "I can't do what I want to your ass right now, but you better watch your back."

Carlton pushed Curtis away and noticed the security guards watching. Looking at Curtis, "Well, in the end, we'll see who's the last man standing."

Curtis grimaced. "Oh yeah, don't drop the soap you li'l pussy." Curtis pushed Carlton and continued on his way, never looking back, only to hear Carlton shouting,

"We'll see, mutha fucka!" Carlton hissed, "We'll see!" His threats fell on deaf ears.

Curtis was still angry from his run-in with Carlton when he reached the institution's workshop. He had an agenda, and had to focus 100 percent on the task at hand. He stepped up to his work station and let his job distract him from his hateful energy for Carlton. One slip up could mean the difference between him getting caught by the guards or getting away with his mission.

Curtis picked up a bottle of T-Eleven, a solution that inmates use to remove the tags off of old license plates, from the counter top and poured some of it in the sink. Curtis cut his eyes in the guard's direction. Positive that his actions appeared normal, he slipped a small plastic Zip Lock bag from under his sleeve. He had someone steal it from the kitchen for him. Inconspicuously, he poured the T-Eleven into the bag and quickly slid the bag back under his sleeve. Curtis nodded at one of the guards, who reacted to the signal by walking over to where Curtis stood.

"What you need, boy?" The guard said loud and disrespectfully.

"I need to use the john, sir," Curtis said, as he slid the husky white guard a couple of twenties.

"A'ight get moving." The guard nudged Curtis in the side with his night stick for appearance. "Watch them convicts, Sarg," the guard said to his partner.

Curtis walked ahead of the hillbilly guard and into the small bathroom, closing the door behind the guard who stood right out front. Curtis quickly pulled the bag from under his sleeve, ensured the bag was closed and ran it under the water to wash off the liquid that was on the outside of the bag. Quickly, he grabbed some thread that he had tied around his wrist. He tied it around the bag tightly. Curtis reached inside his pocket which was filled with Vaseline. He massaged the outside of the bag, making sure it was adequately lubricated. Curtis dropped his pants, and without a second thought, he shoved the bag up inside his rectum, leaving a bit of the string hanging out for him to pull the bag out once he got back to his cell. This was Curtis' only guarantee he had of getting the T-Eleven out of the shop. He flushed the toilet, fixed his clothes and then stepped to the sink to wash his hands.

"Come on boy, let's get moving." The guard looked at Curtis's reflection in the mirror and could see the discomforting expression that he was wearing. Curtis walked over to his area and immediately began to clean up his station. He started to fidget a little from the extra passenger that was riding in his ass like an unwelcome hitchhiker. Curtis was beginning to sweat as the time to leave came closer and closer. Even though he knew the suitcase technique was 99 percent full proof, he also knew that there was a one percent chance that a guard who'd been around long enough could stumble upon the move.

The guards called for the inmates to line up. As Curtis walked in line, he could've sworn that the skinny black C.O. who was scratching his head and looking straight at him, was going to call for a strip search and cavity check. 'Aw shit!' Curtis swiped at the sweat on his fore head.

"Open your mouth!" The guard snapped, "Stick out your tongue." The guard patted Curtis down extra aggressively. "A'ight keep it moving."

Curtis carefully controlled his footsteps, as he walked down the hall towards his cell block. He made it to his room undisturbed and, once in the privacy of his cell, he sat on the toilet and reached for the thread that hung out his ass and pulled the plastic out, washed it off, and poured the liquid inside an empty lotion bottle. With the first half of his mission accomplished, he laid down on his bunk, with both hands behind his head and went into deep thought.

Chapter 16
Mia, Daunte & Jay

"Hi, Baby, are you okay?" Mia asked, as she placed her hand on the glass that separated her from Daunte.

"I'm good."

"Then why haven't I heard from you? Why have you avoided seeing me?" Mia's eyes spoke with volumes of pain. "What's going on Daunte?"

"I'm good, baby. This place has just been stressing me out."

"I know this ain't the best place for you but it will be over before you know it. Baby, you just got to be patient."

"That's easier said than done, Mia. Let's talk about something else." Daunte shifted his weight around, as he spoke with an attitude.

"Daunte, you don't have to take it out on me."

"You right, baby. I'm sorry. It's just, things are crazy. Being stuck in this joint is just getting to me."

"I called Ricky when I didn't hear from you. Have you heard from him or Jay?"

"Why are you calling Ricky, Mia? Is there something you need to tell me?"

"Daunte! What are you trying to say? What is wrong with you?" Mia spit out question after question without giving Daunte a chance to say anything.

"You know what. I need some time, just give me some time." Daunte abruptly stood up and motioned for the guard to escort him back to his cell. "I got to get out of here. Thanks for coming by. I'll talk to you later."

"Daunte, don't walk away from me. Daunte, P-l-e-a-s-e."

Tears streamed down Mia's face, as the other visitors stared.

Daunte's heart was breaking as he turned to face Mia. His heart ached, as he walked away. All he could hear was Mia's last words. "Time for what Daunte?! Time for what?!"

Mia fell back in her seat and reached her trembling hand inside of her pocket- book fishing out some tissue to dry the painful tears. She was completely confused by Daunte's actions and Mia knew that something had to have happened in order for him to be acting so out of character. Mia collected her composure. Hurriedly, she walked out the facility, got to her car and reached for her cell phone which she had left on the passenger seat. Quickly she dialed Jay's number.

"Hello, Jay! Jay is that you?"

"Mia, are you okay?" Jay asked.

"Jay, I need to see you right away. Something is wrong with Daunte. Can I come by and talk to you?"

Mia flipped her phone closed and in less than five minutes she was driving down the main highway headed to Jay's house. She tried to focus, but Daunte's behavior made concentration impossible. She shook her head, as scenario after scenario popped into her mind. 'What could have happened?' she asked herself. The man that I just visited is not the man I've been in love with for the past couple of years. 'Jay, man, I need your help,' Mia thought.

Mia hadn't realized how fast she was driving until she started to see familiar landmarks that told her she was in Jay's neighborhood. The clock on the dashboard told her that the drive that would have normally taken an hour took her forty five minutes. Mia whipped her car into Jay's driveway and while the car was practically still rolling, she hit the pavement running.

Mia ran up the steps with the scenes of her visit still playing in her head. She punched the doorbell. The second Jay opened the door his presence offered her comfort. Mia began to cry a fresh waterfall of fear and confusion.

"Wow! You got here fast Mia!"

"I guess I was driving pretty fast."

Jay comforted her with a hug. He walked Mia over to the

sofa. "Would you like something to drink?"

"No, thank you, Jay. I'm okay."

Jay sat next to her. "What's going on Mia?"

"Jay, something's wrong with Daunte. He hasn't been calling me, he doesn't write, and until today he was refusing my visits. After seeing him, he seemed different. Jay, something's wrong! I can feel it! Something's wrong!"

"Yeah, I know, Ricky told me. He's trying to have it set up so I can go and visit him."

"That place is destroying him, Jay. When I saw him today, there was no excitement in his voice and he appeared to be very detached. I know my man Jay and the person I saw today was not Daunte. Something has changed him."

Jay rubbed his cheek. He wasn't sure what to say. He sat there deep in thought.

"Jay, he accused me of wanting Ricky. It was like he was trying to push me away."

Jay cocked his head in total disbelief. "I can't believe after everything that happened last year, Daunte would even think that. I'll go and see Daunte this weekend"

"Thanks, Jay. I appreciate you doing this for me." Mia was finally beginning to feel a little comfort with Jay. She was looking at Jay and wondered if Daunte would react to him as he'd done with her.

"No problem, Mia, don't worry, he'll be okay."

Silence crept into the living room space, as Mia and Jay each retreated to the solitude of their own private thoughts.

Chapter 17
Daunte & Curtis

"What's up Daunte?" Curtis asked, as he walked into Danute's cell. "How did your visit with Mia go?"

"It didn't go too well," Daunte paused, "Man, I was straight tripping."

"What happened D?" Curtis asked, as he sat across from Daunte.

"Man, I acted like a complete ass." Daunte looked straight at Curtis to read his reaction. "Curtis, you ain't going to believe this, but I made Mia cry. That just goes to prove my point."

"What point, Daunte?"

"I knew I wasn't ready. I shouldn't have started back seeing her again so soon," Daunte trailed off.

"I understand Daunte. I really do. I'm sorry that I pushed you to see her."

"Curtis, lets keep it real, man." Daunte rested his head between his hands, as he gazed at an empty spot on the floor. "What woman is going to want a man after he's been raped?"

"Daunte, if a woman loves a man the way you say Mia loves you, then what happened won't even matter."

Daunte shook his head in total disgust. "I feel so much less of a man."

"Daunte, you have to trust me on this. Believe in the love that Mia has for you. Put all your faith in that."

"I could kill that mutha fucker for what he's done to my life."

"Daunte. Don't worry about Carlton, let it go. I'll take care of him."

"Let it go! Curtis, that man stripped me of my dignity, and

I'm suppose to let it go!"

"Look man, believe me when I tell you this," Curtis looked around to make sure no one was in ear shot of their conversation, "When the time is right, I'm going to take care of Carlton."

"What do you mean, take care of him? Curtis, what are you planning to do?"

"Man, I got a life sentence in this joint, but in your situation, you still have a chance to pick up the pieces and go on with your life, so it's best you don't have any knowledge about my plans…that way if you're ever asked you can say you didn't know anything and you'd be telling the truth."

"Curtis, will you ever have a chance to make parole?" Daunte watched Curtis'expression for some sign of hope.

"Yeah, but I don't think they will ever let me out."

"Hey," Daunte spoke optimistically, "if you were to get a Johnny Cochran type attorney, you never know, he or she just might win you your freedom."

"Shit, Daunte, I don't have anyone out there waiting for me and the mutha fuckas involved with my case don't care if I live or die, for real D. I don't know if I even want to get out. I have no place to go and no one out there to help me."

"Curtis, I will never forget you, man, or what you've done for me. When I get out, I promise you, I'll keep in touch."

"D, the thought is nice." It made Curtis feel warm inside that someone felt that way about him. "But, you will forget about me. I've learned that from experience. That's just how it is in here."

"Curtis, it won't be like that man."

"Daunte," Curtis interrupted his friend, "I wasn't going to say anything cause I wasn't sure how to tell you, but there is something you need to know."

"What is it?" Daunte snapped, this time interrupting Curtis.

"Daunte, I really don't know what Carlton has been doing in this joint or how many times he has done this rape thing before. I think for your sake you should be tested for STD's, as well as HIV.

"What? A fucking HIV test?" Daunte fell back lying flat

out on his bed. "Man you have got to be fucking kidding me."

"D, you have a girl to think about and with the months you have left, you can get tested now, and before you're released you should be tested again."

"Curtis, this is a fucking nightmare, right? Tell me I'm asleep." Daunte clasp his fingers behind his head, immediately standing up. "I'm going to kill that mutha fucker if anything is wrong with me. He's a dead man walking."

"Look, Daunte, don't worry man, you'll be okay and it's just a precaution. I just want you to be smart."

"Curtis, did you get tested when you got raped?"

"Yeah, man, I did. I was okay and you will be too."

"But how?"

"How?" Curtis repeated Daunte's thought, "How what?"

"Do I just walk up to the nurse and say, oh by the way I got raped, would you mind giving me a HIV test?"

"Pretty much…or you can see the inmate psychologist and explain to her what happened. Before you go getting all paranoid, remember everything is confidential so you don't have to worry about your business being spread all over the jail."

"Man, I don't know about that. The first thing the doc is going to think is I'm having sex up in this joint."

"No, man just let the psychologist know exactly what happened without giving up names cause snitches don't last long up in here. And, Daunte, I really do think you need to talk to someone before you explode. All that you're going through can be too much for one person to handle on their own."

"Man my head is fucked up right about now."

"If it'll make you feel better, how about I go with you to see the psychologist."

"Do you think they will let you?"

"Man, I think Ms. Taylor has the hots for me." Curtis smiled. "I'll go and see her, explain the situation and we can take it from there."

"Man, if I have AIDS."

"Stop thinking negative, I promise you everything will be okay."

"I hope you're right."

"Well, it's almost time for bed check and lights out. Get some sleep." Curtis walked over and gave Daunte a friendly hug. As they broke their embrace, Curtis felt something he had never felt towards another man, he felt a physical stirring in the pit of his stomach.

"Thanks again, Curtis."

"No problem, D. I'll see you tomorrow."

Daunte crawled into this bunk fully dressed except for his shoes. Ever since the rape he had been sleeping with his clothes on. He'd just pulled the covers up to his shoulders when the guard yelled, "lights out!" Cells went pitch black except for a small sliver of moonlight that streamed in his room. All he could think about was the impact on his life if he were to be HIV positive. 'I won't be able to have kids. Mia won't love me.' he was thinking, 'I can't live with this. Lord, please don't let this happen to me,' Daunte thought, as the tears ran down his face. He rocked himself to sleep, crying silently through his screaming pain.

Chapter 18
Reese, Antonio, Keith & Mike

Reese, Keith and Antonio joined their teammates on the field for a light practice without protective gear. Everybody lined up to run a play. It was offense against defense. The quarterback handed the ball to Reese, his running back. Reese grabbed the ball and began to cut to the right and headed up the field. Just as he was slowing down, Steve and Zack, two linebackers, hit Reese, knocking him to the ground. Reese dropped the ball extending his arms to break his fall. Steve and Zack stood over Reese as Reese grabbed his arm.

"Damn faggot!" Steve said.

"You better quit bitch or we're going to make you pay every time you step out on the field." Zack chimed in.

Reese took so long getting up that Antonio and Keith rushed over and gave him a hand up. Reese stretched his back and was just about to tell his buddies not to trip when Keith lunged at Steve, knocking him to the ground.

"Oh shit!" Reese jumped between the two. "Keith calm down." Reese pulled Keith off Steve and held him in a bear hug.

"It's all good Keith. Man, I'm a'ight." Reese stared Steve down. "I'm okay – plus he and his boy hit like a bitch."

"Okay, break this crap up!" The coach yelled. "Steve get your butt over here son and the rest of you screw balls hit the damn showers.

The entire team mumbled in disappointment as they walked toward the tunnel, secretly satisfied practice was cut short.

"Man, I ain't taking a shower with that kind of dude," Zack said. He glared at Reese then looked at his teammates, as he gathered his bag and walked out.

"What does he mean by that kind of dude?" Keith curiously swung his head back and forth catching glimpses of Reese.

"Man, Zack is just being the typical asshole." Antonio watched Reese gather his stuff and walk out.

"I'll talk to you guys later," Reese said, as he passed by his buddies.

"I'll be right back, let me go holler at Reese for a minute," Antonio said to Keith. He ran over to catch Reese before he left the parking lot. As Antonio reached Reese, he grabbed his arm. Reese turned and Antonio could see the hurt and embarrassment etched into every crease of his face. Reese tried to hide the pain but it was too great and too much to hide.

"Reese, don't let them jokers chase you outta here. You got just as much right to be here as any of those knuckleheads."

"I can't do it, Antonio." Reese slammed his large gym bag to the ground. "It's just not worth it!"

"Reese, don't do anything rash man. Just go home, relax and put this bullshit behind you." Antonio was determined to make his friend understand that he had a friend in him. "You're not alone Reese," he said, "Beside bru, them losers ain't nothing but a bunch of assholes and haters."

"Thanks, Antonio, I appreciate your support." Reese still felt embarrassed but Antonio's words lightened the mood. "You're a true friend."

"Reese, I told you before, whenever you need me, I got your back."

"Thanks man," Reese said, as he got inside his car and drove off. He was so out of it when he got home, he didn't even notice Mike in the window trying to get his attention as he got out the car.

He walked into the house and unconsciously slammed the heavy wooden door behind him. As he turned towards the living room, Reese noticed Mike hurrying down the spiral staircase.

"Hey baby, how was your day?"

"It was okay, Baby Boy," Reese wrapped Mike in his arms. "How about you?" Reese asked, "How was your day?"

"I talked to Tariff today," Mike said, taking a few steps

back. "He said there wouldn't be any point in coming to visit them because they'll be home in a couple of weeks."

"I thought they were going to be touring straight through Christmas."

"That was the plan, but it appears they will get a two week break, so all the guys will be coming home."

"That's cool, I miss my boyz." Reese looked off in the distance not really focused on what he and Mike were talking about. "It will be good to see them."

Mike took Reese by the hand, and led him to the living room and sat him down on the huge sofa. He could feel Reese's tension and felt it was time to find out what was bothering him. "What's wrong, Reese?"

"Nothing. I'm okay," Reese replied.

"I can feel the tension running all through you. Reese, you haven't been yourself lately. I want you to tell me what's going on, and I want you to tell me now."

"So you think you know me?" Reese stared into Mike's brown eyes.

"And don't you forget it either. Now tell me, what's up?"

"They know. They know and their coming after me."

"Know what Reese? Who knows what and who's coming after you?"

"The guys on the team. They know I'm gay!"

"How?" Mike stared in bewilderment. "Are you sure?" Mike stumbled over question after question without giving Reese time to answer.

"Well, remember the day I went to meet with Antonio? He told me that a source of his who works for the newspaper pre-warned him that a writer was publishing a story about me."

Mike thought back. 'It was that reporter at the police station that day.' Mike looked at Reese. "You said it wasn't over that day when you saw that reporter in the police station. Man, why didn't you tell me? You've been going through this on your own?"

"I don't know. I didn't want you to worry. Some pranksters have been leaving notes in my locker, and I had a run in on the practice field today with the guy who's probably behind the notes and things."

"Reese, I'm your partner. I'm here for you through the good and bad. I always got your back."

Reese realized at that very moment just how much he needed Mike. He was with someone he could trust and didn't have to put up a brave front. Reese could feel his eyes pool with tears of pain, as he stared into Mike's eyes. He knew that Mike could sense the fear that surrounded those tears. Mike gently took his hand and wiped away the tears that streamed down his face. "You'll be okay, sweetheart. You're strong and so am I. There isn't anything we can't get through together."

"You're right, baby boy," Reese leaned over and gave Mike a loving hug, then a kiss. "What would I do without you?"

Mike didn't respond with words, he simply held Reese tighter and together the flames of the two lovers burned as one.

Chapter 19
Larry & Tonya

Larry sat slumped down in his car down the street from Tonya's house, watching her as she got in her car and drove off. Larry picked up his cell and hit the speed dial.

"Good Morning sweetie! How you doing?"

Once Tonya recovered from the shock of hearing Larry's voice, she eyed the neighborhood suspiciously.

"Yeah baby, it's me." Larry smiled inwardly at Tonya's reaction. "I want to see you when I get off work tonight."

"Larry, I told you before that it's over between us. Why do you keep calling me?"

"I love you, girl, and in time you'll feel the same way."

The phone went dead. Tonya hung up on him. Insulted, he glared at his phone in anger. His anger raged like a fire burning out of control. He jumped from his car and began to pace back and forth beside his vehicle while talking to his reflection in the metallic paint job. 'I can't believe this bitch had the nerve to hang up on me,' he was thinking. 'She don't know who she fucking with, I'll kill that dumb whore.'

As Larry paced, he thought back to a time when he and Tonya were kicking it on the regular. He'd locked himself out of Tonya's house. Afterwards, he hid a spare key under a flower pot on the back porch in case it happened again. With anticipation, Larry went around to the back of the house and headed up the stairs and sure enough, bingo, the key was right where he'd left it. He was glad that he never mentioned the key to Tonya.

Larry looked around casually to make sure no one was watching him. He held his breath then tried the key. His attention was suddenly drawn to a beeping sound coming from the living room. His mind raced, as he rushed through the house towards the front door where the alarm pad was. "Six, four, seven, three," he mumbled, the urgency of his footsteps brought him to the point of no return.

Larry typed the four digits into the security system pad cautiously. It was comforting hearing the voice from the system, "system un-armed," it said.

Larry relaxed. He spotted a bowl sitting on a table next to the front door. "This can't be," he whispered to himself. He fished a key ring filled with keys from the bowl and began to try the front door locks. The first and second key didn't work. The third try was successful. The key fit the lock perfectly and now he had the key to the front door as well. Larry reset the alarm system and rushed from the house to his car. He hurried to the nearest Home Depot where he had the two keys duplicated. Within twenty minutes he was back inside the privacy of Tonya's home. 'This shit worked like a charm,' he thought.

Larry re-set the alarm for the second time. He retraced his steps until the final move of putting the back door key under the flower pot had been made. His footsteps had a bounce, as he rounded the corner of Tonya's house and walked up the street to his car. Turning the ignition, a sinister grin crept across Larry's face, as the rumble of his engine turned to a purr. 'If that ain't the dumbest bitch, I ever met.' Larry pressed down hard on the gas pedal and the sound of genuine laughter filled the interior of his ride. Larry was satisfied.

Chapter 20
Ricky, Jay

On his way home Ricky stopped by the local sports bar. The establishment was very large and because of its popularity the place stayed crowded. When Ricky took his seat, he wasn't surprised to see sports fanatics grouped around the large flat screen televisions that hung in just about every available space in the bar.

The bartender was a skinny man with straight brown hair pulled back in a pony tail and a thick mustache that damn near covered his face. He could have been cast perfectly as a bartender in a western movie.

"You been waiting long?" Jay's familiar voice came mysteriously from out of nowhere. "Sorry I'm late, but traffic was crazy as usual," Jay said, as he took a seat across from Ricky.

"Well, at least you made it in one piece, that's a good thing."

"How long you been here?" Jay asked.

"I actually just sat down."

"There must be a party here tonight or something."

"Or something," Ricky started, but his thoughts were interrupted when he saw one of the attorneys he worked with headed in his direction.

Jay saw that Ricky's attention was focused on this older white dude in a suit. "You know that guy over there?"

"Yeah, he's one of the attorneys at the firm."

"Well, looks like he's on his way over."

"Hey Ricky! I didn't know you hung out here."

"I come here every now and then. By the way, this is a very good friend of mine. Fred this is Jay. Jay, Fred."

"Nice to meet you, Fred," Jay said, as he stood up and

shook his hand.

"You guys don't mind if I have a seat for a minute or two. They are about to clear off my table. I'm meeting my son here to watch the NBA game." Fred took a seat before Ricky or Jay could even respond.

"Sure, Fred, no problem," Ricky said, as he watched Jay out the corner of his eye.

Fred waved for the waitress to come over. "A round of beers please and put them on my tab."

"Fred, you don't have to do that."

'How rude is that?' Jay thought, as he forced a smile onto his face. 'Yeah, he does have to do that.'

"Come on, Ricky, I think I can afford a few beers." Fred laughed.

Ricky and Jay smiled at each other before they turned toward the jumbo screen, trying to hide their annoyance. They were talking about the Houston Bullets and showed some snippets of Reese and his head coach. Ricky and Jay both got quiet trying to hear what they were saying. Their attention was broken when the waitress returned with their beers. "Thank you Miss," Fred said to the waitress. "You know they need to get rid of that dude," he said, setting his beer down.

"Why would you say that?" Jay asked, looking directly at Fred.

"Y'all ain't heard," Fred sipped his beer. "I got a couple of clients on the team and there's a rumor going around that the guy is a big ole queer."

"So you believe everything you hear?" Jay asked, trying not to cuss this man out.

"Naw, I don't son, but what I heard about that guy came from a very reliable source." Fred twisted his beer bottle between his hands.

"First of all sir, I'm not your son and what does his sexuality have to do with anything? He's doing very well on the field." Jay pierced Fred with an intense stare.

"That queer you're talking about was one of the top running backs last year; so what if he's gay," Ricky said. "If you look at his stats, you'll see he's a hell of a ball player."

"The best in the league!" Jay said proudly.

"I don't care how good his stats are or how well he runs the ball, the NFL ain't got no place for people like him. I wouldn't want to be on his team," Fred stated with obvious personal conviction.

Jay's anger had reached the boiling point. Ricky could see that Jay was about to explode, and he realized that Jay was keeping his composure out of respect for him.

"Well, if I played ball I wouldn't be worried about a man's sexual preference," Ricky said. He glanced over at Jay and could see that he was about to go raw on this attorney. At this point Ricky didn't care because after Fred's last comment, Ricky was feeling the same as Jay.

Jay was about to say something to Fred when the waitress rescued him.

"Sir, your table is ready."

Fred stood up and extended his hand to Jay. Jay looked at his hand and turned away. Fred then extended his hand in Ricky's direction. Ricky stood up, but instead of shaking Fred's hand. He took a deep breath before speaking.

"Just so you know," Ricky started, "that guy Reese that you were just bad mouthing, is a very close friend of ours. Do me a favor when you get home tonight, Fred. Take a good look in the mirror because you're the only queer I see." Ricky sat back down leaving Fred standing and looking like a fool. "You ready to order, baby?" Ricky asked turning toward Jay.

"Yeah, I am, sweetheart," Jay said, as he looked up at Fred, smiled and winked.

Ricky and Jay both watched Fred turn and walk away without saying a word.

"Hey, order me the usual. I'm going outside to call Mike to find out what's going on with Reese." Jay grabbed his cell phone and headed outside.

"Mike this is Jay. What's up? Where's Reese?" Jay paced back and forth in front of the restaurant.

"Hello to you too, Jay!" Mike responded with a touch of

sarcasm.

"I'm sorry, Mike." Jay was unaware of his rudeness. "How you doing?"

"I'm good, sitting here thinking while Reese is taking a nap. He had a rough day." Mike looked at Reese sleeping. 'He looks so peaceful and innocent sleeping in the fetal position,' he thought. "Things have been kind of crazy for Reese lately."

"So it's true then!" Jay snapped.

"What are you talking about Jay?" Is what true?"

"Ricky and I are out having dinner, and one of the lawyers who work's at his firm, said he heard a rumor that Reese is gay. The asshole didn't have a clue that we knew Reese personally."

"Jay, tell me you didn't do anything stupid?"

"I kept my composure." Jay exhaled a deep breath and for the first time he realized how uptight he was. "I'm trying to be a little bit more mature about things these days so that man can thank his lucky stars for that."

"Good man, I'm proud of you."

"I appreciate that, Mike but I didn't call to talk about me. I called to talk about Reese."

"Reese has been dealing with a lot of pranks and stuff by the players. The word is slowly getting out. Jay, he's trying to put on a brave front but I can see right through it."

"We need to get the boyz together. Reese needs us."

"He needs us now more than ever," Mike said.

"We will figure something out. I love you Mike and when Reese wakes up give him my love. Jay hung up the phone and quickly scanned through his phone book and dialed. "Hello." Jay heard the comfort he was looking for when he heard the sound of Demetrious' voice.

"Demetrious, what's up man?"

"Hey, Jay! What's up with you, chump?"

"Everything is going well. How's Chuck's tour going?"

"Man, it's off the chain." Demetrious felt a rush of excitement fill his chest. "Chuck has a large fan base. He got women throwing their panties on stage."

"Are you serious? If only they knew." Jay laughed.

"For real, so how's the gang doing? Is everybody okay?"

"Well, everybody is doing good, I guess."

"What do you mean, you guess? What's really up, Jay?" Demetrious demanded. He recognized that familiar tone in Jay's voice.

"Well, Mike really didn't get into it to much over the phone. I didn't want to push too much, but the gist of it is, the secret about Reese being gay has gotten out and some of his teammates are trying to get him to quit."

"How did that happened?" Demetrious asked.

"I'm thinking it goes back to that incident at the police station."

Both were silent waiting for the other to speak. "We have one more city to hit, after that we'll get a two week vacation before going on the road again. We'll be home in a few days."

"That's good man, cause I miss you guys and I know Reese can use all of our support."

"I hate to cut you short but a few of the dancers are here for haircuts and I need to trim Chuck up too. He has an interview this evening and there's gonna be a lot of picture taking."

"Love you, D."

"Love you too, Jay, and stay out of trouble. I'll call Mike and Reese this evening."

Chapter 21
Jay, Daunte, Curtis

Jay drove up to the prison's huge gate. A heavyset security guard, dressed in a uniform two sizes too small, waved him to a halt. 'Who the hell is this big sloppy dude?' Jay thought. 'And if something jumps off who in the hell is he going to catch?'

"How can I help you today, sir?" The fat guard eyed Jay suspiciously through the open window.

"I'm here to visit Mr. Daunte Jacobs."

"I need to see your license, son," the guard said sarcastically.

"My name is Jay Reynolds, thank you sir," Jay responded handing the guard his license.

"Follow this road right here, the guard pointed, until you reach a dead end. From there you will be guided by signs, if you can read. You shouldn't get lost." The guard smiled as he gave back the license.

"Good help must be hard to find." Jay snatched his license and drove off. 'Fat Fuck,' he thought.

Jay observed the deplorable buildings that loomed on both sides of the tar road. 'How could anyone expect to be rehabilitated living in these conditions?' He pulled into a parking space across from the south building. Just as he got out of his car, he noticed a large brick tower that looked to be a hundred feet tall, with two guards standing and holding what appeared to be machine guns.

Jay walked across the parking lot and just as he stepped on to the sidewalk a set of double wide glass doors swung open automatically. The first thing to catch his eye was a skinny old white woman who sat at a computer screen behind a desk that looked big enough to swallow up her small frame.

"Excuse me Miss." Jay leaned over the counter.

"Good afternoon, young man. What can I help you with?" The little woman's voice was just as fragile as she was.

"I'm here to visit Mr. Daunte Jacobs."

"What is your name, sir?" The old lady looked around, fidgeting on the keyboard one letter at a time.

"Jay...Jay Reynolds." Jay was becoming annoyed and impatient with the old lady.

"Oh, here you are. Sir, I need to see your identification." Jay pulled out his license once again and handed it to the woman. She glanced at it, and with her trembling hand she returned the ID.

"Sir, do you have a cell phone on you?"

"No ma'am, I left it in my car."

"Ok Mr. Reynolds, just walk through the double doors on the right and stop by the security station as soon as you walk through."

'How could anyone sleep in this place with all the clanging of metal going on?' he thought. Finally making it through, Jay sat anxiously waiting for Daunte to appear.

'It aint no privacy for conversations here,' he thought, as he sat in the booth that had a phone on the wall. Jay tried to get comfortable on the hard plastic chair that looked like it came from a welfare office. The air was filled with the scent of a musty locker room. At the same time everything that Mia had told him was playing over and over in his head.

'Look at this place! How could a sane man expect to hold on to his sanity once he's been subjected to these conditions?' Jay thought, as he started to observe the visitors from all walks of life who came to visit their loved ones.

After about fifteen minutes, Daunte finally walked through the door in his prison issued clothing. Jay smiled when Daunte spotted him. Daunte picked up the phone that hung on his side and motioned for Jay to pick up his.

"I'm probably the last person you expected to see, huh?"

As happy as Daunte was to see his friend, the thought of being raped and the possibility of being HIV positive consumed so much of him mentally and emotionally that Daunte sat across from him totally void of any facial expression.

Jay knew immediately that something was wrong with his buddy and the more Daunte avoided his trademark of looking you straight in the eye, the more apparent it became to Jay that something tragically had damaged his boy.

"Daunte, man look at me." Daunte looked in every direction but the one that would bring him eye to eye with Jay.

Daunte finally raised his eyes up until he and Jay were eye to eye.

"Man." Jay stared in astonishment, "Daunte you look so different, what's going on?"

"Jay, take a look around you. If you had to experience this, you would look different too. Twenty-four-seven, nothing but niggas…Then again maybe you wouldn't." Daunte regretted what he'd just said no sooner than it left his mouth.

"I talked to Mia. She's is really worried about you." Jay ignored Daunte's sarcastic remark.

"I told her I'm okay," Daunte snapped, "She just won't leave well enough alone."

"Daunte, this is me you talking to. I know you, and something is different about you. Are the inmates here giving you a hard time?" They both sat in silence; unspoken words filling the space between them.

"Daunte, talk to me, man! What's going on with you?"

"I told you Jay!" Daunte shifted in his seat. "Everything is fine, shit! Why you keep pressing me?"

"Now I can see what Mia was talking about. You're snappy, irritable and just down right nasty."

"What do you mean, Jay?" Daunte was getting paranoid that Jay might put everything together. "I just want to get out of here, man."

"Yeah, this place is turning you into somebody completely different. It's in your eyes, it's in your posture and it's in your disposition. You have a sadness in your eyes, a sadness that I've never seen before."

Jay waited for Daunte to come out of his shell but when Daunte wouldn't speak, Jay continued to press. "Daunte, you're trying very hard to hide something from me and you want to know why I say that?"

"No, but I'm quite sure you're going to tell me. What the hell are you, some kind of psychologist now? You know what's going on inside my head?" Daunte leaned forward in his chair. "Well, let's trade places, Mr. Psychologist, and you try living like a caged animal. Let's see how you would feel after being in here for twenty-four hours!"

"Daunte, you're right. I can't even imagine what you're going through in here," Jay said, as he eyed his surroundings, "but what I do know is that we are best friends and I'm here to help you in any way possible. And through all the things that have kicked off in the past, I would have hoped we'd grown up and learned from it so that we could leave the past, in the past."

"Jay, believe me. I have put the past to rest," Daunte said sincerely. "All I am trying to do now is to get through this shit and back to my life with Mia."

"That's good, Daunte, but remember what got you here. It's that temper of yours. You need to get it under control! So, again I say, talk to me. Tell me what's got you all bent out of control!"

Daunte debated coming clean with what Carlton had done to him. Finally, he looked up and lied. "Jay, there ain't nothing wrong. I'm just not used to this kind of shit."

"Okay. I'll accept that for now." Jay stood up and looked down at Daunte intensely. "But understand this, I'll be back soon. Real soon and when I get back, I want answers to what's really going on because the Daunte that I know wouldn't have just sat there and looked a friend in the eye and flat out lied."

'Damn!' Daunte was thinking, 'He knows I'm lying.' He hung his head in shame. "Jay?" Daunte's voice was barely above a whisper.

"Yeah bruh" Jay responded, "What's up?"

"How is Mia?" Daunte asked.

"She's worried about you. Mia is really upset." Jay sat back down. "Daunte how do you think she is?" Jay didn't wait for Daunte to respond, he continued. "She doesn't know what to do to help you. She loves you, but you're pushing her away and it's killing her mentally, physically and spiritually."

"I know, Jay and I'm sorry," Daunte said, as he thought about how he treated her during their last visit.

"I'm not the one you should be apologizing to. And another thing, if you're worried about Mia and Ricky, don't be." Ricky and I are very much in love with one another, beside if Mia was going to cheat on you, which she wouldn't, but just for the sake of argument, believe me, it would not be with Ricky." Jay saw Daunte begin to let his defenses down. "Daunte, look at what happened the last time you assumed that Mia was cheating on you. That girl loves you, D and she's proven that. Hell, you both worship the ground that each of you walks on."

"I know, Jay, but I've been straight trippin man. Mia is my world and there's nothing I wouldn't do for her. My life and death is solely for that woman plus I know she's got my back." Daunte tried to crack a smile for Jay's benefit.

"Okay, I'm in a bad place right now. I'm trying to get back to my old self, it's just hard."

Jay wasn't sure what Daunte meant, but he knew he felt bad about the situation. "Just don't push the ones that love you away," Jay said.

"When did you become so wise and mature?"

"Over the last year, I guess I've learned a lot from my friends and I've learned how to forgive. Don't get me wrong I'm still a work in progress."

"I guess we're all a work in progress."

"Yeah, D. I just got to get my mouth under control. It's taking some time, but I'm working on it."

They both shared a laugh at Jay's revelation, then Daunte became serious again.

"Jay, can you do me a favor?"

"Sure D, what do you need?"

"Could you call Mia for me and tell her that I'm sorry and tell her," Daunte swallowed to hold his emotions in place, "Tell Mia that I love her."

"I think she needs to hear that from you directly. Mia

needs to hear that straight from you." Jay eyed Daunte to see if he understood where he was coming from. "What I will do, Daunte, is tell her to be expecting your call."

"Yeah, you're right. That's exactly what you should do." Daunte understood. "Thanks. I appreciate that."

Jay stood up just as the correctional officer signaled to all visitors that visiting time was over.

"Oh! Yeah, Daunte!" Jay yelled out to Daunte, as he was being led away. "Don't forget about what I expect the next time I come to see you."

"Expect. What do you expect?"

"Answers and remember that friends are good listeners."

"I gotcha, Jay."

"Keep your head up D," Jay said, as he watched the guard lead him away.

Daunte walked back to his cell with one thought on his mind. 'How would Jay have accepted the truth about his being raped?' Daunte just kept wishing that someone would wake him from this horrible nightmare. His thoughts were interrupted by the sound of Curtis' voice.

"How did your visit with Mia go?"

"It wasn't Mia, it was my boy Jay, the guy I told you about."

"Oh yeah, the gay dude."

Daunte knew Curtis didn't mean anything by his comment, so he ignored it. "He came to check on me for Mia and he also wanted to let me know how worried Mia has been over me."

"Did you tell him about the rape?" Curtis was curious to hear.

"Curtis, I can barely say it to myself, so how do you expect me to tell him. I hope this Ms. Taylor, you speak so highly of can help me because this is wearing me down. I feel like I'm about to snap. I can't eat. I can't sleep."

"Daunte, don't worry about it. Ms. Taylor is very good at her job. She helped me when I couldn't help myself."

"I hope you're right Curtis." Daunte didn't want to talk about it anymore. "Hey Curtis man, I'm going to go to my cell and chill out for a while. I'll catch up with you later okay."

"A'ight man. I'll see you later."

Daunte lay across his bunk and began to think about Mia the minute he was alone. He couldn't help but think about all of what Jay had said to him about Mia. She was definitely his ride or die chick. The thought of how Mia had stuck by him through everything was amazing. Daunte also didn't want to think about where he would be if Curtis wasn't there helping him. 'Thank God for Curtis' help. If it wasn't for him, I probably would have killed dude by now.'

Chapter 22
Daunte, Curtis & Carlton

After hanging around in the recreation room for a while, Curtis decided to head to Daunte's cell and see how he was doing. He knew that Daunte was taking this rape incident hard and he knew the more time Daunte had to think about it the more he would wallow in self pity.

"Hey-yo, Daunte!" Curtis said, as he stood out side of Daunte's cell calling his name.

Daunte was so wrapped up in his thoughts that he didn't even hear the echo.

"Daunte!" Curtis shouted.

Daunte snapped his head around to face Curtis. "Man, I'm sorry. I was deep in thought."

"You still thinking about the rape?"

"Man, I'm trying not to, but I can't seem to shake it."

"Daunte, man, don't focus so much energy on that shit. Like I told you before, everything is going to work out just fine. I know the feelings and the thoughts you're having. I did the exact same things that you're doing now. You're still going to see Ms. Taylor aren't you?"

"Curtis, man, I don't know how I feel about giving a woman a blow by blow account about how some freaky mutha fucka got his rocks off pounding me in the ass."

"I'm telling you she will make this easy for you. She has a way of connecting with you. It's hard to explain."

"I hope you're right."

"Man, Curtis is always right," Curtis said, flashing a smile, as he bragged on himself. "Now let's get out of this cell and go pump some iron. It will help you release some of that pent up frustration.

"Yeah, I guess you got a point," Daunte said, as he stood up.

"Besides, that flabby body of yours could use the help," Curtis joked.

"Who you calling flabby?" Daunte grabbed Curtis in a bear hug.

The two laughed and headed to the gym. 'What the hell is happening to me?' Curtis thought as he looked and saw that the small encounter with Daunte got him aroused.

An hour or so later a voice boomed across the intercom asking all inmates to report back to their cells. Curtis grabbed his shirt, as he and Daunte headed back to their cells. When they reached the recreation room their moods changed as they caught a glimpse of Carlton.

"Well, Well, Well, look at what we have here fellas, the happy camper and his bitch!"

"Fuck you, Carlton!" Curtis glared angrily.

"Fuck me!" Carlton responded mockingly, "Naw man," he said, "I already did that to your boy! Was it good for you?" Carlton asked, as he licked his lips.

Daunte lunged at Carlton, with both fist balled into tight knots. He was blinded by his anger and was prepared to murder Carlton if that was what it would take to get some satisfaction, but Curtis grabbed Daunte's arm just in time.

"Daunte, man, fuck that joker, he just trying to provoke you, but don't worry, I'll be handling some business with him real soon."

"That ass was nice and tight, just like a virgin getting hit for the very first time." Curtis ignored Carlton's last statement to Daunte. "Matter of fact," Carlton continued to fuel the situation with a fiery torment, my dick gets hard just thinking about that good ass of yours."

"Carlton, you fucked up bitch and you don't even realize it," Daunte shouted, "But you will, mutha fucker, your ass is going to see the light."

"OOOh, I'm supposed to be real scared!"

"Yeah! You should be. What I got in store for your ass don't even come in no package bitch, but you gonna get one hell of a surprise."

"Man, I will fuck you up!" Carlton said, as he stepped within inches of Daunte's face, looking at him menacingly. "You don't know who you fucking with!"

"Fuck with me nigga." Daunte took a step and got all up in Carlton's face, then turned to walk away.

"Just let me know when you ready for some more dick!" Carlton said, as he and his buddies pushed past Curtis and Daunte.

Curtis and Daunte watched Carlton and his crew walk down the tier until they all turned and went into Carlton's cell. Curtis turned to Daunte. "Yo, D, what the hell you talking bout? What plans you got in store for him?"

"Shit, Curtis, I ain't talking about nothing. It just sounded like the right thing to say. You're the one that said don't let them know they got to me. But one day his ass is gonna be mine. Well, maybe not his ass." Daunte couldn't help but chuckle at what he had just said.

"Anyway, don't worry man, I got this. Carlton won't even see it coming," Curtis said. The look on Curtis' face told Daunte that there wasn't room for questions or objections.

The next morning Daunte sat outside of Ms. Taylor's office looking around. 'Where in the hell is Curtis?' he wondered. 'He suppose to be here with me. I can't do this by myself.' Just as Daunte looked up, the guard brought Curtis through the door.

Curtis could see that Daunte was a ball of nerves. "I told you I would go with you man."

"Bru, I was worried for a second."

As the door to Ms. Taylor's office opened up, the guys became quiet. "Hello Curtis," she said with her soft feminine voice. "You must be Daunte. Nice to meet you. Please let's go into my office."

Daunte looked at Ms. Taylor and thought she looked too young to be a head doctor. Her hair was long and flowing. She reminded Daunte of Mia. She stood about 5' 8" inches tall, and when she walked the movement of her body demanded attention.

You could tell the black pant suit she wore was tailored for her and only her.

"Come in, gentlemen, have a seat."

Curtis nudged Daunte. "Go ahead man. Don't worry. It'll be okay."

"Curtis, nice to see you again. Hopefully everything is going well with you," she said, as she touched the rim of her reading glasses with her perfectly manicured nails.

"I'm doing okay, Ms. Taylor. I hope all is good with you too."

"I'm glad to hear that Curtis, and all is well with me to." Ms. Taylor shifted her gaze to Daunte. She wanted to start on safe territory. "Mr. Jacobs do you like sports?" Ms. Taylor started the conversation with general questions. It was her way of getting Daunte to open up a little bit.

Daunte was thrown off by her question, but it did work. Daunte mentioned he was a Dallas Cowboy fan when he saw the autographed picture of Terrell Owens on her wall. As they talked, she said she was a big fan of his and at the last game she went to, she was able to get an autographed picture. She saw that Daunte was getting comfortable. "I see you're only with us for a short time Mr. Jacobs. What are your plans when you get out of here."

"My plans are to marry the woman that I love as well as get my life back."

"Sounds good Daunte. I wish more guys in this place had things planned and organized before leaving here."

"I have strong motives that encourage me."

"What's your motivation?"

"I have a beautiful woman waiting for me and I can't wait to get back to her." Daunte was opening up a little more. He had even forgotten Curtis was in the room. All his attention was focused on Ms. Taylor.

"That's good, Daunte. I'm sorry, you don't mind me calling you Daunte do you?"

"No ma'am, that's fine."

Ms. Taylor shifted to a more professional demeanor. "Daunte, I don't usually allow other inmates to sit in on a session with a client, but since Curtis is here at your request, I'll permit it."

"Thank you." Daunte replied, "I really appreciate it."

"Why don't you fill me in on why you're here today?"

Daunte immediately became uncomfortable. "Ms. Taylor, I apologize for wasting your time." Daunte got up to leave.

Curtis grabbed his arm. "Go ahead D. You can do this." Curtis looked at Ms. Taylor for some support.

"Daunte, let me reassure you that anything that you discuss with me will stay in this room. Her Doctor's face took on a loving mothers concern. "Have a seat Daunte, and start where ever you feel most comfortable," Ms. Taylor said, "You can trust us." She shifted her eyes to Curtis then pointed to herself.

"I was in the shower." Daunte paused, taking in a deep breath of courage. "These guys," he continued, "They came in the shower. Daunte couldn't go on as the degradation of being punked brought a tear to his eye.

"Daunte." Ms. Taylor called his name, "Did these guys…did they rape you?"

Daunte slowly, in a painstaking effort, let his head bob up and down in agreement.

Curtis could see the pain his buddy was feeling as he sat back fighting his own emotions, but he knew he had to be strong for his boy.

"Daunte, how did that make you feel?" Ms. Taylor asked.

"What kind of question is that?"

"Daunte, I can't even imagine what your going through, but I am here to help you get through this and on with your life." Ms. Taylor clipped the end of her thought and waited for Daunte to fill in the empty silence that came.

"Okay, Ms. Taylor," Daunte whispered. "I definitely need some help."

"Daunte the first step in getting past all this is realizing that you need help. We need to schedule you for twice a week sessions. Then I'll schedule you to have a HIV test immediately. If it's negative the first time then we will wait six months and have the test again and if that one is negative you should be fine. I know this is a lot to digest, but do you have any more questions?"

"No, not right now." Daunte's gaze was steady.

"Daunte, at some point you should give me the names of the inmates so we can deal with them accordingly."

"I'm sorry, Ms. Taylor, but the one thing I have learned in here is snitchers don't survive."

Ms. Taylor gave Daunte a knowing look that implied she was well aware of the rules and retribution that they lived by. 'And the punishment for snitchers,' she recalled, was death.

Curtis chimed in. "Ms. Taylor, Daunte here actually should be in another cell block. He shouldn't be housed with the type of prisoners in our area. He was told they were looking into it, but nothing has happened yet."

"Really? Okay, I will look into that and see what I can find out."

"Thanks, Ms. Taylor." Both responded in unison.

"Daunte, if you have any questions before our next session, don't hesitate to contact me, I have an open door policy. Besides the more you're open with me the quicker the healing process will be."

"Thanks Doc, for being so understanding," Daunte said, shaking Ms. Taylor's hand.

Chapter 23
Curtis & Carlton

Early the next day, Curtis walked into his cell from another day of work in the prison Tag Shop. He lay down across his bunk and glanced over at the bottle of lotion that was a third full of the T-eleven liquid. A couple more trips and the bottle will have just enough liquid in it to do what he had planned. The plastic bag he had inserted in his rectum had leaked inside him. Now he was sticking ointment up his ass three times a day to fight the irritation. 'Carlton you're ass is going to pay,' he thought.

Curtis drifted off to sleep, then woke up suddenly.

As his eyes focused, he felt a chill down his spine when he noticed Carlton standing in the door of his cell. Immediately he positioned himself in a strategic defense position.

"What the hell you doing here?"

Carlton just stood there and threw Curtis a kiss.

Curtis got up in Carlton's face. "Don't bring your ass over to my cell anymore!" Curtis snapped. He wanted to yank his new archenemy by the throat.

"What!" Carlton never flinched. "What the hell you going to do, bitch, if I don't move?"

"Carlton man, your ass is going to burn in hell by the time I get finished with you. Your ass owes a debt that my niggah and I are going to make sure you pay in full." Curtis spat out a ball of phlegm in Carlton's face. "I can promise you that."

"Aw, so now you done grown some balls?" Carlton smirked at Curtis' insult. "Think you running shit," Carlton said, as he slowly wiped the spit from his face. "I'm the one who always ran the show and you need to know ain't nothing changed. Curtis, you just like your bitch ass friend Daunte. When you decide to come at me, bru you better come correct 'cause, I ain't gonna be fucking with you," Carlton said leaning over, trying to give Curtis a peck on the cheek.

Immediately, Curtis leaned back. "No mutha fucker! You save those kisses for your boys."

"I'll be seeing you around niggah."

Curtis could feel the adrenaline rush. He knew Carlton had to be stopped. He caught a glance of the bottle of lotion. 'It's time for me to put my plan into action and fuck Carlton's life up,' he thought.

Chapter 24
Ricky, Jay & Wil

It was an early Saturday morning. The slight breeze coming through the crack in the window caused the blinds to move letting the sound of the neighbor's lawnmower filter through.

"So what do you want to do after work?" Ricky asked, Jay as he sipped his coffee.

"I can't believe I have to work today and on a Saturday of all days."

"Yeah, man, I know, but at least it's not a whole day," Ricky replied.

"Why don't we go and pick out new furniture for that spare room after I get off."

"That's a good idea," Ricky said, as he took a bite of his toast. "I can drop you off at work, and you can call me when you're finished, then I'll come pick you up, we can go have some lunch, and check out some furniture."

"Sounds like a plan," Jay said, as he picked up his ringing cell phone and took a glance at his caller ID. "Wil again!" He became a little irritated.

"Is everything okay, Jay?" Ricky keyed in on Jay's irritation.

"Yeah. Everything is cool. Why you ask?"

"You look tense. Who was that on the phone?"

"Oh it was nobody. I'm okay." Their conversation was interrupted again, but this time it was Ricky's phone.

"Hello." Ricky pressed the phone to the side of his head. "This is Ricky."

Jay got up and began to clear the table hoping that Ricky would just drop the questions about his last call.

"Who was that?" Jay asked.

"That was that dude I work out with now. He was checking to make sure I was still going to workout this afternoon," Ricky said, as he stood up and took his dishes over to the sink where Jay stood.

"Do I need to be worried about this dude?" Jay's insecurity crept through.

Ricky slipped his arms around Jay's waist and kissed him deeply and passionately. "Now, does that seem like you have something to worry about?"

Jay smiled at Ricky's attempt to reassure him.

"You may have to be concerned about other things, but another man ain't one of them. You stuck with me." Ricky nibbled on Jay's bottom lip. "Oh yeah, man, I was so proud of you the other night for keeping your composure when that colleague of mine started poppin off all that nonsense about Reese."

"You're a good influence on me and I'm trying to approach life's situations with more maturity."

Ricky pressed his growing manhood against Jay's thigh. "See what you done did. We better get you to work or you may not have a job next week."

A half hour later, Rick dropped Jay off at work then headed to the gym. Just as Ricky pulled into the gym's parking lot, he became distracted by a honking horn. It was Wil climbing from his car.

"Hey, my man! You ready for a good workout?" Wil asked, as he approached Ricky's car.

"Yeah. You know it, man!"

"Well, let's get in and get it on," Wil said, as he slid his arm around Ricky's neck.

Ricky felt an uncomfortable chill wash over him.

"Oh snap!" Ricky camouflaged his reason for slipping Wil's grip. "I left my workout gloves in the car."

"You definitely will need those."

Ricky walked back to his car and opened the truck pretending to be looking for his gloves. He took a couple of deep breaths in an effort to shake the queasy feeling that crept through his body from Wil's touch. He closed the trunk and walked back over to where he had left Wil standing. He kept some distance between himself and Wil. The two men headed for the gym entrance and Ricky used the moment to clear his head of the thoughts that he was having about his workout buddy. 'Man I need to stop tripping,' he thought.

Ricky and Wil walked, with hurried footsteps, to the locker room to change clothes. Ricky started to undress, but was completely unaware that Wil was admiring his honey brown skin. Ricky had a well-chiseled body. Wil could see why Ricky's jeans hugged his ass and thighs so perfectly.

Wil peeped the crotch area of Ricky's low cut, tight fitting briefs. He noticed the silky strands of pubic hairs peaking over the rim. Wil's dick started to grow rigid. 'Damn this man is sexy,' Wil thought.

"Hey, Wil!" Ricky felt that uncomfortable feeling he had in the parking lot earlier. "Are you okay?" he asked.

"I'm cool, man." Wil snapped out of his trance. "Why you ask?"

"It just seems like your mind is someplace else and besides that, you're staring at me."

"Oh naw, it's all good Ricky. I was just daydreaming." Wil had one agenda and that was to get back at Jay. 'What better way to get back at Jay than to sleep with his sexy ass man?' Wil thought.

"Well, Ricky, let's get our workout on 'cause I got this real hot date with this bad honey I met." Wil figured that would throw him off. He knew he had to proceed with his plan with the utmost caution.

Chapter 25
Larry, Barbara & Tonya

The room was dark and the wind was stirring the curtains around slightly as Larry lay across Tonya's bed enjoying the breeze coming through the window. He spotted her nightgown lying on the arm of a chair a couple feet from the open window. Larry stood up, crossed the room and when he picked up the sweet scented material, he pressed it to his nose and inhaled deeply. The scent on the gown became intoxicating to him. He started to reminisce about the times that he had made love to her. Larry walked back over to the bed, laying the gown neatly across it. He imagined that it was Tonya herself lying on the bed, waiting for him to mount her. Larry's dick started to grow hard and the sensation drew his hands to the area. He began to rub his manhood with a sexual yearning that called his name over and over. He eased down his zipper and wrapped his dick in his fingers and began to stroke it. The more he stroked, the more he thought about Tonya and the harder his penis got.

Larry was captured mentally and physically. All of a sudden, he felt constricted by his jeans. Larry caught the clasp of his pants between two fingers and clipping the button with professionalism his jeans dropped down around his ankles. He stepped out of the pants, one leg at a time, and climbed back on the bed and rubbed the nightgown right in the place where Tonya's breast would be if she were actually wearing it. His fantasy had taken total control, and the more his imagination told him that Tonya was beneath his touch, the more aroused he became. His dick was brushing against the mattress, sending sensation after sensation through out his body.

Larry's moans of gratification were getting louder and

louder, as he continued to masturbate while lying on the bed, with one leg thrown across the night gown. He could feel his dick oozing some of it's nectar out on the nightgown.

"Ah shit baby, you feel so good!" Larry said out loud, getting closer and closer to a climax.

Larry jerked the thickness of his penis harder and harder until more and more of his nectar climbed to the surface. He moaned and groaned. The waves of sensation allowed the head of his dick to swell like the steam in a tea kettle about to erupt. "Aw, shit!" Larry's dick exploded, spewing hot semen all over Tonya's nightgown and bed. He collapsed, exhausted on the bed, as if he and Tonya had just engaged in a session of lovemaking. Within minutes, Larry had dozed off to sleep.

A couple of hours had passed when Larry finally woke up disoriented and confused about his surroundings. He finally realized that he'd fallen asleep in Tonya's bed. He jumped out the bed, grabbed his clothes from the floor and rushed to the bathroom to wash up. Larry grabbed a washcloth from the drawer and in a rush to clean himself up splashed water all over the floor and counter. Rushing to wash off his dick he heard the front door open. He jerked his pants on and threw the washcloth in the hamper. Walking in the bedroom, he grabbed his shirt off the floor and slowly crept to the top of the stairs where he heard voices coming from the living room. 'Tonya and that bitch Barbara are downstairs,' he thought.

Larry could faintly hear their conversation from where he stood, so after buttoning up his shirt, he tiptoed down to the middle of the staircase where his position allowed him to hear better.

"I don't remember leaving that light on," Tonya said, as she plopped down on the sofa.

"Girl, you've had so much on you're mind lately, you could've thought you turned it off."

"Yeah, must be my hormones and this morning sickness shit is not cool at all."

"Have you heard anything else from that trifling ass Larry?"

"Not since that morning when he called me while I was on

my way to work. He said he was out of town, but knowing his ass he was probably lying. I just hope he keeps his ass wherever he is."

"Be thankful he doesn't know you are pregnant because you really would have some shit on your hands."

"Barbara, please, I can't even image what that fool would do if he knew I was pregnant and the child could possibly be his."

"Well, we don't have to worry about that," Barbara said, as she yawned. "I'm tired girl. I think I'm just going to stay here tonight."

"Head on upstairs. I'll be up as soon as I turn on this porch light and lock up down here."

Tonya walked over to the front door to turn on the alarm system while Barbara headed upstairs.

"Barbara!" Tonya called out.

"Yeah, girl!' Barbara yelled, from the top of the steps.

"Did I turn the alarm system off when we walked in the door?"

"I don't know, Why?"

"It's off, but I just don't remember turning it off when we walked in," Tonya said nervously.

"We were running our mouths as we came in. I think you might have turned it off." Barbara felt Tonya was just being her forgetful self. "I'm going upstairs and get ready for bed."

"Okay. I'll be up in a second," Tonya said, as she tried to remember them coming in over and over again in her head. Shrugging her shoulders, she turned on the alarm system and headed in the kitchen for some water.

Drinking her water she heard Barbara scream. "Barbara are you a'ight! Barbara are you all right?" Tonya yelled out, as she headed upstairs.

"I'm fine! I'm fine!" Barbara said, as she looked up and saw Tonya walking in.

"What's the matter? You scared me half to death with that screaming," Tonya yelled.

"It's all this water on the floor I stepped in. Girl, I can't stand wet socks on my feet."

"Girl, you scared the shit out of me," Tonya said.

"I'm sorry. Are you peeing on the floor now?"

"Go to hell trick," Tonya said, laughing.

"What's all this water on the sink?"

"I must have done that," Tonya said, as she walked over to the chair and to grab her nightgown.

Barbara came out of the bathroom and noticed Tonya searching for something. "Girl, what you looking for now?"

"I could have sworn I left my nightgown here on this chair and now it's not here anymore."

"You sure you left it there? You know how your mind been lately. You need to get some sleep," Barbara said, as she climbed in the bed.

Tonya felt chill bumps all over her as she looked around the room. "Is it cold in here to you, Barbara?"

"No. I'm fine. If you're cold close the window."

Tonya took a look out the window and the streets were dark except for the lamps and porch lights on. Tonya grabbed an over-sized blue cotton t-shirt from her top drawer. Tonya turned off the lights and sat on the side of her bed. She looked around the room in a calculating manner. She knew something was just not right, but for the life of her she just could not put her finger on it. She thought about all the little mishaps that had been happening to her lately, and she knew something in her home was amiss, but she didn't know exactly what.

"Tonya, what's wrong now?" Barbara asked, as she sat up in the bed.

"I'm not sure. I have this strange feeling but it's unexplainable." Tonya pulled the covers back and crawled into bed. Before either woman could talk about Tonya's suspicions both women were comfortably sleeping. The room fell quiet and all that could be heard was the tick tock of a wall clock.

Larry waited a solid hour before he eased himself from under the bed dragging the nightgown that Tonya was looking for.

He bumped into an arm dangling over the mattress. "Oh Shit!" Larry quietly reprimanded himself in a hushed tone. He inhaled the scent of the nightgown once more before carefully laying it back on the chair where it was earlier.

Larry stood next to Tonya's bed watching both women as they slept. Unexpectedly, Tonya coughed and rolled over facing Larry. Larry jumped, looking for cover in the darkness that bathed the room. He noticed that Tonya hadn't opened her eyes. Larry crawled along the floor and grabbed the nightgown, balled it up and stuffed it inside his shirt. He didn't want to leave evidence of his visit. Larry eased back on the floor and slowly crawled on his belly until he was outside the bedroom and stood up once he was in the safety of the hallway.

He took one last look at the sleeping women and tiptoed from the upstairs hallway and down the staircase. Before Larry left, he disengaged the alarm system, turned out the porch light, and walked off leaving the door unlocked.

Early the next morning Tonya woke to a sliver of sunlight that peeked through the curtains of her bedroom. She yawned, swung her feet to the floor. She glanced over at Barbara to see she was still asleep. Tonya stretched, as an overnight full bladder guided her footsteps towards the bathroom.

"What the fuck!" Tonya noticed some dirt on the carpet.

"Morning, girl." Barbara was now awake. "What's the matter?"

"There's some dirt on the floor and it looks like a man's footprint." Tonya scratched her head wondering how the footprint could have gotten there.

"Girl, stop tripping! It probably came from one of Antonio's late night booty calls. Plus, by the looks of things, you ain't cleaned up in a minute."

"I guess. You could be right," Tonya said, as she remembered the multiple orgasms she had the last time Antonio came over. "I just wonder why I never noticed it before."

"Well, think about it as we get dressed," Barbara said, as she threw back the bed covers. "I want some pancakes from I-HOP."

The girls showered and changed. As they both headed downstairs, Tonya stopped at the closet in the foyer to grab a pair of tennis shoes and they headed out the door. Neither noticed that

Barbara had just swung open the front door without unlocking it or that the alarm had been turned off. Tonya did remember to lock the door. As they got in Barbara's car, neither noticed Larry's car as they drove by.

Chapter 26
Reese, Demetrious & Tariff

Reese sat at the kitchen table sipping on a protein drink. 'Is my career over?' he thought. His thoughts were interrupted by the sudden vibration of his cell phone. Reese smiled when Demetrious' name appeared on the caller ID.

"What's up, man? How you doing?" he asked with excitement.

"Sup, man. Been a little busy is all. Everyday I remind myself to call you, but hey you know how it is."

"Yeah. I know how it can be, not enough hours in a day."

"Naw man, you my boy and I want to always be there for you whenever you need me," Demetrious said sincerely. "So tell me what's happening?"

"I don't want to burden you with my troubles. You already got a full plate and you don't need me adding to it."

"Bearing the burden of a friend means having a friend in the end. Now what's going on with you right now?" Demetrious persisted.

"Have you talked to Mike?"

"No, I haven't, but I've talked to Jay. He kinda filled me in a bit."

"Mike must have talked to him 'cause I haven't talked to Jay. Anyway the rumors about my sexuality are starting to surface," Reese said letting out a long sigh. "I've been getting some harassment from a few of the players on the team and I'm just not sure how much more I can take."

"I'm sorry to hear that, Reese. What can we do to help?" Demetrious wasn't sure how the boyz could help Reese on this one.

"I don't know," Reese said, as he cradled his head in his

hand.

"Reese, man, Chuck's schedule is pretty much set, but we have a break coming up. Tariff and I can be there in a New York minute. Man, all you have to do is say the word."

"That's my boy," Reese said with a smile. "You guys always have my back and I love ya'll for that."

"We love you too, Reese and don't forget to give Mike our love." Demetrious waited for a second to see if Reese had more to get off his chest. "A'ight man, remember, day or night we're here for you. So promise me you'll call if you need anything."

"I promise, man. I will."

Demetrious sat in the same spot for a moment replaying the conversation he'd just had with Reese. 'We need to fly back to Houston. Our boy needs our support,' he thought. Demetrious jumped off the bed, headed to the elevators and down to the lobby.

"Hey you! What took you so long?" Tariff asked Demetrious, as he exited the elevators.

"We need to talk," Demetrious said, as he grabbed Tariff by the hand and lead him to the big cushion chairs.

"What's wrong, Demetrious?" Tariff's soft brown eyes stretched wide with concern.

"It's Reese."

"Reese! What's wrong with Reese? Is he okay?" Tariff asked, rising out of his seat.

"Calm down, T." Demetrious grabbed Tariff's fingers, pulling him back to his seat. "Reese is fine. It's nothing like that. Don't worry."

"Then what?"

"There's a rumor about Reese going around."

"A rumor! What rumor?"

"It's gotten out that Reese is gay and now he's being harassed by some of the guys on the team."

"We were all afraid this was going to happen and knowing Reese, he's probably having a hard time," Tariff said. "We need to go home."

"I was thinking the same thing, but what about Chuck and the tour?"

"My assistant can handle things while we're away and I know Chuck will understand. I'll go find Chuck and Tyrell and let them know what's going on."

"I'll get on the phone to get us out on a flight first thing in the morning."

Chapter 27
Tariff, Demetrious, Mike, Reese, Jay & Ricky

Within an hour of their flight landing, Tariff and Demetrious headed straight to Mike and Reese's place to surprise them. The limo pulled up to the curb in front of the black and white house. As soon as the driver put the car in park, Tariff broke the silence of what seemed like a long ride.

"I just don't understand this world or people," Tariff said, as he stared out the window.

"Understand what?"

"Reese is one of the top running backs in the country, an overall likeable guy and he gives so much back to the community," Tariff said. "You would think people would focus on other things besides who he sleeps with."

"I don't understand it either, but I guess it's true how the old sayin' goes."

"What old sayin' is that?" Tariff asked.

"Something like," Demetrious recalled what he'd heard a man say one day, "A man who doesn't have an open mind, is a man who is afraid of change."

"Demetrious, do you think things will ever change? Not only for us, but for the rappers, athletes and actors in our country? I mean really! When you think about it, what does a person's sexual orientation have to with how effectively they're able to perfect their craft?"

"I agree with you one hundred percent, Tariff. If our society continues down this same path of discrimination, there'll be a whole lot of brothers and sistas who'll live out their lives on the down low."

Demetrious and Tariff sat in silence until the chauffer opened the limo door. Tariff gave the driver instructions on what time to pick them up, as Demetrious walked up to the door and rang the bell.

Mike looked out the window to see who was ringing the bell. His face lit up and he swung the door open. His eyes sparkled with delight! The three men, Demetrious, Tariff and Mike embraced each other as a group, without a spoken word.

"What are you guys doing here?" Mike asked.

"Our boy needed us, so we caught the first flight out and here we are," Tariff said.

"Wow! Man, you guys are the best," Mike said, as he stepped inside, practically dragging Tariff and Demetrious into the house. "Reese is going to be so happy to see you two."

"Where is Reese?" Demetrious asked.

"He's in the study watching some T.V. He's been kind of down this morning, but I know this will definitely cheer him up."

Mike led the guys to the study and pushed the door open. Reese's back was to the door. Mike walked around the soft brown leather sofa and sat down next to Reese with a wide grin plastered on his face.

"Sup, Baby Boy?" Reese asked, with a look of confusion. "Why you smiling so hard?"

Demetrious walked up behind Reese and covered his eyes before Mike could answer. "Guess who?"

Reese jumped to his feet, recognizing the voice. He turned around and, to his surprise, there stood his best friend. Reese grabbed both Tariff and Demetrious, squeezing them tight while Mike rubbed his back affectionately.

Mike turned away, momentarily, to wipe the tears that had suddenly appeared in his eyes. Mike heard the doorbell once again and headed to the door. He peeked out the window and saw Jay and Ricky standing there.

Before Mike could get the door completely open, Jay stepped in.

"Are they here yet?"

"You knew they were coming?"

"Who do you think called them?" Jay walked pass Mike and followed the sound of the voices he heard.

"Hey, Ricky!" Mike said giving Ricky a hug. "How are you?"

"I'm good man. The question is how are you?"

"I'm good, and starting to get even better."

Finally, everyone gathered in the study. "So where's Tyrell and Chuck?" Reese asked.

"Chuck couldn't get away because of the tour and Tyrell stayed to help him out." Demetrious explained. "But they send their love and they will be home soon."

The guys spent the next hour catching up and talking about Chuck's tour. Jay had always been outspoken and could not hold it in anymore, "So Reese, what's," he started, but was cut short when Demetrious pinned him with a glare.

"What D." Jay continued, "Isn't Reese the reason we are all here?" Jay stated demandingly. "We don't need to keep avoiding this."

Deep down they all knew that Jay was actually right to bring up the issue that had in fact, brought them all together. Reese felt somewhat relieved that Jay had spoken out the way he did. Everyone sat in silence as Reese expressed what he'd been experiencing since the rumors about him being gay started to surface. Ricky and Jay both spoke up about what happened in the Sports bar with Ricky's co-worker.

"Jay, you didn't do anything crazy did you?" Tariff asked.

"Actually," Ricky laughed. "Jay was a trooper. I addressed the issue."

"Now that I would've liked to see, Jay quiet. That's a Kodak moment." They all had to laugh.

Reese, thinking about all that was happening, suddenly became outraged. He stood up reaching the full height of his 5'10 muscular frame and slammed his glass into the dry fireplace.

A shocked silence descended on the group of friends. No one could recall ever seeing Reese lose his temper to such a monumental degree.

"They're not going to make me quit!" Reese shouted then dropped down in his seat. His sudden and intense release of anger had left him exhausted.

Mike went over to Reese and sat down beside him on the arm of the chair. Reese buried his head in Mike's lap. Mike tenderly rubbed the top of his head. Demetrious walked over and stood close by. "Reese don't let anybody take your dreams away from you. Football is your life. You fought so hard to get here. If they can't deal with you because of your sexuality then that's their problem. Reese, we are all here for you. Everyone in the room loves you and we're here to support you."

Reese looked up at the guys. "I know, and I appreciate all of you. I thank you guys for the support and everything. As long as I got my man and my boyz on my side, I'll be okay. I'm so glad you guys are here. Now I know, I'll be okay."

* * *

Several hours later Jay and Ricky headed home. Taking the scenic route, they noticed that the sky was clear and black. The only thing that you could see was the moon giving off a glow. Both enjoyed the smooth sounds of Phyllis Hyman and realized they had been riding, just enjoying the mood. Ricky glanced over at Jay and noticed he was deep in thought.

"A penny for your thoughts," Ricky said.

Jay smiled, "I was just thinking how lucky I am to have you and to have true comrades like the guys that make up our circle. I feel so sorry for those who don't have or even know how it feels to experience such love."

"I feel lucky too, baby." Ricky said, as he pulled into the driveway. "Here we are, home sweet home."

Once inside, Jay headed for the kitchen and Ricky bounced up the stairs to hit the shower before going to bed. 'My God it's after midnight,' Jay thought, as he looked at the clock on the stove. Jay turned off the light and pushed his way through the swinging door and headed up the steps. The sound of the doorbell stopped him in his tracks. Jay looked up the stairs, as he heard the shower running. 'Who in the hell could be ringing the doorbell this time of night,' he thought.

Jay peeped through the security hole and was stunned by what he saw. He wiped his eyes to make sure he wasn't seeing things. He snuggled his face close to the door once more and eyed the man standing on the other side ringing the bell once again.

"Damn it!" Jay hissed. 'What the hell does he want?' He swung open the door. "Man, you just don't get it, huh! What part of leave me the hell alone don't you understand?!'"

Wil just stood there swaying from side to side taking a sip of alcohol from his red cup and spilling its content on his white tee shirt. "Can I come in please?" He said, as he put his hand inside his black sweats.

"I think you came to the wrong house man!" Jay spoke each word distinctively.

"Aw, come on Jay," Wil said, as he pulled out his hard erect manhood. "I miss you man."

"Man get the fuck off my porch or I'll call the cops on your tired drunk ass!" Go the hell home!" Jay slammed the door and locked it.

"Was somebody at the door?" Ricky asked, as he appeared at the top of the stairs wrapped in a towel.

"It was nothing. I was just making sure the door was locked," Jay lied, but wasn't sure why.

"Well, come on upstairs. We got an early day and I got something for you," Ricky said, walking away dropping his towel.

Wil staggered drunkenly back to his car. Sliding into the driver's seat, he pulled out his cell phone from the leather case about to fall from his waist. He punched in Jay's phone number, but it went straight to voicemail. 'Damn it!' Wil continued to scroll through his phone and came across Ricky's number. He paused, but the thought passed quickly. 'Naw not yet.' Tapping the phone log a couple more times, he came to another name and number. A smirk crossed his face as he dialed the familiar digits. Pressing the send button, he waited for an answer.

"Hello." Wil said sounding like a drunk imitating a player.

"Do you mind if I come over?"

Wil started his car, flipped the phone close, and headed in the direction of his late night booty call. A short time later, Wil pulled up in front of the house. 'Why in the hell would anybody put pink shutters on their house?' He thought.

Wil reached in his pocket to make sure he'd remembered to grab his box of condoms. Making his way to the front porch and the door bell, he could hear within seconds the door locks being tripped hurriedly. The door slowly opened and Wil smiled at his sexual encounter for the night. "Sup, you?" Wil asked, with a heavy drunken slur. "I got here as soon as I could."

Chapter 28
Reese & Antonio

The locker room vibrated from the loud buzz of football players getting ready for an intense practice in unusually scorching heat. The coach walked out of his office and observed all the chatter going on. He spotted Reese standing in front of his locker wrapping his wrist while talking with Antonio. The all pro defensive end, Keith Perry, stood a few feet away admiring his abs in the full length wall mirror.

'Everyone in this room should've been dressed and out there on the field fifteen minutes ago.' the coach thought. He kicked over the garbage to get everyone in the locker rooms attention. "Before you ladies take the field there's something I want y'all to hear and I'm only going to say this once." Coach Smith slowly looked at each man until his gaze had touched each one individually, "I don't know what's been going on in these practices and in this locker room, but the one thing I do know is whatever differences you guys may have with one another, I don't want to see them expressed on the field or in this locker room! As a matter of fact, I don't want to hear about them period, on or off the field. As far as I am concerned, you are a team, twenty-four-seven, and as long as I am the coach of this team that's the way it's going to be. Do I make myself clear?"

"Yeah, Coach." The guys answered in unison.

"Reese, I want to see you in my office and the rest of you guys hit the track and give me five laps," Coach Smith said and turned and walked to his office.

Reese closed his locker and headed in the direction of the coach's office. He entered the small cluttered office and closed the door. Coach Smith settled in his high back brown leather chair and asked Reese to have a seat.

"Reese, I've heard the rumors that have been floating around about you." Coach Smith's monotone was flat, but that didn't stop Reese from feeling like his heart had just been yanked from his chest.

'This is it,' Reese thought, 'My career is over.' Reese was about to defend himself when the coach stopped him.

"Reese, you're one of my best players, and I commend you when you're out there on that field. Your performance is spectacular and you always give this team 100 percent." Coach Smith continued, "Reese, I want you here, and I hope you're not about to quit on me. I can't say that I even know what you're going through because I don't." Coach picked up a silver picture frame that sat on his desk turning it to face Reese. "You see this?" Coach Smith said in a whisper. "This was my son when he was sixteen years old. He was a star athlete and in my heart I believed one day he would play in the NFL. The coach's vision started to become blurry as his emotions tried to take over. "When he was in high school some guys on his team heard rumors that he was gay. Every day at school they would tease him. I told him he needed to man up. It was my way of ignoring it." Coach Smith stared at the photo intensely, "I ignored my son's pain. I didn't want to accept the fact that my son was gay. I never even asked him. One morning, like every other morning, I went into my son's room to wake him up for school. The only thing different this particular morning, from all the others, was that my son didn't wake up."

Reese could see the pain the coach was feeling. The confirmation was the lonely tear that glided down the coach's face.

"Reese, my son committed suicide. He left a note addressed to me on his night stand, and still to this very day I can't forget how the note ended."

"What? What did it say, Coach? Coach, what did it say?"

"It said, 'Dad, I'm sorry. I didn't mean to disappoint you.' Coach continued, "I will carry that to my grave, and I will never forgive myself for ignoring my son."

They both sat silent before the coach finally spoke. "Reese, all this could have been avoided if I would've put my foolish pride to the side and talked to my son." The coach laced his fingers together. "My stubbornness cost me my son. Reese, I have never told any other coach or player this story. I tell you this story and I'm telling you what I should have told my son. You have some ignorant people out there caught up in other people's lives and business because deep down they're probably not happy with theirs. So Reese, don't quit."

Reese didn't know what to say so he just sat there for a moment, quietly absorbing everything the coach had told him. "I'm sorry about your loss, Coach."

"Thanks, son." Coach stood up and smiled. "Don't ever let anyone make you feel bad about being who you are. Now you need to go out there and show those guys what you're made of." The coach said, as he reached back inside his drawer and pulled out a sealed envelope and handed it to Reese.

"What's this coach?

"I found it one day after practice next to your locker. It must have fallen out your bag."

Reese hurriedly opened the envelope to find a picture that he and Mike had taken when they were in Miami. 'I thought I had taken all the pictures out of my bag, I guess I must have over looked this one.' Reese turned to leave and then looked back at the coach. "So Coach, you knew all this time and you didn't say anything?"

"Yes, son. I've known for a while."

Reese turned slowly to the door to leave. "Thanks again, Coach."

"You're welcome, Reese." The door slowly closed as Reese walked out. Coach reached into his pocket and pulled out the handwritten note that his son left for him on the saddest day of his life.

"Son, you didn't disappoint me. I disappointed you and for that I'm the one who is sorry."

Chapter 29
Ricky & Wil

Ricky took a quick glance at his watch and, sure enough, his stomach was right on que. 'It's lunch time a'ight.' he thought. Ricky plucked the cordless phone from its hook and with one punch connection, he buzzed the office secretary.

"Yeah Lisa, I'm about to go out and grab a bite. If you could hold my calls I'd appreciate it." Ricky then dropped the phone back on the cradle, grabbed his suit jacket and headed straight for the elevator. A few minutes later Ricky nodded his head at the doorman's courtesy, as he headed out of the building.

'Beautiful day,' Ricky thought.

Ricky walked up to his favorite deli and grabbed his lunch. Since it was an exceptionally beautiful day, he decided to eat in a park across the street from the deli.

Ricky headed toward an empty bench. He was stopped by a homeless man who reeked of an offensive odor.

"Hey, Mista, You got any change?" The old toothless guy asked. His dirty hand was covered with a dirty holey glove.

"Yeah, Pop!" Ricky reached in his pocket and handed the guy a crisp ten dollar bill. "Make sure you get something to eat, sir."

"Thank you, sir! Thank you, sir!" The homeless man said, as he walked away.

Ricky sat down and watched the old guy, as he headed into the convenience store next to the deli. Ricky felt really good about giving the man the money when he saw him come out the store with what appeared to be a loaf of bread and juice. He wished he could do more for the homeless.

The park was a pleasant setting, with well manicured, green grass and strategically placed trees lining the entire park. In the center of the park was a large water fountain. Ricky took a deep breath feeling relaxed. 'I'm so glad I'm not caught up in all that traffic,' he thought, as he watched the cars snaking along at a snail's pace. A familiar voice caught Ricky's attention.

"What's up, Wil? What brings you on this side of town?"

"Oh man, I work right up the street," Wil replied taking a seat next to Ricky.

"That's cool. I thought you told me you worked across town," Ricky said.

"Normally, I do." Wil's mind was racing, looking for a believable lie. "But I had something to take care of over here at our satellite office."

"It's such a beautiful day today," Ricky dismissing the doubt he had. "I decided to get away from my office for lunch instead of eating at my desk." Ricky licked the sweet after taste of his lunch from his fingers.

"I feel you," Wil started then his cell phone chimed an interruption. "I'll call you back," he told his caller without even saying hello. "Sorry about that man. That was one of my ladies."

"One of your ladies?" Ricky laughed. "So how many of them do you have if that was just one of them, Mr. Playboy?"

"Naw, man, it ain't like that. She just some old girl named Barbara I met who think I got money."

"Oh, so you the money man too?"

"Naw, man I was house sitting and met this girl while hanging out one night and I took her to my boy's place and I guess she thinks I got deep pockets." A huge smile parted Wil's soft lips into a genuine smile. "You should have seen her when she got inside my boy's car. To this day she thinks it's mine."

"Wow, man! Some women out there are like that," Ricky said.

"Ricky, man, she started asking me all these questions about where I work and everything. So I just let her believe what she wanted to believe. I just tap that ass here and there when I can't get it from where I want," Wil said, as he shot Ricky a seductive smile.

'Is this brother flirting with me again,' Ricky wondered, as he turned his focus toward the water fountain.

"So how 'bout we meet after work for drinks?" Wil asked, invading Ricky's thoughts.

"As much as I'd like to, Wil, I can't." Ricky quickly came up with an excuse. "I'll be working late tonight, but maybe later this week."

"Well, it will have to be after I get back in town."

Ricky felt relieved. "Business or pleasure?" He asked.

"Hey man, its business, but I always try to get in my pleasure."

"So I guess I'll be working out solo,"

"Yeah, I was going to hit you up on your celly and let you know but since I ran into you. Will you be able to manage without me?" Wil asked.

"I think I can manage," Ricky said, as he noticed Wil's attention had been drawn to a brother in a dark suit impatiently trying to cross the street. "Well, I need to get back to my office, Wil. I'll see you at the gym when you get back."

"A'ight man. I'll check you later," Wil said.

Ricky got up and headed back to work. A few steps later, Ricky looked back only to find Wil's attention still in the direction of that brother crossing the street.

Chapter 30
Barbara, Tonya & Antonio

Tonya wanted to freshen up before Antonio arrived for their dinner date. Stepping out of the shower, she wrapped her dripping body in a towel. Wiping the steam clinging to the bathroom mirror, she was able to peep at herself as she let the towel drop to the floor.

'Oh my God, look at this weight I'm starting to put on,' she thought, looking at her once very flat stomach. 'Even my breasts look fuller than they used to.' Tonya glanced at the clock on the bathroom wall and realized it was getting late. Thirty minutes later, she walked downstairs and headed to the kitchen to prepare dinner.

'I wonder if I'll still have to cook after I become the wife of an NFL player?' Tonya wondered, dropping a cube of butter into a pot of steaming broccoli. Tonya shook a small seasoning dispenser over the chicken, as her mind continued to entertain thoughts of the future. 'I've got to find out what it is that a man like Antonio is looking for in a woman he'd want for a wife.' Tonya flipped the chicken and her thoughts over at the same time. 'When I find out, I'll have ole boy down on one knee.'

Bing Bong. The door bell jingled and interrupted Tonya's thoughts. Tonya glanced at the clock on the stove as she grabbed a dish towel, dried her hands and headed to the front door. 'That can't be Antonio. It's too early,' she thought. The thought of it being Larry caused her knees to buckle. "Lord please don't do this to me."

"Who is it?" Tonya called out still a good four feet from the door.

"Girl, it's me. Barbara Open the door!"

"I started not to answer," Tonya said.

"Why not?"

"Because I thought it might be Larry."

"When was the last time you heard from him?"

"I haven't. That's what scares me."

"Well, maybe he's found some other woman's life he can fuck up. Anyway, I would have called, but I ran out of minutes on my cell." Barbara made a beeline for the guest bedroom that was just off the kitchen. "Besides, I had to pee real bad and you were closer than me trying to make it home."

Tonya drifted over to the stove to check on the chicken and broccoli.

"Girl, what you cooking? It smells good!" Barbara yelled from the slightly closed bathroom door.

"Well, my man Antonio is on his way over here, as you sit there on your throne."

"HA! HA! Bitch!" Barbara flushed the commode and washed her hands.

"So now he's your man, huh? You go girl! I ain't mad atcha! They say the best way to a man's heart is to know your way around the bedroom and kitchen and by the look of things you got the sex down. Oh yeah, and you better know a little bit about sports while you at it."

"So Barb, tell me about this mystery man," Tonya said, sitting down across from Barbara.

"Honey, it was the fourth of July in this camp. That brutha came over the other night," Barbara's face split into a huge smile, "and, girl, he got bank!"

"Oh yeah?" Tonya's happiness touched the corner of her eyes. "Well, maybe we both hit the jackpot this time."

"Umm. Girl. I almost forgot." Barbara's excitement shifted gears. "Guess who called me the other night?"

"Who? Girl, tell me! Who?"

"Your man's friend, Keith," Barbara said, as she licked her lips.

"Why did he call you? What's up with that?"

"What you mean? He's calling me cuz he want some of

this good candy! He's taking me out for dinner and drinks!"

"So, are you gonna go?"

"Girl, are you trippin' or something? Of course I am. I'd be some crack head shit if I didn't." Barbara couldn't help but laugh at what she just said. "That man has probably got more money than my mystery guy. And speaking of money, has Antonio come clean with you about him being an NFL player?"

"Not yet," Tonya's reply was flat and unemotional, "and as far as I'm concerned, I'm going to let him keep right on believing that I don't have a clue. He will have to tell me eventually." Tonya rubbed her stomach and her face sparkled like a star. "I'm sure he won't want to keep no secrets from his baby's momma."

Tonya reached for her vibrating cell phone. Looking at her caller ID she placed her index finger in front of her mouth to hush Barbara, letting her know it was Antonio.

"Hey, baby. You on your way?"

"Yeah, I'm on my way." Antonio's voice boomed through the speaker on her phone. "See you when I get there."

"Well, I guess that's my clue to leave," Barbara said, as Tonya flipped her phone closed. "Plus, I need to stop by the beauty supply store and pick up some hair."

"Barbara, your hair looks fine as it is."

"I know. I just want to rock me a ponytail for my date to-morrow." Barbara got up and headed toward the front door. "I'm out girl. Have fun. I'll talk to you tomorrow."

*   *   *

An hour later Antonio was relaxed and sitting in Tonya's living room surfing the channels on the TV, while Tonya put the finishing touches on their dinner. Antonio immediately turned the volume down on the TV and hit the captions key. The sports commentator was talking about the team, and it showed Reese, Keith and Antonio on the screen during their workouts on the field. Antonio turned to make sure Tonya was still in the kitchen. The screen behind the commentator became a picture of just Reese. Antonio became nervous when the announcer started to address the gay rumor about Reese.

'Damn the rumors about Reese are really staring to get out now,' he thought.

Antonio whipped out his cell and immediately dialed Reese. After a few rings the phone went straight to his voicemail. Looking over his shoulder to see that Tonya was still in the kitchen, he left a message for Reese. "Hey, this is Antonio, I just saw ESPN, we need to talk ASAP," Antonio whispered in the phone, finished up his message and quickly shoved it back in his pocket.

"Is everything okay?" Tonya asked, as she emerged from the kitchen.

"Yeah, everything is fine. I hit the caption button on this remote control and I was trying to take it off. It distracts me." Antonio answered.

"I hope you're ready to eat. Dinner is ready."

"Good, because I'm hungry!" Antonio stood up. "Can I help you with anything?"

"No, you sit down and finish watching television. I'll bring everything out. You sit and relax."

"Thanks, babe." Antonio sat back onto the sofa's fluffy cushions. "What do you have to drink, babe?"

"I got some Kool-aide and a couple of forties in the fridge."

'Did she offer me some welfare sweet water or a Forty?' Antonio thought, as he laughed to himself.

"I'm good, babe," he lied, "I'll just have a glass of water."

Tonya finally appeared from the kitchen with two plates of food and two glasses filled with water perched on a television tray.

Antonio attacked his food like he hadn't eaten all week. "You must have been hungry! Your plate is clean already!" Tonya said, pleased that he obviously liked her culinary skills.

"Yeah, I had a hard workout today so a brutha was hungry."

Tonya curled up in Antonio's arms on the sofa, as they started to watch a movie she rented. Tonya heard a slow heavy snore from Antonio and realized he had fallen asleep. Tonya gently nudged Antonio, "Why don't you go upstairs and get in bed."

"I'm sorry, babe. I didn't mean to fall asleep on you. It's

just been a rough day and you fed me that awesome meal."

"Well, you go ahead upstairs and get in bed and I'll be up in a bit. I'm just gonna clean up these dishes and put the food away."

Antonio headed upstairs, as Tonya started to tidy up downstairs. Half an hour later Tonya checked the front door, turned on the porch light and took one final look around before finally heading upstairs. Tonya stopped in the doorway of her bedroom and was struck by Antonio's physique, as he lay across the bed. She began to have sexual fantasies by just looking at how Antonio's blue silk boxers hung over his pecan brown muscular legs.

Antonio laid there sleeping with his semi hard dick head peeking through the opening of his boxers. "What are you staring at?" He asked, waking up with a slight grin on his face.

"Why don't you get out those clothes and give your man some of that good lovin'?"

Tonya smiled, "I thought you were sleepy."

"Yeah, I was, but I'm up now," he said, as his erection started to get harder.

"Let me turn out the lights," Tonya said feeling just a little self conscience about her body since becoming pregnant.

"Why? You never wanted the lights turned out before."

"I'm starting to pick up weight from the pregnancy. You may not find it attractive."

"Well, I think you look sexy as hell carrying my little man."

"And what makes you think it's a boy? It could be a little lady."

"As long as it's healthy it doesn't matter whether it's a girl or boy. Now come on over here and put a smile on your man's face."

Tonya walked over and he pulled her down on top of him and kissed her passionately. Tonya grabbed the remote and turned on the CD player. The room was filled with the sounds of the Whispers. Tonya and Antonio were finding their sexual groove when she thought she heard the front door open and close.

"Antonio!" Tonya swung herself into a sitting position. "Baby, did you hear that?"

"Hear what?" Antonio crawled into Tonya's lap and started to suck on her breast. "I didn't hear anything."

"Antonio, I'm not kidding! I heard the front door open and close. Could you go check, please?"

Antonio stood up fully erect. "You sure you want me to go check?"

"Yes."

Antonio didn't really want to lose his grip on the moment, but he knew if he didn't go check things out, Tonya's fear would spoil the night. Antonio headed downstairs and walked over to the front door which was locked and undisturbed. "Since I'm already down here I might as well get me some water," Antonio mumbled.

"You okay down there?"

"Yeah, babe, everything is fine." Antonio sat the glass on the kitchen counter and headed back up stairs. 'Your hearing things woman,' he thought.

Tonya's smiled faded when he came back in the room and she noticed his erection had gone down.

"Now where was I?" He asked, as he started to massage her breast, both unaware that an intruder was lurking in the darkness of the house.

Larry sat unnoticed in a reclining chair in a dark corner downstairs. He watched enviously, a minute ago as the man he'd watch arrive earlier came down the steps in a pair of boxer shorts. Larry began to creep upstairs when the all too familiar moans of sexual intercourse drifted from the bedroom where he once slept. He stood deathly still and just listened to the sounds of his woman making love to another man.

Larry slowly backed down the stairs and slipped into the kitchen for a moment of quiet that would let him think. After replaying a couple quick scenarios, he decided on a plan and method of revenge. Easing open the drawer, where Tonya kept her knives, he picked up the biggest butcher knife, and headed back upstairs.

The closer Larry got to Tonya's bedroom, the stronger the stench of sex burned his nostril. He crept closer to the bedroom's doorway with his attack plan in motion. Taking that final step, he could see Tonya in one of their favorite positions, but instead of that man being him, Tonya rode the thick penis of another lover.

"Oooh yes, baby, ride this dick!" Antonio said, as Tonya threw her head skyward and smacked her own butt cheeks together on each downward stroke. "Call me daddy, baby...call..." Antonio moaned, as Tonya bucked her ass harder and harder. Antonio, was so into Tonya and her hunger, for his dick that he was oblivious to his surroundings. He never noticed Larry standing dead center of the bedroom door watching him fuck the woman that Larry so loved.

As Antonio started to rise; Larry immediately stepped back into the darkness in the hallway. He watched as Antonio continued his sexual escapade. Larry began to feel the desire of arousal touch his loins as Antonio turned Tonya on her stomach, nudging her wordlessly until she was in the doggy style position.

Antonio penetrated Tonya with ease at first and let her readjust to the size of his dick, as he screwed her from the back. As he felt her pussy gradually expand, he began to bang her forcefully. She started to beg all over again.

"Oh! Tone, go faster! Yeah, baby, that's it!" Tonya grunted, "Smack that ass, baby." Tonya reached behind her and finding Antonio's hand she guided his index finger straight to her burning desire. Antonio took the hint and with an urgency to match Tonya's thrust, he rotated his finger on her clitoris causing Tonya's entire body to shiver.

Larry stepped back into the doorway watching as anger gripped his soul. He was so mad that he didn't even realize that he squeezed the butcher knife blade with such force that it had cut into the flesh of his palm, nor did he see the droplets of blood as they splashed on the carpet.

He couldn't take it. He had seen enough and embarrassment began to replace the anger that drove him. He pushed the knife in his back pocket and with a stomach full of envy he went back downstairs trying to tune out the sexual encounter replaying in his mind. The bright color of Antonio's jacket caught his attention. Picking up the jacket, he rifled though each pocket until he found something. 'This right here will at least let me know who this niggah is fucking my woman,' he thought, as he looked through the wallet.

"This dude must got some money," he mumbled, as he noticed all the platinum and gold express credit cards along with a thick wad of fifty dollar bills. Taking a few, he continued and slowly pulled out the driver's license. "Antonio C. Johnson. I got all I need right now," Larry said to himself, as he wiped the droplets of blood that were on the wallet from his cut and placed it back in the jacket.

Larry tossed the jacket back on the sofa and headed for the front door. Opening the door to his car, Larry took one final look in the direction of Tonya's bedroom window. "I'm going to take real good care of that li'l bitch and her boyfriend soon," he hissed the thoughts into the night's cool air, as he saw the silhouettes of their bodies walking by the window.

Chapter 31
Keith & Barbara

Keith headed out to pick up Barbara, intending to pump her for information. As he drove through her neighborhood, it reminded him of a time and place he tried to forget. Homes in desperate need of repair and others completely run down. Keith cruised the trash littered streets eyeing the lawns of homes that resembled mini jungles with over-grown weeds and vines. By the numbers on the houses, he could tell he was only a block or two away from Barbara's house. The last time he came by he was so drunk he really didn't remember much, plus it was so long ago. 'These young kids today,' he thought, as he noticed a couple of young girls who couldn't be any older than fifteen or sixteen, their stomachs hung low with pregnancy. 'Babies having babies and young men chasing the false glitter of life only to end up in jail, or dead before they reach the age of eighteen.'

Keith finally pulled up in front of Barbara's house, as the smell of marijuana wafted into his car window. He picked up his cell phone from the car console to dial Barbara's number. He had no intention of getting out of the car, as he locked the doors in his Benz. Barbara's phone went to voicemail. "Yeah, you got me. I'm busy right now, so please hit me back up."

'I know damn well this girl better be home,' Keith thought tossing the phone on the passenger seat. Keith put his car in gear and was ready to leave when he heard his phone vibrating.

"Hello," he said trying to restrain his anger.

"Hey! I see your car out front. I'm coming," she said.

'Lord have mercy, what kind of talk is that?' He thought, as the sound of her voice made him cringe. "Okay."

Minutes later, her front door opened and Barbara appeared.

Keith chuckled as his eyes rolled when he saw the black miniskirt that was so short you could see what the hoochie broad was thinking and the leopard print shirt that was suppose to match the skirt was so small she could have borrowed it from the young girls he had passed on his way over. 'Well, at least her hair looks nice,' he thought.

"The things we do for our friends. I sure hope Antonio appreciates the hell I'm about to endure. Keith watched her, as she walked to the car. 'I surely won't get out the car and open her door,' he thought. 'God, please don't let any of the guys from the team see me out with this woman.'

Antonio looked over at Barbara, as she hopped in the car bobbing her head to a melody that must've been playing inside of her head because the radio in the car was turned off. 'Man this is going to be a long night,' he thought.

Keith pulled off for a twenty minute ride that was pretty much conversation free. He plotted how he would approach his task without raising any suspicion. Keith turned into the restaurant parking lot. 'I guess I should give this trick the whole act and open her car door.' After he parked, he slowly walked over to the other side and opened her car door. The first thing he saw when Barbara swung her legs to the ground, was a fat patch of black pubic hair that appeared moist. 'This is a nasty trick!'

"Come on baby," he said politely, but his true thoughts were, 'I had to be one horny brutha to fuck this chick.'
Barbara and Keith headed into the restaurant and were greeted by a slender hostess wearing a tight-fitted, black dress. Keith was turned on immediately by her.

'That's the kind of woman I want.' Keith noticed the expression on the hostess' face when she looked at Barbara. It was like she had just smelled the stench of sewer. She still greeted them politely and quickly seated them at a table that was deep in a corner of the restaurant. Keith discreetly threw her a wink and thanked her for seating them. Barbara caught the smile that the hostess shot her date for the night. 'Yeah girl you look good and all, but you flirt with my man again, and I'm gonna beat you down in this joint,' she thought, as she made sure the waitress saw her roll her eyes.

Keith returned to the mission at hand and ordered a bottle of Dom Perignon. "Do you like Dom?" Keith asked.

"I'm not really a wine drinker," Barbara responded, giving Keith a sister gal look.

"Girl, you are funny!" Keith slightly chuckled, "Dom is not a wine, it's champagne."

"Oh, okay." Barbara leaned back in her chair smiling, "Champagne? Hell yeah, bring it on!" Barbara took notice of the restaurant and how nice the place was. "This place is really el-oglant."

'Did she just say e-l-o-g-l-a-n-t?' Keith asked himself. It took every thing in him not to laugh.

"Yeah, it is e-l-o-g-l-a-n-t," he said mocking her.

'If he was a really big baller, he would of ordered us some Crystal instead of some ole Don priron or whatever he said,' she thought, 'but I guess Champagne is Champagne.'

Keith made small talk until the waitress came over with the champagne on ice with two crystal glasses. The waitress popped the cork and poured it into champagne flutes. Barbara grabbed the glass and quickly gulped it down slamming the glass back on the table. The waitress grabbed her pen and pad, took their orders and left.

Keith sat back, relaxing, sipping on his same glass. He filled her glass every time it was empty.

"If I didn't know better, I'd think you were trying to get me drunk."

"No, I just want you to enjoy yourself. Only the best for you!"

"I just want to make sure you don't try and take advantage of a sister 'cause I know how you football players are."

'Trick slipping up already!' He thought. Keith waved the waitress over and ordered a gin and tonic. "Would you like more champagne or do you want a real drink?" He asked her.

"Well, I'll have a gin and tonic too." As the waitress walked over, a waiter walked over with their food. Two gin and tonics later, Barbara was slurring even more.

'This looks like the time for me to get the information I need,' he thought.

"I see you a real party girl. You know how to have a good time."

"Yeeeeeah! This girl heeere loves to party!"

"So how often do you and your girl Tonya hang out at the club where you and I met?"

"Oh, we go there all the time. That's where all the baaaal-llers hang out at!"

Keith laughed lightly. "Where all the ballers roll. What kind of ballers you talking about?"

Barbara took the last sip of what was left in her glass. She took it to the head as she tipped her head back until it was completely empty. "You know basketball players and football players, like yourself."

"Can't pull nothing over your eyes I see."

"Hellll naw. Can't no one pull anything over on a sister!"

"I see. So you and your girl, Tonya, trying to get paid."

"HOLD up Kee...Keith!" Barbara burped loudly. "What's up with all the questions?"

"Oh nothing. Just making small talk that's all."

"Kee...Keith that's some bull shit! You just trying to pump a girl for information to see what I know about you and your boy. What's his name?"

"Calm down, girl! It's all good. I mean my boy and your girl are going to be getting married and since she is having his baby, we're going to be hanging out more. So I'm just trying to get to know you better, that's all."

Barbara was starting to get loud and the customers all started whispering and looking at the table. The hostess walked over and Keith knew what she was about to say.

"Can I just get the check please?" Keith was embarrassed.

Before Keith could say anything else, the hostess handed him the check. Keith immediately pulled out his credit card and handed it to her and watched her as she hurriedly walked away.

"Come on! Let's get you out of here!" Keith said, as he stood up to grab her before she stood up. "I think you had one too many drinks."

"Keith, are you going to fuck my brains out like you did the last time?" Barbara spoke so loud that all the patrons started to shake their heads.

The hostess came back over with their bill. Keith signed it, grabbed his card and escorted Barbara to the car.

*   *   *

Barbara passed out in the car on the ride back to her house. Keith cussed himself every time he looked over at her, passed out, in the passenger seat of the car. Pulling in front of the house, Keith tried waking her up, but she was completely out.

"Now, I gotta carry your stank ass into the house," he said, to a passed out Barbara.

Keith rummaged though her purse, finding the keys to the house. Keith hopped out the car and walked up to the house, unlocked the door and headed back to the car to get Barbara. He carried her into the house. He slowly looked around the house, recalling things from his last visit. Keith finally made it to the bedroom and laid her cross the bed. Her eyes never opened, as he began to completely undress her. Keith had her totally naked. 'What next? I still need to get more information from this girl,' he thought glancing over at the condoms that sat in the open on top of her night stand.

Just then an idea popped in his head. He grabbed the box of condoms pulled out one package. He told himself that his actions were all in the name of friendship. Ripping the packet open, he went into the bathroom and flushed the condom down the toilet. He took the condom wrapper and placed it on the nightstand next to the bed, on the side where Barbara slept. Keith quickly got undressed and jumped into bed next to Barbara. Lying in bed, he realized how tired he was and drifted off to sleep within seconds.

The next morning, a bright sun seeped through the cracks in the curtains of Barbara's bedroom she started to stir. For a moment, she was disoriented. She jumped up, as she saw the open condom package on her night stand. "Oh, my head," she said, cradling it like a sick child. "Where are my clothes? How did I get naked? What did I do last night?" She asked herself silently, not knowing the answers. Suddenly, she heard a moan. Turning toward the sound, she saw Keith lying in the bed next to her. Slowly, she lifted the covers and saw he was just as naked as she was. So hung over, all she could do was smile at the morning erection he had. Barbara creep into the bathroom reached into the medicine cabinet and grabbed a few aspirin.

She gingerly got into the shower and proceeded to spit up three times, from all the champagne she drank on an empty stomach. As she emerged from the bathroom, she found Keith up, slipping on his slacks. 'Damn, look at that chest and those abs,' she thought.

"Lady, you are some kind of animal!" Keith smiled knowing that nothing happened between them. "Are you always that aggressive?"

"Well, you ain't that bad yourself," Barbara said, though she couldn't remember anything about last night.

"You wore me out! Put a brother straight to sleep!"

Barbara's face burst into a bright smile, as she thought about how she now had Keith by the balls. Especially, since he used the condoms from the box on her night stand. She thought her game was airtight, especially since she poked holes in each pack of the condoms on the stand before heading out last night. But little did she know that she had just been played. She had finally met her match.

Chapter 32
Reese, Antonio & Keith

'Damn, it's hot out here,' Reese was thinking, as he sat on the sideline watching Coach Conte work with the defense. Wiping the sweat from his face, he noticed a few of the players who had congregated around the Gatorade table. They looked in his direction, slapped each other five and shared whispers.

Reese was looking for a distraction from his self consciousness, when out of the corner of his eye, he saw Antonio storm across the field angrily, with Keith right behind him. 'I wonder what's up with them two?' he thought. Reese got up and headed in the direction of the only two guys who didn't judge him. Reese walked past the group that was just whispering about him. As he walked by, he fell to the ground. Someone had stuck their foot out tripping him. Reese fell flat on his face.

"Looks like Ms. Thang here can't walk in heels!" Said Flash, who got his nickname for being one of the fastest receivers in the league.

Reese, sat for a second. Got up and brushed the grass off his bottom lip.

Antonio noticed what had just happened and headed in Reese's direction. "Leave it alone, man." Keith grabbed Antonio by the arm. "Don't get involved," Keith told him, when he saw Antonio headed to Reese's defense.

"How can you say that, Keith? Reese is our boy and I'm going to help him out. Now, let go of my fucking arm!" Keith stood there and watched Antonio walk away.

"That was real immature," Reese said, as he shook his head at the group of guys.

"What you going to do about it, faggot?" Flash said, all up

in Reese's face.

The insult cut Reese to the bone. Without a thought, he leaped on Flash and began to land hard punches to his face and body. Flash's buddy Reno grabbed Reese around the neck in a choke hold. Reese broke his hold, flipping him over his shoulder and slamming him to the ground so hard Reno lost his wind.

Antonio made his way over, pushing everyone out the way. "Reese, man you a'ight? What the hell is going on here?"

"Nothing going on Ant," Reese said, shaking the hand that he had landed on Flash's jaw.

"Come on, let's go, man. These jokers ain't worth getting kicked off the team."

Reese started to walk away and then turned back around to look at Flash and eyed his friends. "Next time, you better think twice before you call someone else a faggot. Not one of you is man enough to make me quit. What I do off this field, in the privacy of my own home, is my own business. I am here to stay, so you might as well get use to it. Oh and just so you know, I'm not now nor have I ever been interested in dating any of you chumps. Sorry if that disappoints you." Reese spit out.

Reese looked around at the guys one final time before he made eye contact with the coach. The Coach gave him a slight head nod. The trainer walked over to Reese to check out his hand and saw how fast Reese's fingers were swelling.

"Hey, Coach, I think we need to take him in to the locker room and get an X-ray of his hand," the trainer yelled over.

"Reese, go on ahead in the locker room and get that taken care of."

"Sure, Coach."

The Coach turned around to the group of players standing around.

"As for the rest of y'all, get back on that field and practice."

The coach called over the assistant coach. "Take over until I get back. And you two, in my office now." Coach walked Flash and his buddy to his office.

In the locker room the trainer finished wrapping Reese's

hand. He only had a minor sprain. Nothing was broken.

Antonio walked over, "You sure you're okay Ali?"
Reese left out a laugh, "Yeah, man, I'm good. Thanks for having my back. You're a real good friend, but you better get back out there."

"Well, as long as you're okay," Antonio said, as he started to leave.

"Hey, Antonio!" Reese called, as he was walking out. Antonio turned around, "Thanks again, man, I really appreciate you for being such a good friend."

"No problem. Just go home and take care of that hand. And whether they know it or not, this team needs you," Antonio said, as he disappeared out the double doors.

Reese showered and quickly headed home. Pulling up in the driveway behind Tariff and Jay's cars, he sat in the car for a minute replaying what just happened.

Mike greeted him at the door, "Sup, man?" Mike immediately noticed the ace bandage on Reese's hand. "What happened to your hand?"

"It's nothing, just a sprain," Reese said, giving Mike a peck on the lips.

"How did you sprain your hand?" Mike asked.

"I was kinda in a fight," Reese said, as he walked toward the kitchen.

"A fight! What do you mean you kinda got in a fight?" Mike asked, following behind him into the kitchen.

"Reese, what happened?" Tariff asked, as Reese entered the kitchen.

Reese looked over at Mike and then Tariff. Demetrious and Jay sat calmly at the table waiting for Reese's answer.

"A couple of the players decided that they wanted to try and punk me."

"Punk you how?" Demetrious asked.
Jay echoed Demetrious' question only with an angry attitude. "Punk you how?"

Demetrious gave Jay a knowing look. "I was wondering how long it was going to be before the old Jay reappeared."

"I walked past a group of players and one of them decided to trip me and when I got up they called me a faggot and some other things, but it's over now,"

"Well, I hope somebody got an ass kicking," Jay said, grinning.

Reese ignored Jay's comment and looked over at Mike who was shaking his head.

"Baby Boy, I know what you're thinking. But it's going to be okay."

"Will it, Reese? Will it really be okay?" Mike asked, as he walked out of the kitchen.

Tariff walked over to Reese and ushered him over to a chair. "Have a seat, man."

"I need to go talk to Mike and make sure he's all right," Reese said.

"You can talk to him in a minute. Just listen to me for a second. You can't blame him for being worried about you and what's going on. He has worried about you ever since you got hurt back in college and he still worries about you. That's just how he is. He's very protective of you, Reese."

Demetrious and Jay sat next to Tariff. "Reese, you have to understand how Mike feels," Demetrious said.

"I know he's worried about me, but I can't just sit back and let these guys get away with this shit. I can't let them have the satisfaction of thinking that they ran me off. I'm not going to let them take away my dream."

"Shit, I know that's right! I just hope you kicked some ass!" Jay said.

"Jay, man, would you chill out with that!" Demetrious said.

Jay rolled his eyes at Demetrious and grabbed his keys. "Reese, man, I love you and I'm proud of you for sticking to your guns. Let me know if you need anything and tell Mike I'll call him tomorrow," Jay said, as he went to the front door and left.

Mike walked back into the kitchen and put his arms around Reese's waist.

"Are you okay, Baby Boy?" Reese asked Mike.

"I'm cool. I'm just worried about you."

"I know you're worried about me and I'm sorry," Reese said, as he wrapped his arm around Mike's waist.

"I know. I know. Is your hand okay?"

Reese let out a chuckle. "I'm fine compared to the ass whooping them guys got!"

Demetrious and Tariff stood by the kitchen door. "Well, we're going to get out of here and let you two enjoy each other."

Chapter 33
Chuck & Tyrell

Chuck settled into the comfortable limo seats. Since his concert in Dallas was cancelled, he decided to rent a limo to take him and Tyrell back to Houston. He was terrified of flying, so every chance he got he would ride instead of fly. He sat and watched footage of the concert in Los Angeles while Tyrell slept in the seat next to him. He glanced out the window and saw the mileage sign that showed they were only ten miles out from Houston. Chuck took Tyrell's hand and stroked his cheek, as Tyrell stirred a little.

"Hey, sleepy head!"

"Hey, yourself!" Tyrell said with a slight smile. "How much further do we have before we get there?"

"Ten more miles and we're home."

"I can't wait to see the guys."

"You miss them, don't you?" Chuck asked.

"I do."

"I'm sorry, baby," Chuck said rubbing his hand.

"Sorry for what?" Tyrell asked, leaning his head on Chuck's shoulder.

"For keeping you away for so long. I know how close you guys are and how you all ain't use to being away from each other for long periods of time."

"No need to be sorry, baby. You're my man and you need me as much as they do. Trust me when I say they understand that I'm here for you, and I'm still there for them too."

"I love you so much," Chuck said, as he stared into Tyrell's eyes. "What did I do to find such a special man?"

"Who says that you found me? Maybe I found you," Tyrell said, with a huge grin on his face.

"How about we found each other," Chuck said.

"I'll take that. Look, baby we're home!" Tyrell said with excitement.

The driver had stopped the limo and was making his way around to open the door. Afterwards, the driver grabbed their bags out of the trunk. Tyrell ran up to the door and walked into the house. "Hello house! We're home!"

Chuck could only laugh. "Ty, you are a clown! I'm going to run upstairs and hit the shower."

"Okay, I'll be up in a minute. I just want to grab something to drink. You want anything?" Tyrell asked.

"No, I'm cool. See you in a minute." Chuck shot Tyrell a seductive smile.

Fifteen minutes later, Tyrell finally made it into the bedroom. He heard the shower running and smiled as he heard Chuck singing. Tyrell walked in the bathroom, and leaned against the doorway and watched Chuck through the glass. He became aroused, as he watched Chuck shower is muscular body. 'Thank God for glass showers,' he thought.

Chuck always kept his body tight. His six pack abs had "FOR LIFE," in gothic letters tattooed across his stomach. He also had a cross that outlined his back. Tyrell continued to admire Chuck's body. Chuck lathered his perfectly round ass and thick muscular legs. Chuck turned to find Tyrell watching him. He smiled, flashing his pretty white teeth. "So are you going to watch, or are you going to join your man?" He said, as he opened the shower door. Tyrell quickly undressed, as he saw Chuck's manhood rise. Closing the shower door behind him as he got in, his lips were immediately drawn to Chuck's. Passionately they kissed, as the water from the shower massaged their bodies. Tyrell turned him and started to lick the lining of the cross on his back. The more Tyrell licked the harder Chuck got.

Minutes later, Chuck turned around to look at his partner through the streaming water. "Baby, I love you," Chuck said.

"I love you too, man." Tyrell said, as he passionately

started to kiss him.

Chuck turned Tyrell around and pressed his body against the wall of the shower. Chuck nibbled and sucked Tyrell's ear, making his way down to Tyrell's ass. Lick after lick made Tyrell moan. Chuck became more turned on, as he heard Tyrell's cries of passion. As Chuck started to stand, he slid his manhood firmly against Tyrell's hard body.

"I want to make love to you baby," Chuck seductively whispered in his ear.

Turning off the water and opening the shower door, they headed to the bedroom. They fell on the bed kissed each other passionately. Tyrell reached for the bottle of baby oil that sat on the night stand, squeezing the bottle squirting oil all over their wet bodies. As their bodies rubbed together, the sensation of their manhoods rubbing against each other turned them on even more. Sounds of excitement filled the room.

Tyrell maneuvered Chuck on his back. He took Chucks's tool inside his mouth. Chuck's moans became intense.

"Hold up baby! Hold up Baby!" Chuck said as he caught his breath. Chuck reached over grabbing a condom and the lube…

*   *   *

An hour or so later, they both re-showered and headed out the door. They hadn't told any of the guys that they were coming back early. They wanted it to be a surprise. Tyrell had spoken to Demetrious earlier and he said that he, Mike, Reese, Tariff and Jay had made plans to go out to dinner and wished that he and Chuck could be there. As soon as they parked the car, Chuck was swarmed by a few fans who recognized him. He signed a few autographs and took pictures with some who used their camera phones. One girl shoved her phone at Tyrell and asked, "Will you take a picture of me and Mr. Chuck?"

Tyrell grabbed her phone and took the picture. Chuck thanked his fans and he and Tyrell headed into the restaurant to surprise the guys. When they got inside it was crowded and the waiters and waitresses were buzzing about here and there. It was hard to spot the group. Finally, Chuck spotted them sitting at a table near the window.

"Look, Ty! There they are!" Chuck said, as he pointed in their direction.

"What are the guys celebrating?" Chuck asked, looking around at all the stuffed deer heads on the walls.

"Ricky won a big case and wanted to take everyone out for dinner and this place is down the street from his office. The truth is, when I called Jay the other day, I mentioned to Ricky that we might be coming home early and he suggested that we make it a surprise." Tyrell said.

As they walked over to the table, Ricky was the first to spot them.

"Is there room here for two hungry souls?" Chuck asked, as they reached the table.

The guys turned and looked up into the faces of their friends. They embraced each other and made room for Tyrell and Chuck to sit down. All the commotion they were making caused other patrons to stop and stare at them. The guys were so excited about seeing Chuck and Tyrell they didn't really notice they had become the center of attention. They were just happy to see them and finally, after only a few months they were back together as a complete group.

An hour after eating and drinking, Chuck tapped Reese and asked if he could talk to him privately for a moment. Chuck and Reese walked to a lounge area that was near the bar.

"It's good to see you, Chuck, and to have you and Tyrell home."

"Well, it's good to be home. I missed you guys. I know Tyrell has really missed you guys too," Chuck said.

"We missed you guy's too."

Chuck stared over Reese's shoulder to see if anyone was close by and able to hear their conversation.

"I've heard about everything that's been going on. How are you holding up? I can't imagine what you're going through. I don't know how I would handle this type of situation if the shoe were on the other foot."

"Thanks, man," Reese said, as he smiled at Chuck.

"If there's anything that I can do, by all means, let me know. You know I don't' have a problem cracking a couple of heads if that's what it takes," Chuck said, in a serious tone.

Reese broke out in a laugh. Chuck had to laugh as well. Although he had only been apart of the group for about a year, Reese felt like he'd been around forever.

"Man, all I can say is that I'm glad you're on my side."

"I respect you, Reese, and you are a good person. We need more brothers out here like you. I don't have a problem telling anyone that."

Reese stood up and embraced Chuck. "Thanks, man. That means a lot to me. We need more brothers like you, too. But we better get back before Mike and Tyrell call the police and report us missing," Reese said, as they started walking back inside to the table.

As they approached the table, the guys were gathering up their things.

"You guys get lost or something?" Mike asked with a laugh.

"Yeah, I thought we were going to have to call the police!" Jay chimed in.

Jay was glad that everybody was back together. He had an uneasy feeling that they were going to need each other.

"Are you okay?" Ricky asked looking at Jay.

"Yeah, I'm fine, for now."

"What do you mean, for now?"

"I'm not sure. I just have this feeling that we're going to need to lean on each other now more than ever."

"Come on, Jay, just enjoy your friends right now. Stop worrying so much," Ricky said.

Chapter 34
Jay & Daunte

Jay kept his word and went back to see Daunte for some answers. When he arrived at the guards desk, after going through all the check points, the guard, sitting behind his desk, told Jay, "I'm sorry, sir, but he's not expecting any visitors." Jay was furious and as the old Jay was beginning to surface, he knew that this was not the place for his antics.

"Is there anyway that he can see me? It's very important that I see him today," Jay said, all the while fuming inside.

"I'll see what I can do, but if he's not seeing visitors, then it's his choice," the guard told Jay.

"Anything you can do will be appreciated," Jay said, as he sat down in a chair to wait for Daunte. A few minutes later the guard returned and told Jay to have a seat in the visiting area and Daunte would be right out. Jay took a seat and tried to calm himself down before Daunte came out. A few minutes later, Daunte appeared with a guard in tow. He sat down in front of Jay without so much as a hello.

"What's going on, Daunte? Why were you not going to see me?" Jay asked glaring at Daunte.

"I wasn't going to come out, but my boy talked me into it," Daunte said.

"What do you mean you weren't going to come out? Man, what is really going on? I told you I would be back to get some answers. Now is the time for you to come clean and tell me what's really going on."

Daunte couldn't look at Jay. He could see that Jay was agitated and upset.

"Talk to me man, tell me what's going on. I'm not leaving

until you do." Jay was getting more and more upset with Daunte's silence.

Daunte looked at Jay with sad and hurt eyes. Jay could see and feel his pain.

"I…I can't, Jay. I can't do this now! I wish you could understand that!" Daunte said, as his eyes became misty.

"You have to make me understand! I can see there's something you want to tell me, you're just holding back!" Jay said, in a frustrated tone.

"I don't know how to tell you." Daunte said.

"Just spit it out, man. I'm here for you!"

After some more prodding from Jay, Daunte finally told Jay about how he was raped and that he was seeing the prison therapist to help him through it. When he finished hearing about what happened to Daunte, Jay slammed his fists on the table and stood up. Everyone in the room stopped talking.

A guard came over, "Is everything all right over here?"

"Yeah, everything's fine," Daunte said, while looking at Jay.

Jay composed himself and sat back down in the chair across from Daunte.

The guard walked away, but stood close by. The conversations in the room resumed. For quite some time they both just sat quietly. Jay's thoughts were running wild. He had heard stories about men getting raped in prison, but after talking to Daunte, the reality of it sunk in. Now Jay completely understood where all of Daunte's behavior and attitude towards Mia came from.

"You haven't told Mia, have you?" Jay asked.

"No, I haven't. How do I tell the woman I love more than anything in this world that I was raped?" Daunte whispered, trying not to let the guard know what happened.

"Mia loves you man, just as much as you love her, probably even more. She is a very strong woman. If you ask me, she would want to help you get through this. You should at least give her the chance," Jay said.

"Man, it was hard enough telling you, Jay. How can I look her in the eyes and tell her that I was raped? How can I? Please tell me how! My manhood was taken away from me."

"He may have violated you physically, but he can only take away what you let him," Jay said, with compassion.

"I could kill that niggah!" Daunte said, as a tear rolled down his cheek.

In all the years that Jay had known Daunte, he didn't think he had a tear in him. He was always so strong. Seeing him in this weakened state was heartbreaking.

"Does anyone else know about this? You told me about the therapist, but do the inmates know?" Jay asked.

"Yeah, there is one dude who knows. He's been a real good friend to me. He's helped me a lot," Daunte said with a sniffle.

"What can I to do to help?" Jay asked.

"Jay, you being a good friend to me is all the help I need right now. Just knowing that you support me and have an understanding is helping me, but there's something else that I haven't told you," Daunte said, looking down at the table.

Jay's eyebrows rose, "What else is there? You haven't killed anyone have you?"

"No, nothing like that, man. I'm trying to do my time and get the hell out of here. Believe me, if I had the chance that niggah and his boys would be dead. The other thing that I need to tell you is that I had to take an HIV test."

"You had to take what?" Jay couldn't believe what he had just heard. "This can't be happening. This has to be some kind of joke," Jay said, as he laid his head down on top of his hands. "When will you get the test results back?" Jay asked.

"I'll get the results in a few weeks," Daunte said.

"I am so sorry that you've had to go through this alone."

"I'm not alone completely. I have my boy in here and I have you and that's the most important thing," Daunte said as he smiled at Jay. "I know I need to tell Mia, but it's going to have to be when I am more comfortable with this myself, not to mention, I haven't gotten the test results back yet. So can you cover for me?"

"I got you, man. Don't worry."

They were interrupted by the guard who tapped Daunte on

the shoulder. "You have about five minutes left."

"A'ight, thanks, man," Daunte said, to the guard before he turned and walked away.

"Jay, do me a favor, man. Would you call Mia and tell her I'll call in a couple of days and tell her that I love her."

"I will man," Jay said, as he stood up to leave. "Keep your head up man, and stay strong. I know you're a strong man and you will get through this. I'm here for you. Anything I can do, just let me know."

"Thanks, Jay. You don't know how much this all means to me," Daunte said, as Jay walked away.

Jay got back to his car and leaned his head back. He was having a hard time processing everything that Daunte had told him. Jay sat there for over thirty minutes before he could start his car to head home.

Chapter 35
Larry, Antonio & Keith

Larry had been waiting outside of Tonya's house for hours, waiting for Antonio to come out. He had been following Antonio for over a week. In that time, he had discovered that Antonio was an NFL player for the Houston based team. It was only a matter of time before he would spill the beans about the real father of Tonya's baby. When Larry looked up, he saw Antonio coming out of Tonya's house wearing baggy sweats, a gym bag over his shoulder and his cell phone up to his ear. He waited for Antonio to get into his black explorer and pull off. Larry waited a few minutes, before he started to follow Antonio. Fifteen minutes later, Antonio pulled into a Starbucks. He got out and went inside. Larry pulled into the parking lot a few spaces down from where Antonio parked and waited, but Antonio didn't come out. Heading inside, he found Antonio sitting at a table drinking coffee and reading the newspaper. He shot Antonio a look and headed for the counter and ordered a large regular coffee and a slice of lemon cake. After paying the cashier, he walked over and sat down at an empty table near Antonio. Larry thought out his plan before he approached Antonio.

"Excuse me, but aren't you Antonio Diggs who plays for the Houston Sabers?"

Antonio smiled, "Yeah, that's me."

"Wow! Who would have thought that I would run into an all star like you in Starbucks?" Larry asked.

"I'm meeting a friend of mine here."

" I have followed your career since your college days. I've seen you play in almost all of your games, well, that is the ones that I could catch on TV." Once Larry found out exactly who Antonio was, he'd done some research on him. He knew all about both his college and his professional playing career.

"I have two sons and it would make their day if I could get your autograph for them. They would love it!" Larry could lie at the drop of a hat.

"Sure, man, I can do that for my number one fan! I could probably get them some tickets to one of the games. You could be a special guest!"

"You do that and my sons would vote me father of the year!" Larry said between chuckles.

"No problem. I enjoy my fans. They're the reason that I'm who I am today. Any time that I can give back is an honor for me."

"What's up, man?" Keith asked, as he walked up to Antonio and Larry, interrupting their conversation.

"Well, I took up enough of your time and I see your friend is here. Besides my coffee and cake are getting cold," Larry said, as he walked back over to the table where he was sitting before he started talking to Antonio.

Keith sat down in the chair where Larry had been sitting.

"So, what's up man? Who was your friend?" Keith asked.

"He was a fan that's all. Anyway, we're not here to talk about him. What was so important that you had to get me out of bed so early in the morning?"

"I took your girl's friend out on a date the other night and got her smashed."

"Okay and what does that have to do with me?"

"If you'll give me a chance, I'll tell you what it has to do with you," Keith replied sarcastically.

"Well, the girl can't hold her liquor. After about two bottles of champagne, she was singing like a canary."

Antonio and Keith were unaware that Larry was listening to their whole conversation.

"Antonio, I think that your girl knows you're a ballplayer and I bet you my bonus check that the baby she's carrying isn't yours!"

"Come on, man, why are you going there?" Antonio asked, with irritation in his voice. He was really looking forward to being a father, especially since his own father hadn't been in his life when he was growing up. He knew deep down inside that there was a possibility that he may not be the father, but he didn't want to believe it.

"So what am I suppose to do?" Antonio asked Keith.

"I have another date with her coming up. Give me a little time and I will get all the answers I need. I just have to get her drunk again, but not to the point that she passes out."

Larry sat and listened to everything they said, already knowing that he was more than likely the father of Tonya's baby. 'Everybody is onto these two tramps. I guess I wasn't the only one being played,' he thought to himself, as he walked pass Antonio and Keith and exited the coffee shop.

Chapter 36
Mia, Daunte & Curtis

Mia rolled over in the bed. She stared at the digital red numbers on the clock, 3:00 a.m. Turning back over, she looked at the neatly fluffed pillow where Daunte's head would normally rest. Reaching over she gently rubbed the pillow. 'Daunte, what is happening to us? God, I miss you!' The ringing phone broke the silence. "What the hell? Who could this be?" She asked herself, as she looked at the caller ID. The number wasn't one that she recognized. She picked up the phone and the voice on the other end was very familiar. Immediately, she started to smile. "Daunte, is that you? It can't be, what…"

"Hey, Baby Girl, it's me!" He said.

"But how?" Mia tried to ask but was interrupted by him.

"I was thinking about you, baby and how I treated you last time we talked. I miss you and love you so much."

"I know, baby, but how are you able to make a phone call this time of morning?"

"One of the guys here on the block is sleeping with one of the prison guards and he got her to sneak him a cell phone in here. So I gave him a few dollars and he gave it to me for the night," Daunte explained.

"Are you serious? You won't get into any trouble will you, baby?"

"No, Baby Girl, I got this under wraps. I have a few people looking out for me."

The phone was quiet when neither spoke for a second. Finally, Mia said, "Baby, you know you can tell me anything. I know there's something wrong. Talk to me."

"Baby, there is something wrong and I'm working it out.

Jay came by to see me and we talked. He's helping me out,"
Daunte continued, "Regardless of what I'm going through that
doesn't excuse the way I acted towards you. You have been my
best friend and lover and you've never let me down. I'm sorry,
Baby. I am really sorry."

"I know you are, Daunte. When can I come see you and if
it's me your worried about, don't. I'll be here waiting for you to
come back to me. You proposed to me!" Mia smiled, as she
looked at her engagement ring. "You're stuck with me!"

"I'm stuck with you, baby girl." Daunte smiled, as he realized that this woman meant everything she said. He loved her
more than ever.

As Daunte laid there in his cell, the room dark, he looked
out to only see the security guards walking back and forth and the
small night lights cascaded through the block. Daunte's free hand
made its way to his hard, erect dick. The sound of Mia's voice
truly turned him on.

"What are you thinking about, Daunte?" Mia asked, in a
seductive whisper.

"I was thinking how good it would feel being inside of you.
Baby, you done woke your friend up from his sleep."

Mia smiled. "You got kitty over here wanting you to
scratch." Mia spread her legs. The thought of Daunte made her
long for his touch. She inserted one finger after another until the
feeling of wet juices started to run. She reached over and grabbed
her plastic friend, switching it to the on position. The sheer vibration started her to moan. Daunte listened, rubbing down on his
dick.

"My dick hard over here." Daunte pulled his dick out and
started to stroke it. The more Mia moaned the more Daunte
moaned being careful not to be too loud. He didn't want the
guards to hear. By this time Mia had all 9 inches of her plastic
friend up inside her. Moving her hips from side to side she pushed
it in as deep as it could go.

Mia's moan got louder and Daunte could feel the pre-cum
in his hand. Daunte finally felt warmness all over his hand. He
looked and there was cum all over his hands and thighs.

"Now, Baby Girl, you ought to see what you made me do."
Mia smiled. "Well, it's wet over here too, baby."

"Well, baby looks like this cell phone is about to die.
Looks like I wore out the batteries. As much as I hate to, I got to
go. Plus, I need to clean myself up. Love you girl and I will call
you next chance I get," Daunte said.

"Okay, baby, be careful for me. Hurry up and come home
to me," Mia said, before hanging up the phone. Mia smiled as she
lay in bed. Finally, getting up out of bed she headed to the bathroom and took a shower. Getting back into bed, Mia's attention focused back on the clock which now read four thirty. Within
minutes, Mia had dozed back off to sleep.

Chapter 37
Keith, Barbara & Wil

Keith sat in the living room watching television and sipping on his glass of champagne, as Barbara made the finishing touches to dinner. He wasn't sure what she was cooking, but the aroma of the food was starting to make him hungry. 'Well, at least it smells like she can cook,' he thought to himself. Finally, sitting down to eat, Keith was surprised at how well the food was seasoned. He cleaned his plate completely and even had a second helping. After dinner Keith knew he had to play along to get the information he needed. He offered to help her clean the dishes and put them away. Keith opened another bottle of champagne and just as he expected, the ghetto girl started to drink. The first sign of her having too much to drink was her dropping the plate on the floor. She laughed, as she looked at the many pieces that sprawled across the kitchen floor.

"Move back girl, I don't want you to cut those pretty feet of yours." Keith couldn't believe what he had just said, but he knew he had to play the game.

"Ahh! That's so sweet of you, baby. I guess the champagne shot to my head."

"No, baby, it wasn't the champagne, the dishes are just slippery. I almost dropped one myself," Keith lied. He didn't want her to stop drinking.

"So you trying to get me drunk so you can take advantage of me again," Barbara said.

"No, I wouldn't do that to my girl. Shit, I hope I do get lucky again tonight."

"Oh, so I'm your girl now? That's what I'm talking

about!" She said, spilling her champagne.

"Why don't you clean these dishes later and watch a movie or something with me now!"

"A'ight, go and turn on the television and I'll grab another bottle of champagne out of the refrigerator and I'll be out in a minute!"

Keith headed into the living room, flicking through the channels on the television. He stopped when he saw a picture of Reese. Turning the volume up so he could hear, he didn't even notice Barbara walking up behind him. She flopped onto the sofa next to him. "That brother is a faggy!" Barbara replied.

"I know that dude!" Keith said, with a slight bit of irritation.

"You're not on his team are you?" Barbara asked.

"What you trying to say?" Keith was even more irritated. "I hope it ain't what I think it is, 'cause a brother here loves him some pussy!" Keith grabbed his dick thinking it was proving his manhood. "I don't know nothing about being a faggy and I damn sho don't hang around them."

"So how do you know him?

'Damn this is going to be like taking candy from a baby. Shit I didn't even have to bring it up. She set the stage. Now it's time for me to find out some things,' he thought to himself.

"Stop tripping! Why you trying to act dumb?" Keith asked. "You and your girl knew my boy Antonio and I played professional ball." He knew he could ask now cause her words were starting to slur.

"Kinda. We thought you might be, but we weren't sure," Barbara said.

"See, now why you trying to play with a brutha's intelligence? I'm not mad cause you got a brutha over here whipped!"

"My boy, Antonio and I, knew y'all were peeping us out at the club that night. We were just playing along," Keith lied.

"For real? Y'all knew? You lying Keith! Oh my God! You didn't know for real." Barbara was spilling her guts and not even realizing it.

Keith heard all he needed to hear. As he was about to

speak, the doorbell rang. He looked at Barbara. "Aren't you going to answer the door?"

"Oh yeah, hold on for a second. I'll be right back."

"While you're getting that I'm going to run to the bathroom," Keith said.

Barbara opened the door and to her surprise there stood Wil. She could smell the weed. It hit her like a tone of bricks. "Wil, what are you doing here? How dare you show up to my place without calling first!"

"I've never had to call this time of night before. Should I start now? You got some other niggah in there or something?" Wil asked.

By this time Keith had made it to the front door. "Is everything okay?" Keith asked.

"Naw man, everything's not okay," Wil said.

"What seems to be the problem?" Keith asked.

Wil swayed from side to side a bit before starting to speak. "Barbara, here, all of sudden wants to be shady and don't want a brutha to come in. Any other time, your girl here is willing and ready to fuck!"

"So I see." Keith said.

Barbara stood there like she had gotten caught with her hand in the cookie jar.

"Bru you can come on in. You guys don't have to worry about me. I'm outta here. All I have to do is grab my jacket." Keith headed into the living room and grabbed his jacket. "From the looks of things you two deserve each other." Keith walked up from behind. "Excuse me Barbara."

Barbara stepped aside with her arms crossed and her mouth twisted.

Keith walked pass and then looked back. "I found out all I needed to," he said, as he looked at Barbara with a grin on his face. "Now I just need to call my boy."

Keith left Wil and Barbara standing there. Barbara stood there and looked at Wil. 'I guess there's no need to let a good piece of dick go to waste,' Barbara thought, before speaking. "So are you coming in or you gonna just stand there?" Barbara asked,

as she noticed Wil staring at Keith as he walked away. Wil didn't
answer at first, so she repeated herself.

"So, you coming in or what?!"

"Who was that guy?" Wil asked.

"Just some guy who's full of shit! Why you ask? You trying to meet him or something?" Barbara spit out.

"Shit, that works for me!" Wil said, as he rubbed his dick.

"Damn, not you too!"

"Me too what?" Wil asked.

"So I see you're a faggy too!" Barbara said, as she
slammed the door shut in Wil's face. Immediately, she walked
over to the phone and dialed Tonya. Before Tonya could say anything, Barbara spoke. "Girl, I'm on my way over 'cause we got serious problems!" Barbara said, hanging up the phone not even
giving Tonya a chance to ask questions.

She grabbed her purse and keys and jetted out the door
driving like a bat out of hell. Barbara pulled up in record time.
Barbara looked up at the house and could see Tonya's shadow in
the window. Removing her keys from the ignition Barbara noticed
someone leaving out of Tonya's house. She figured it was Antonio
and just decided to wait for him to leave. As the person got closer,
she saw that it was Larry.

'This dumb bitch! She ain't going to get enough of this
fool until he hurts her.'

Barbara sat patiently and watched Larry as he got in his car.
She waited until she could hardly see his tail lights. Quickly get-
ting out of the car, Barbara dashed into the house after noticing
Larry had left the door unlocked.

"Tonya, where the hell are you? I thought you were smarter
than that. When will you learn?" Barbara yelled out, as she
walked around the house.

Tonya appeared from upstairs. "Girl what are you shouting
about and how did you get in here?"

"How could you, Tonya?"

"How could I what, Barbara?"

"How could you keep sleeping with that trifling ass
negro?"

"Who Antonio?"

"No girl! I mean Larry."

"Barbara have you lost your mind? I haven't seen or talked to Larry, let alone slept with him."

"I just watched Larry walk out the house."

"Larry has not been here Barbara. What the hell is wrong with you?"

"Wrong with me? What's wrong with you? I can't believe you're going to stand there and tell me I didn't see Larry leave!"

"Again, how did you get in here? I locked that door when I came in!" Tonya said.

"Your trifling ass boyfriend left the door unlocked."

'It's all beginning to make sense,' Tonya thought. She remembered the footprint, the water on the bathroom floor and the front door being unlocked when she knew she had locked it. Fear took over as she sat slowly in the chair.

She looked up at Barbara. "You're right, you did see Larry."

"Why did you just lie and say he wasn't here, Tonya?"

"Because I didn't know he was here," she said, as she looked up at Barbara.

"Tonya, I don't understand!"

"I think Larry must have a key to my house and he's been coming and going without me even knowing it!"

Barbara fell into the chair beside her. She knew Tonya was not the type of friend who would lie to her. "So you mean to tell me that his dumb ass been having the run of your house whether you're here or not?"

"If that's the case, he probably knows that I am pregnant, and suspects that he is the father. Oh My God, Barbara, that has to be it, I know deep down inside he has to know!"

"SHIT! SHIT! He's not the only one that knows everything!"

"What are you talking about?"

Barbara got up and sat next to Tonya and told her about every thing that happened earlier at her place. They both sat quietly. Finally, Barbara broke the silence. "We've come too far and

I 'ain't letting no jail bird or dumb jock ruin my plans for the future. You can take that to the bank!"

Chapter 38
Curtis, Carlton & Daunte

As Curtis headed to Daunte's cell, he saw Carlton and his boys chatting with some guys that he hadn't seen before. 'Those guys must be new. Carlton must be trying to recruit them to do more of his dirty work,' he thought. It became very routine for them to head out together to eat breakfast. Reaching Daunte's cell, he notice him looking out the window. He had a letter he was holding down to his side. Curtis called out to him, but Daunte's mind was somewhere else. "Daunte!" Curtis called out again. Daunte turned.

"Sup, Curtis?" Daunte was actually smiling. Something he hadn't done much in a long time.

"Looks like someone had a good conversation on the cell phone," Curtis smiled.

"Yeah, man. It was a good call," Daunte said, as they both laughed. Daunte reached under his pillow and handed Curtis the phone. "Let your boy know that the next time I talk to my girl I'll have her send your boy a money order to cover it."

"That'll work. I'll let him know. So is that a letter from your girl I see in your hand?" Curtis asked.

"Damn, man! I almost forgot!" Daunte said, as he lifted the letter to show Curtis. "No man, it's a letter from my boy, Jay. I told you his boyfriend was an attorney right?"

"I remember you telling me something like that. What about it?"

"Well, his boy was able to pull some strings and looks like I will be getting out of here in a couple of weeks. Turns out I will have to wear some type of ankle bracelet. I'll have to spend the rest of my time on house arrest," Daunte said, as he smiled from ear to ear. "Even though I'll be on house arrest at least I can spend that time with my girl and not between these gloomy walls. Excluding you, of course."

"Wow, man, that's great! I'm happy for you!" Curtis said, trying not to sound so solemn.

"What's wrong?" Daunte keyed in on Curtis's demeanor.

"Don't get me wrong, I'm happy for you, bru. Things won't be the same without you here."

"I'm gonna miss you too, Curtis. I don't know how I would have made it if it hadn't been for you. But man, I'll write and check up on you from time to time. I'll definitely come out to visit you too."

"Sure you will, man." Curtis had heard so many people in his life promising to stay in touch. After a while, they all went on about there lives and he figured Daunte would be no different, but he was happy for Daunte.

"I see I'm going to have to show you, man. We are always going to be friends. I cherish friendships, man. You've done a lot for me," Daunte said with a warm smile. "I have more to tell you."

"What's that?" Curtis asked.

"I told my boy everything!"

"Everything!" Curtis asked, as he walked over closer to Daunte.

"Everything, man! I told him about the rape and the possibility of me being HIV positive!"

"How did he take it?"

"He took it just like I expected it. He was hurt. I didn't even know if he would still go back and talk to his attorney friend about getting me out of here, but he did."

"Dawg, sounds like to me he's a true friend!"

Daunte started to stare out the window again and then looked at the letter. "Yeah, man, a true friend!"

"Man, all this good news. Let's go celebrate over breakfast. I'm hungry. We can't be late!" Curtis said, "I am really happy for you! I better not see you back in here!"

"Don't worry, man. I ain't trying to see no prison walls no time soon!"

As they headed to go get something to eat, they saw Carlton.

Carlton noticed Daunte and Curtis headed in the direction of the cafeteria. He grabbed his boys and headed off to meet them. "So where you girls headed?" Carlton said with sarcasm.

"Move out the way niggah!" Daunte said, as Curtis pushed him past Carlton.

Curtis stepped in between the two. "Carlton, you need to back off before I kick your ass like I did last time!!!"

"I'll deal with you niggas later," Carlton said, as he started to walk away, then stopped in his tracks, Carlton shot Daunte a quick smile before speaking. "Nothing gets past me in this joint. Don't think you're going to be released just like that. I want your ass here with me!" Carlton said, then threw him a kiss.

Daunte looked at Curtis, forgetting that he had just seconds ago told Curtis about his letter. "Why you tell him I was leaving?"

"I haven't said anything to that dumb ass niggah, Daunte. I just found out from you."

"Oh yeah, I'm sorry, man. How do you think he found out?" Daunte asked.

"Man, he works in the mail room! He probably read your mail!"

"Shit man!" Daunte said, as he started to pace. "This niggah gonna mess up my getting out of here."

"Daunte! Calm down!" Curtis said, as he put his hand on Daunte's shoulder.
"That niggah ain't gonna mess up nothing. I promise you that." Curtis tried to sound reassuring. "So let's just go and get something to eat and make an orange juice toast to your getting out of here!" They both laughed. Curtis knew whatever plans he had for Carlton had to happen soon and very soon.

Chapter 39
Reese, Antonio, Larry & Mike

Antonio lay in his queen size bed. Grabbing the remote control, he pointed to the flat screen television that hung on the wall. Hitting the guide button on his remote control he saw that it was 7:00 a.m. Antonio hopped out of the bed and walked over to the wooden dresser. He looked in the mirror and noticed that it was time for him to get a haircut and shave. Hopping back in bed, he picked up his cell phone and saw that he had missed two calls, one from Tonya and the other one from Keith. Retrieving his messages, he notices that Tonya's voice sounded a little upset. She said that she would be at Barbara's house for a few days. The next message was from Keith. His voice boomed through the phone. "Hey man, this your boy. We need to talk. I got some information for you." Dialing Keith's number, he was interrupted by the ringing of his home phone. Looking at the caller ID, he saw it was Reese.

"Morning, man!" Reese said, "I hope I didn't wake you."

"Naw, man, I'm cool! I was just checking some voice messages. I was just about to call Keith."

"What's up with Keith, man? He's been kind of distant. I called him a few times but he didn't return any of my calls," Reese said.

"Really? That's odd. Ain't no telling what's up with that dude. I think he got too much going on," Antonio said, but had some idea about the cause of Keith's distance.

"I guess. Anyway, I was calling to see if you wanted to hit the gym early today. My boy's father is coming in town and me and the fellas are going out to dinner tonight."

"What time did you want to hit the gym?" Antonio asked.

"How about in a couple of hours? That will give me a chance to eat and shower and stuff."

"A'ight man, I'll see you there." Antonio said.

Antonio thought about Tonya's message again and immediately dialed her number. After a few rings it went to voice mail. "Sup? This is Antonio. I fell asleep last night. Sorry I missed your call. About to head out to the gym in a bit. I'll call you when I get back in."

Antonio hopped out of the bed and headed straight to the shower. 'Damn!' I was suppose to call Keith back. Shit, I'll call him on the way to the gym.' Finally dressed, Antonio got in the car and headed to the gym. On the way he had to stop, pick up his coffee, and get something light to eat. After ordering his coffee and blueberry muffin, Antonio sat down and opened the paper.

"Antonio, what's up with you, man?"

Looking over the paper, Antonio spoke. "Hey man! How are you this morning?"

"I'm good. Had to stop and get my morning breakfast before hitting the gym," Antonio said, as he took a bite of his muffin. "What was your name again, bru?"

"It's Larry. The name is Larry."

"Oh, okay so you come here every morning, Larry?"

"No. Two or three times a week. I like this spot."

"I'm normally here everyday about this time and I've never seen you in here before," Antonio said.

Larry was always good at thinking on his feet. "I usually come later in the morning, but now that my work hours have changed, I just come a little earlier."

"Oh, okay, I see."

"Well, Antonio, I'm going to grab me something to eat and head on out. It was a pleasure running into you again."

"A'ight dude!" Antonio watched Larry as he grabbed his coffee and waved to him as he left out. 'That cat seems really strange to me,' he thought to himself. Antonio looked at his watch, finished his coffee and muffin and headed out to the gym.

*   *   *

Reese pulled into the gym parking lot, grabbed his gym bag and walked inside the gym. Only about three or four of the players were there working out. Nodding at the guys, Reese walked up to his locker. Opening his locker, a woman's high heel shoe fell out, then he noticed a dress, which he snatched, ripping it from its hook! Grabbing the other shoe, he wrapped them in the dress and threw them in the garbage can, knocking the can over. The other players stopped and looked over at Reese as he picked up the can. Reese looked around the room, turned and headed back to his locker. Unzipping his bag, he started throwing the contents into the locker. Not caring about the noise he was making.

"Bad Morning?" Antonio asked, walking up behind Reese.

"Naw man. Some niggah in here call himself being funny by putting some high heels and a dress in my locker."

"Sounds like a bitch move to me. Whoever's putting this shit in your locker, if you ask me, he's the punk!" Antonio continued loudly. "'Cause if he was any kind of man, he would do it in your face, and not hide and do this shit!" Antonio was now getting pissed.

"Let's just work out and get the hell out of here, 'cause somebody's gonna make me hurt them!" Reese said.

Antonio and Reese worked out for a few hours. Finishing, they hit the showers, got dressed and headed out to their cars. Antonio had parked right next to Reese. After chatting for a minute, they got in their cars. Just before Reese pulled off, Antonio blew his horn. Reese rolled down his window.

"Yeah, man, what's up?" Reese asked.

"Your passenger door!"

"My passenger door? What about it?"

"Someone painted it pink!" Antonio said.

Reese sat still for a minute. Then he started to beat the steering wheel with his hands. Antonio didn't know what to do or say. "Reese! Reese!"

"What?! "

"Calm down! Beating the steering wheel ain't gonna solve the problem!"

Reese got out of the car and walked around and looked at the door on his silver Benz, which now had a pink door.

"I got to get out of here, man. I'll holler at you later!" Reese said, as he walked around to the other side of the car slamming the door as he jumped in.

Antonio sat there and watched. He waved to Reese as he drove off. Antonio was really feeling bad for Reese. 'I hope he doesn't quit. We have got to find out who is doing all this bull shit.' Antonio sat there for a moment before finally driving off.

Chapter 39
Mike, Reese

Mike walked in the room, as Reese lay across the bed. Reese didn't move he just laid there staring at the ceiling. Mike walked around the bed.

"Scoot over," Mike said, as he sat down. "What happened?"

Reese sat there quietly before finally sitting up. "How would you feel if I told you I was thinking about quitting football and doing something else?"

Mike sat and just stared at Reese. He could see all this was taking a toll on him.
"What else would you do?"

"Sports casting maybe. I really don't know."

"Why are you thinking about quitting in the first place?" Mike asked. "Did something happen again today?"

"Somebody put some heels and a dress in my locker." Reese shook his head. "I just don't know if it's worth it." Reese didn't even bother to tell him about the car door.

"Reese, how could you say that? You're living your dream. Do you know how many people don't get that chance?"

"I know. Ever since I was a kid, every chance I got, I watched or played football." Reese got quiet for a second. "You know the most important things in the world to me are you, the gang and playing football, but now this dream is turning into a nightmare. I know I have a good life."

"So then I need to ask you, are you going to let some immature knuckle heads come along and take that away from you? You'll always be looking back, mad at yourself because you gave up!"

"You right!" Reese said, as he leaned over and put his arms around Mike.

Mike smiled, as Reese smiled back. "We better get up and get out of here so we can pick your dad up from the airport on time," Reese said.

"So, you ok now?" Mike asked.

"I'm ok."

"Good, 'cause now I need to ask you a question."

"What's the question?" Reese asked.

"Was it at least your color?"

"Was what my color?"

"The dress and shoes they left in your locker!" Mike laughed.

Reese couldn't help but laugh before he spoke. "No! It wasn't my color, but it was your size!"

Mike grabbed at Reese and he jumped up out of the bed from the other side. Reese ran to the bathroom door. "I'm going to go and take my shower."

Chapter 40
Mike & Reese

Mike and Reese made their way to the airport to pick up Mike's father. The three headed to a restaurant to grab a bite.

"So Dad, how do you like staying in Maryland with Uncle Angelo?"

"Son, I tell you I was a little worried about moving there, but my brother needed me. I just hated leaving you here."

Mike smiled at his father's comment. He knew that was his father's way of saying I miss you.

"I knew my other sons would be taking good care of you. Matter of fact, where are they?" Mike's father asked, as he looked around the restaurant.

Just as Mike was about to speak. His father saw them walking through the door. "There they are," his father said.

Mike turned to see his boyz walking through the door. One by one, they hugged Mr. Green.

"How are you Mr. Green?" Jay asked, as he sat down.

"I'm doing good son. I miss you guys."

"We miss you too, Mr. Green." Chuck chimed in.

"You know I've been keeping my eye on you, making sure you been behaving. You were on some show doing an interview. It was on the BET Channel, I think. They were talking about your tour and how well it was going. I'm proud of you, son."

"Thanks, Mr. Green," Chuck said, smiling from ear to ear.

Mr. Green noticed everyone had big smiles on there faces. He had his back to the waitress walking towards him he was carrying a birthday cake with lots of candles. All the guys started to sing Happy Birthday. Mr. Green started to feel warm all over. He felt so much love from the guys and he was so moved.

"You guys remembered," Mr. Green finally spoke.

"Mike, wouldn't let us forget," Tariff said chuckling.

"He reminded us at least 100 times a day," Demetrious chimed in.

"That's my boy!"

"Speaking of your boy, Mr. Green, we were thinking about having a guest house built on the property once things are straight in Maryland with your brother," Reese said

"Yeah dad. It would be nice having my father close by," Mike said.

"You guys don't need an old man like me hanging around."

"Sure we do!" Tyrell said.

"I'll feel like I'm imposing or in the way," Mr Green said.

"No, you won't Dad. You will have your own car and own place! It'll just be on our property!"

"Well, Mr. Green, you take some time and think about it and let us know." Reese said.

"That's right, Mr. Green, we will give you about one hour to think about it!" Jay said. The group burst out in laughter. Demetrious grabbed Jay and laughed. "You ain't changed a bit!"

"Where's Ricky?" Demetrious asked.

"He should be here any minute. He's been working on a case for a friend plus he had to go by the house and pick up all the gifts, from us, for Mr. Green," Jay replied.

"Friend! What friend of yours and what case?" Demetrious asked.

"You remember Daunte? Mia's fiancé."

"Yeah. Is Daunte okay?" Demetrious asked out of concern.

"No. But I'll tell you about it later."

"Well, if I can do anything, let me know."

"Thanks, Demetrious, you're the best," Jay said, as he gave Demetrious a hug.

"Did I miss the party?" Ricky asked, as he walked up smiling, carrying bags of gifts.

"Ricky!" Mr Green exclaimed, "I was wondering where

you were!"

"Work, Sir. But you know I wouldn't have missed your birthday for anything. We've missed you. It's good to see you again!" Ricky smiled, as he gave Mr. Green the gifts.

The night went on as Mr. Green opened the gifts one after another, while lots of laughter and toasts were made. As the night finally came to an end, Mr. Green raised his glass, the boys got quiet. "I just want to thank each and everyone of you guys. Each of you have become a very important part of my life. Thank you for looking after my son. Continue to help each other and keep that bond that you all share so dearly. Never! I mean never let no one come in and destroy what you all have built. You've become each other's lifeline and life support. A bond truly unbreakable," Mr. Green continued. "Reese you are a very special man. Keep your head up and be strong. No matter what people say or try to make you feel. You are a role model that most of the kids in this world need in their lives today. I raise my glass high and say this from the heart, I love each and every one of you, as though you were my own sons. I am proud of all of you. Keep being you and never change."

The guys all hugged each other. "I love you's," filled the room. They all gathered together, finally, with a group hug. Mr. Green felt warm inside as he watched them. He decided to take Mike and Reese up on their offer to move back home. This was his family too and they were going to need him."

Chapter 41
Barbara, Tonya & Larry

Tonya and Barbara both sat quietly in front of Tonya's house, thinking about the plan that the two had come up with. The street lights were dimly lit. They both listened to the faint sound of a dog barking down the street.

"Tonya, are you sure you ready for this?"

"I don't know."

"You don't know? Damn Tonya! This man is sneaking in your house, hitting on you when he feels like it, and stalking you! What the hell you mean, you don't know?
We've been planning this for the last few days! If we don't take care of this now, this niggah's gonna end up killing you! Do you want Larry to spoil the plans we've been making over the years?"

"No, I don't," Tonya replied.

"Well, get it together girl!" Barbara spit out.

"Call Larry and tell him to meet you at your house."

Tonya hesitated, and then dialed Larry's number. "I need to meet you at my house. I'll be home in about an hour." She hung up the phone without giving Larry a chance to ask questions..

Barbara and Tonya headed inside the house and immediately went up to her bedroom. Tonya sat quietly on her bed, in her bra and panties, while Barbara sat peeking through the curtains, looking for signs of Larry. The sweat on Tonya's forehead was evidence that she was nervous about what was about to happen. Looking at the clock, she realized it had almost been an hour since she'd called Larry. Barbara's quick movement told Tonya that Larry had finally arrived. Tonya removed her bra and panties and jumped in the shower long enough to get her body wet. Barbara got inside the closet and left the door cracked so she could see what was going on. Tonya's heart was beating a mile a minute, as she stood in the doorway waiting for Larry to make his way up-stairs. The melody of the doorbell sounded throughout the house. Both heard the front door downstairs open. Barbara moved further back in the closet, as she heard the sound of footsteps. Tonya ran into the bathroom and waited a few minutes giving Larry time to walk into the bedroom. Finally, making her way to her room she dropped her towel and scream as she saw Larry sitting on her bed.

"How did you get in here?" Tonya asked, as she bent to grab the towel to cover her body.

"I rang the bell and got no answer. I knew you wanted to see me, so I figured you left the front door unlocked for me." A mischievous smiled started to form on his face.

"No, I didn't leave the front door unlocked. I checked it myself when I got in."

"Well, maybe you thought you did," Larry said, as he walked over and sat in the chair.

"Larry, I know you have been coming in my house and sneaking around."

"You tripping. Why would I do something like that?" Larry was calm and cool, it was almost scary.

"Barbara saw you walking out of my house the other night."

"That bitch is seeing things." Larry was tapping his feet. Tonya knew that when Larry tapped his feet or hands, it meant he was lying. Tonya started to get angry. This man had violated her privacy and she knew Barbara was right. He had to pay. Her anger took over but she remained calm.

"I'm going to have you arrested."

"For what? You are such a stupid bitch!" Larry stood up and walked in her direction. "Let's say I did come by, how you gonna to prove anything? It's your word against mine. Why don't you call your new man?"

"My new man?"

"Did you actually think you could keep that from me? Let me see what is his name again? Hmm, Oh yea, Antonio!"

"Get out my house Larry! Get out!"

"Calm down, Tonya! You wouldn't want to hurt that baby

you're carrying!"

"What baby? You're out of your mind, Larry!"

"No! You're out of your mind if you think I would let you pawn my baby off on some other dude!"

"It's not your baby Larry!" Tonya yelled.

"From what I understand, you don't know who the baby's father is. You disgust me, whore! I heard you and your little hookah girlfriend discussing your plans."

"So you lied. You have been coming by my house."

"I guess I did. So what you gonna to do about it? I know you and your girl's entire plans and I'll be the first to tell your little NFL player boyfriend. Hmmm, maybe I'll go by his house and tell him myself!"

"You wouldn't!"

"I would. I know where the niggah stays. Maybe we will talk about it over coffee. I'm quite sure he would want to know what you two bitches are up to!"

Larry walked over to Tonya, slapped her in the face, knocking her to the floor. Reaching down, he ripped off her towel. Pulling Tonya off the floor, he threw her on the bed. Tonya's scream could be heard throughout the house.

"I'm going to give you something to scream about, you stupid bitch!" Larry said, as he started to unzip his pants.

"Shut up!" He said, with his hand raised high above her face. "I'll break your fucking jaw!" Tonya laid back down. Getting out of his pants, he used his legs to nudge her legs apart. He mounted her ramming his dick inside her as she began to scream Barbara's name.

"Get off of her! You sorry ass excuse for a man!" Barbara yelled.

Larry quickly turned, and was face to face with the barrel of a gun. Slowly, he stood up making sure not to make Barbara nervous. Tonya quickly got up and went and stood next to Barbara.

"You okay girl?" Barbara asked her.

"I'll be okay." Tonya said, as she wiped the blood from her mouth. "How could you let him go that far Barbara!"

"We have to make sure it appeared to be attempted rape. Call the police and tell them we just killed a rapist."

Larry looked at both the girls. "Do you really think you can get away with this?"

A smirk came across Barbara's face. Never taking her eyes off of Larry and holding the gun pointed directly at him.

"How does this sound to you Larry? Tonya was in the shower and when she came into her bedroom, she found you here, uninvited. Sounds like a break in to me. She tried to run back in the bathroom. You grabbed her and started to beat her and attempted to rape her." Barbara continued. "See Larry, you set the perfect stage without our help."

"You Bitch! That's not going to work!"

"Shut up niggah and let me finish. Of course, I was in the other room asleep and you didn't know I was there. I heard Tonya scream, I ran in here and found you on top of her about to rape her."

Larry could not believe what he'd just heard. He looked at Tonya, as she stood there trembling, tears running down her face. They all stood there, quiet for a moment. Finally, Barbara spoke up, "So you see Larry, we are going to get away with it!"

"You made one mistake Barbara," Larry said.

"What would that be Larry?"

"Tonya could never shoot me." Larry smiled.

"Yeah, you're probably right. That's why I'm going to do it! See, Tonya can be weak at times. But me, I've never been weak, especially when it comes to getting what I want. So if you shut the fuck up, I'll tell you the rest of the story. You see, I saw your gun sitting on the night stand. The gun has to belong to you, Barbara or I wouldn't dare own an unregistered gun. Plus it has your finger prints all over it.

"My prints aren't on that gun. I never touched it."

"Tonya knows that and I know that. Once you're dead, I'll put the gun in your hands and make sure your prints are all over it! Doesn't matter, that mine are on it, cause I picked it up and shot you! Self Defense nice and clean."

"You don't have the guts to shoot me, BITCH!" Larry

yelled, and started to laugh.

Barbara looked over at Tonya. Larry lunged at Barbara, the gun went off. Tonya covered here ears. Larry fell to the bed holding his chest. He tried to get up. Barbara fired again. Larry hit the floor like a ton of bricks!

"Is he…Is he dead?" Tonya asked.

"Check his pulse, Barbara told Tonya!"

Tonya walked over. She was afraid to touch, fearing he might get back up. She put her fingers under his neck and had her answer. Barbara, he's dead!"

Barbara stood there. She had never killed anyone in her life. The gun dropped to the floor. Tears started running down her face. Tonya picked up the phone and dialed 911.

"911, what's your emergency?"

Tonya was scared.

"What's your emergency?" The operator repeated. "HELLO!"

Tonya whimpered into the phone. "My girlfriend just shot this guy who was trying to rape me. We need some help." Tonya said, as she grabbed a piece of cloth and put the gun in Larry's hands making sure his finger prints were on the weapon. She looked over at Barbara who just sat their stunned and crying. Tonya had no choice but to take over.

"Maam! Maam! The police are on their way!" The operator said.

It seemed like everything was moving slow. Tonya walked over putting her arms around Barbara. Barbara couldn't believe that she had just done the unthinkable, taking another's life. Minutes later they both heard the sirens and could see the flashing red lights coming through the window. The footsteps told them that the police were on their way up the stairs.

Both officers walked in with their guns drawn. The heavier of the two officers walked over to Barbara and Tonya, while his partner attended to Larry. Looking up at his partner, the cop shook his head from side to side, informing his partner that Larry was dead. The officer noticed blood coming from Tonya's swollen lip. He grabbed the walkie talkie off his hip. "Where are the paramedics?" His baritone voice filled the room.

"We're right here!" One of the EMT's, said, as they entered the room.

The officer looked up. "This one is dead, but she looks like she has been beaten," he said pointing to Tonya. The other woman, I think is the shooter. She doesn't appear hurt just shaken up a bit."

The officers took the girls out of the room to get them away from what had just happened. The heavier officer stayed with Tonya and his partner went with Barbara, to question them separately about the incident.

The EMT sat attending to Tonya while the officer asked her questions about what happened. Tonya repeated the story to the officer, just as Barbara had told the story to Larry. 'I hope Barbara remembers the story if they question her,' she thought.

The other officer continued to try and get Barbara's story. He could see she was too upset. The officer went and got Barbara a glass of water.

"Ma'am, I know this is difficult but I need you to calm down and tell me what happened."

Through sniffles and tears, Barbara managed to replay the events to the officer, just as she had earlier to Larry. The officer took Barbara into the living room with Tonya. They both sat there consoling each other. Tonya listened to the officers talking. They both looked at their note pads, comparing stories. Tonya felt relieved when she heard the officer say it sounded like it was self defense. Looks pretty cut and dry. The paramedics came back in with a stretcher. They both looked at Tonya.

"We need to take you to the hospital just to make sure everything is ok. The baby appears to be fine but we should take precautions."

"You sure my baby is ok?" Tonya asked,

"Everything looks fine, ma'am. It's just a precaution," the EMT said.

Barbara finally calmed down. "I need to go with her, is that okay?"

"Yes. That's fine."

Chapter 42
Antonio & Keith

Antonio sat at his usual spot having his coffee and muffin. He placed his muffin down to answer his cell phone that vibrated in his pocket. He had missed two calls.

"Niggah, I know you saw I called. I knew you would be here," Keith said, as he walked up and took a seat across from Antonio.

"Naw man, my phone was on vibrate. I was just about to check my messages."

"Well, I have been calling for a reason. I went out with your girl's friend again. Man, I was right. Your girl knows that you play for the NFL. I got Barbara drunk, and she sang like a bird!"

Antonio leaned back grabbing his head. "Are you sure?"

"Why would I lie man? I'm looking out for you! I'm willing to bet that the baby she's carrying probably ain't even yours!"

Antonio was becoming agitated, he had gotten used to the idea of becoming a father, and now this fool was telling him everything was a lie.

"Let me school you bru. You got some women out here who will move heaven and earth just to get a few pennies in their pocketbooks. Don't get me wrong now buddy, you have some women out here that are a true blessing. Good, Wholesome, and Independent. Where there's good, there's also bad. These two bitches, man, they are part of the bad," Keith tried to explain.

Antonio was starting to like Tonya. But, if he found out that she was playing him all this time, she would have hell to pay, and he would make sure of it.

Antonio's cell phone vibrated again. Grabbing it off the table, he looked and saw it was Reese. "Hey Reese! What's going on? Let me call you back in a few. I'm sitting here talking to Keith," Antonio said, before hanging up the phone.

"Speaking of Reese, every time I pick up a sports magazine or turn to the sports channel, they're talking about him being gay," Keith said.

"I know our boy needs us to stick by him and help him get through this," Antonio replied.

"Naw, man, speak for yourself. I mean Reese is okay, but I ain't down with that gay shit. You might want to back off being so close to that niggah too, before people start calling you gay."

"You joking right?" Antonio asked.

"Do it sound like I'm joking?"

"Reese is your boy too!"

"Reese is your boy. He was my boy until this gay thing came up. If it was up to me, I think he should be kicked off the team. Maybe he'll give up and just quit!" Keith said.

Antonio could not believe what he was hearing. He sat there quiet for a second, then he looked up. "Why would he quit, and why should he give up?"

"I'm just saying, all those things that've been happening!"

"What things are you talking about?" Antonio was furious but he wouldn't let Keith see his anger. 'Could this dumb ass niggah, sitting in front of me, have anything to do with the stuff that was happening to Reese?' Antonio asked himself. The more Keith talked, the madder Antonio got. Immediately, he thought back to the day someone left the note and tampons in Reese's locker. He remembered seeing Keith and one of the other guys walking by him laughing about something.

"Why you so quiet man?" Keith asked.

Antonio welcomed the ring of his cell phone. "Let me get this call right quick. Hello," he said without even looking at the caller ID.

"What happened? When? Are you okay?" Antonio spoke into the phone.

Keith sat there wondering what happened and who he was

talking to. "What's going on?" He asked, as Antonio hung up the phone.

"That was Tonya, She's at Barbara's house. Something really bad happened last night, so I need to go and see what's going on." Antonio got up and immediately headed out the door.

Keith followed close behind. "Come on Antonio, don't fall for that! I betcha the two of them hookahs knew I was going to talk to you, and planned this shit!"

Antonio ignored Keith and headed to his car. Just as Antonio was about to get to his car, Keith grabbed his arm. "I'm telling you bru, listen to what I'm saying. I would not steer you wrong. I'm looking out for your best interest." Antonio just stood there, waiting for Keith to finish.

"Look Keith, I hear what you're saying and I appreciate everything you're doing and have done. But no matter what, the possibility of that child being mine, still exist. So I have to be sure, before I make my next move!" Antonio walked pass Keith and opened his door. "I've got to go! We'll talk later!"

Keith stood there and shook his head, as Antonio drove away. "Man, you being played, and you too stupid to even realize it. I'm done with this shit. You get what you get. I warned you."

Antonio pulled up to Barbara's house within minutes. All he could think about was his child. He immediately ran up to the door and rang the bell.

"Where's Tonya?" He asked, walking pass Barbara, like she was nobody. Antonio never really liked her. He felt that Barbara was just a bad influence.

"Is the baby okay?" He asked.

"How about, is Tonya okay?" Barbara spit out.

Ignoring her question. He headed towards the noise he heard in the bedroom.

"Hey you! Are you okay?" Antonio asked, as he saw her picking up the remote control she had just dropped.

"Yeah, I'm find and the baby is fine," Tonya said

"So what happened?"

Tonya told him the whole story. She referred to Larry as someone she dated last year. He couldn't believe what he had just

heard. The conversation with Keith and his suspicions about
Tonya went right out the window along with the thought of him not
being the father.

"Get some rest baby and I'll be back later to check on you."

"You promise?" She smiled.

"I promise."

"Antonio, I…"

"What, baby?"

"Nothing. I'll talk to you later." She smiled

Antonio walked away, wondering what she wanted to say.

Chapter 43
Wil, Jay, Chuck & Ricky

Early Saturday morning, Wil walked in the kitchen and grabbed the box of cereal off the top of the refrigerator. He shook the box to see how much he had left and poured some into the bowl. Sitting down and starting to eat, he scrolled to Ricky's name in his cell phone, then proceeded to scrolled to Jay's number. He decided to eat his cereal before making his call. Ten minutes later, he called Ricky.

"Hey man. You working out today?" Wil asked.

"Yeah, man that's cool. But I thought you were out of town or something?"

"Things came up so I didn't make it."

"Oh, a'ight! I'll meet you at the gym around noon."

"That'ill work! Talk to you later." Wil responded.

Wil hung up the phone, grabbed a banana and put it in his pocket. He then dialed Jay's number, but not without blocking his number.

"Hello." Wil listened to Jay speak into the phone. Hearing the noise in the background, he knew Jay was at work.

Wil immediately hung up and dialed Jay's desk. "This is Jay. May I help you?"

Wil hung up the phone a second time. Jay leaned back in his chair. He looked at his cell phone and then his desk phone. 'What was that all about?' he thought.

Wil drove up to Jay's house and saw the black Denali parked in the driveway. Walking along the side, he took the banana out of his pocket and stuck it inside the tail pipe of the truck. He trotted back to his car, continuously looking back, making sure Ricky hadn't come out. Wil parked up the street, far enough away to see when Ricky came out.

Ricky walked out and headed to the truck. He put the key in the ignition and tried to start it, but the truck wouldn't start.

"Shit! What the hell is wrong with this damn truck? I just had it serviced."

Ricky sat and waited a few more minutes before trying to start the truck again, but no luck. Ricky grabbed his cell phone to call Wil.

"Hey Wil, I seem to be having car trouble. So looks like I'm going to have to skip the gym."

"I'm already on my way. I can swing by and pick you up," Wil offered.

"I don't want to put you out of your way."

"Not a problem, where do you live?" Wil asked.

"I'm over near the fox five news station. 6011 Charles Street…"

"No shit! Man I have to pass that way going to the gym anyway. So it's no problem. I'll key it in my GPS." Wil smiled to himself. 'This is going to be a piece of cake?'

"You there man?" Ricky asked breaking Wil out of his train of thought.

"Oh, my bad man, I was keying in your address. I should be there in about ten minutes," Wil said.

"A'ight man. I'll see you then," Ricky said, as he got out the truck and headed back into the house.

Wil drove up to the house, hopped out and walked over to the truck to remove the banana from the tale pipe. He then walked over and knocked on Ricky's door.

"You here already?" Ricky asked, as he tried to step out the door.

"Yeah, man, but I need to use your bathroom first, and I need to make a quick call. On the way over, my cell phone died on me while I was talking with my girl."

"Sure man, the bathroom is right down the hall on the left and when you come out just use the phone in the kitchen. I'll be right back. I just remembered I left something upstairs."

Wil smiled, as he watched Ricky trot up stairs. He noticed Ricky's cell phone sitting on top of his bag. Quickly, he grabbed the cell phone and pushed it down in the chair. Wil was ready to put his plan into motion. He walked over to the kitchen phone and made his call.

"Hey baby, what you still doing home." Jay said, as he answered his cell phone.

"Ahh, doesn't that sound sweet?" Wil asked.

"Wil! What the hell are you doing at my house and where is Ricky?"

"Oh, he's in the shower. So I guess you didn't know he and I have been kicking it for a while. I really like Ricky. I just thought you should know. I tell you man, this bed feels good." Wil really tried to lay it on thick. Wil disconnected the call. Picked the receiver back up and left the receiver on the table. Jay slammed down the phone.

"You finished your call?" Ricky asked, as he walked into the kitchen.

"I finished. I had to call my girl, that's all man. She been tripping a lot lately. I had to call and let her know that I didn't hang up on her, and that my phone died. You know how sensitive women can be."

"Yeah, okay. Well, let's get to the gym so I can get back and get somebody to look at my truck."

"I'm ready if you are."

Ricky and Wil both headed out the door. Ricky, unaware that he didn't have his cell phone.

Jay continuously dialed the house phone getting a busy signal, and immediately he tried Ricky's cell phone, but no answer. He dialed it again, but still no answer. 'How could Ricky cheat on me and with Wil?' he thought to himself. Tired of dialing the cell phone, Jay slammed it on his desk. Driving like a mad man, Jay finally pulled up in front of the house, parking behind Ricky's truck. Jumping out of the car, he ran into the house. Up the stairs and down the stairs he ran, checking every room. The more he looked, the more beads of sweat rolled down his face. His heart pounded faster by the minute. "Ricky! Ricky! Where are you?"

Jay walked into the kitchen only to find that the phone was on the hook. Sitting next to the receiver was a key chain that he had brought for Wil a few years ago. Wil had conveniently left it there for Jay to see. Jay picked it-up and slung it across the room. Sliding down the wall, Jay fell to the floor, the tears streaming down his face. Jay walked over to the phone and dialed Demetrious. After a few rings, the call went to voice mail. Jay hung up and then dialed Tyrell's house.

"Yo!"

Jay tried to hide the fact that he was upset. "Hey Chuck. Is Tyrell there?"

"Naw man, he's out with Demetrious and Tariff. Jay, are you okay?" Chuck could tell something was wrong.

"I'm okay man. Just have Tyrell ..." the flood gates opened as Jay couldn't hold his emotions in any longer.

"Jay, what's wrong!? Man, what's wrong!?"

"I don't know where to start."

"Jay, where are you right now?" Jay whispered.

"I'm at the house."

"Stay right there and I'll be right over. You hear me man? Jay do you hear me?"

"Yeah, Chuck. I hear you. I'll be here."

Chuck hung up the phone and grabbed his keys and cell phone. Putting on his seat belt, he dialed Tyrell. His phone went straight to voice mail. "Hey baby it's me. I'm on my way to Jay and Ricky's house. Jay is really upset. I'll call you once I find out what's going on. Love you."

Chuck pulled up to Jay's house. As he walked up the driveway, pass Ricky's truck, he saw that the front door to the house was open. Chuck walked right into the house. "Jay, where are you?"

"I'm right here," Jay said, as he sat on the floor.

Chuck sat next to Jay. "What's wrong bru? What's going on?"

"Ricky's having an affair with my ex-lover!" Jay blurted out.

"Naw, man, not Ricky! That man's a punk when it comes to you! You must have misunderstood." Chuck tried to sound re-assuring.

"My ex-lover called me on my cell, from here, on the house phone."

"What did Ricky have to say about all this?"

"I haven't talk to Ricky. I called him a million times on his cell phone and he didn't answer," Jay said, as he looked down at his own cell phone.

"Ricky loves you man. He loves you more than anything in this world. When he talks about you or looks at you that man has stars in his eyes."

"I love him too Chuck," Jay continued, "that's what makes this so hard."

"Then, if you love him, like you say you do, you need to trust him and trust in what the two of you have built. Ask yourself this question, could the man that you fell in love with, the man that has grown to love you, be unfaithful to you?"

"No…I don't know, but, where is he? Why isn't he answering his phone?

"I don't know Jay, but there has got to be a reasonable explanation," Chuck said, as he sat down in the chair.

Chuck felt a vibration, standing up and reaching under the pillow he pulled out a cell phone. "Maybe this is the reason he hasn't called you!" Chuck handed Jay Ricky's cell phone.

"Why is his cell phone here?" Jay asked.

"I'm not sure, but I'll sit here with you, man, until Ricky gets back home. So why don't you go upstairs and get yourself together before he gets here."

Jay headed up stairs. He needed an aspirin, all the drama had given him a headache. Jay turned and smiled. "Thanks, Chuck. Tyrell is lucky to have you."

Chuck blushed. "No problem man. But can you do me a favor."

"Sure, what's that!"

"Tell Tyrell that," Chuck said, with a chuckle.

"I think he already knows," Jay said, as he headed up the stairs.

Chuck reached into his pocket and pulled out his ringing cell phone. "'Sup you?"

"Hey everything okay? I just got your voice mail," Tyrell asked out of concern. "Is Jay okay?"

"He will be okay. I'll tell you about it tonight."

"A'ight. But you sure everything is okay?"

"Don't worry, your man got things under control. I love you and I'll talk to you later."

* * *

An hour or so later Chuck saw Ricky and this guy get out of a car. He watched the two as they walked up the drive way. 'Ricky, I hope I was right about you,' he thought to himself.

"Chuck! What's up man? I didn't notice your car out front. Where's Jay? Is everything okay?"

"Jay went to get something from upstairs. He should be down in a minute," Chuck said, not taking his eyes off of Wil. "So who's your buddy here?" Chuck asked.

"Oh man, excuse my rudeness. This is my workout buddy. His name is Wil. My truck wouldn't start earlier and he gave me a ride to the gym."

Wil reached out his hand. Chuck just nodded. He didn't like the vibe he got from Wil.

Wil started to feel a little uneasy. "Ricky, I will talk to you later, man. I really need to get going."

"Why you in such a hurry, Wil?" Chuck asked. "Sit down for a minute or two."

"I wish I could but I really need to be going," Wil said, as he headed to the door.

"Why you in such a rush to leave, Wil?" Jay asked, as he appeared from upstairs.

Ricky was now confused. "Jay, how do you know Wil?"

"Oh, so you mean to tell me that Wil didn't tell you?"

"Tell me what?" Ricky asked, as he walked over to Jay.

"Well, Wil here is my ex-lover. He called me earlier today from here to tell me you and he were sleeping together."

"Sleeping together?" Ricky asked.

"Are you?"

"Am I what, Jay?"

"Sleeping with Wil?" Jay asked, as he looked at Ricky.

"How can you ask me that, Jay? You should already know the answer to that question! I would never cheat on you!"

Jay walked away from Ricky and over to Wil. "Do you want to know why Wil and I split? Why don't you tell them Wil!"

Wil just stood there.

"I see the cat got your tongue, Wil," Jay said. "Wil thought it was cute to try and control me! Wil put his hands on me twice."

Ricky moved in Wil's direction. Chuck grabbed Ricky's arm.

"Wil has been calling me over and over again trying to get me back. I've told him that I would never take him back. I also told him that I was in a loving relationship," Jay said.

"I even found text messages in his phone from guys he had been sleeping with while we were together. So you see Ricky, Wil became friends with you to get back at me. He's been using you all this time!"

Wil lunged at Jay. Jay took a step back and swung, knocking Wil to the ground. All his pent up anger came rushing out. Jay was ready to kill Wil. Wil had crossed the line and Jay was fed up. Ricky and Chuck tried repeatedly to grab Jay's arms. Finally, they were able to pull him off of Wil. Wil fell to the floor wiping the blood from his lip. Slowly, he got up off the floor and backed up toward the front door.

"You won this round, Jay! But this is far from over! You haven't seen anything yet! You're going to regret the day that you ever laid eyes on me!" Wil said, as he rushed out the front door.

Chuck walked up to the window, checking to make sure that Wil was gone. He watched as he sped off.

Closing the curtain, he looked at Ricky and Jay. "I'm out of here to let you guys talk. Jay, remember what I told you."

"I will. Thanks Chuck," Jay said.

"Yea, thanks Chuck!"

Jay turned back around and looked at Ricky. "I'm sorry, I should have trusted you and not given up on us so easily."

"You're right! You should have." Ricky gently pushed Jay

away. "Jay, I love you man and I've tried to show and tell you that. You have to trust me. If you can't do that, how can we have a life together?"

"Ricky, I love you, man. I'm sorry! Can you forgive me for being so stupid?" Jay asked.

Tenderly, Ricky took Jay's hand, placed it under Jay's cheek and raised his head so that their eyes met. "Man, I love you more than anything in this world. I would never cheat on you. I care about you too much. Just always remember that I love you and I am here to stay. As long as you remember that, we'll be okay," Ricky whispered, as he and Jay sealed their truce with a kiss.

Wil pulled in his drive-way. He pulled down the mirror in his car and saw the swelling of his jaw and the small cut on his top lip. 'This is far from over. Jay hasn't seen the last of me,' he thought, slamming the mirror closed, as he leaned back in his seat.

Chapter 44
Daunte, Mia, Curtis & Carlton

Daunte headed out to meet with Ms. Taylor, one last time. He couldn't wait to get out of the joint. His release was going to be bittersweet. He was glad that he was getting out, but he didn't know how he was going to be able to tell Mia about the rape and the HIV test. 'I know she is going to want to have sex. Should I tell her or should I not?' His thoughts played over and over in his head. Daunte looked up and realized he was standing in front of Ms. Taylor's office door. Knocking on the door, he finally heard her voice inviting him in.

"Hey Daunte. How you feeling today?" She asked.

"I'm cool…"

"I hear some hesitance in your voice. What's the problem?"

"My problem!? My problem!? How am I going to explain to my girl why I can't have sex with her?"

"Daunte, you can still have sex. You just have to use protection. But also, you should also share with her what's been going on with you."

Daunte stood and started to pace back and forth. "Daunte, if she loves you, she'll be there, right by your side."

"I just don't know." .

"Daunte, we can test you again today and give you the results today. After we tested you last time, we got funded to use the swab test."

"The swab test. What is that, Ms. Taylor?"

"We take a cotton swab, wipe it around inside your mouth and we'll have the results in twenty minutes or so. If you test negative, you can be tested again in about six months and if the results are negative you should be fine."

"I don't think I wanna know right now!"

"Why wouldn't you want to know? At least you'd know sooner than later," Ms. Taylor said.

"I guess you're right. A'ight, let's do it."

Ms. Taylor walked around her desk and grabbed a pad out of her desk. "Take this note to the infirmary and they will take care of you."

"Thanks, Ms. Taylor."

"You're welcome Daunte, and don't worry, you'll be okay."

"I hope you're right. So what about the test I already took?"

"Those results will probably come in after you have left and I will call you personally." Ms. Taylor tried to put him at ease.

"Thank, you," Daunted responded, as he headed out the door.

"Daunte."

"Yes ma'am."

"As much as I like you, I don't ever want to see you in here again!"

"Don't worry Ms. Taylor, I don't want to see you again either!" They both had to laugh.

"Good luck!"

Daunte headed to the infirmary and had his test done. He didn't want to wait around for the results. He decided to head back to his cell and wait. Daunte started getting angry, as he headed back to his cell. 'How did I end up in this situation?' He thought to himself. 'I should be married and at home with my wife, awaiting out first child. Now, I'm not even sure if I can have that dream.' Daunte looked up. 'Lord, if you get me out of this, I promise I will do better,' he whispered to himself.

"Daunte! Daunte!" Curtis called out to him.

Daunte turned and saw Curtis, as he trotted in his direction.

"Daunte, what's wrong with you. Didn't you hear me calling you?"

"I'm sorry man. I was deep in thought."

"My friend, you will be out of here in a couple of weeks,"

Curtis said, as he patted him on the back.

"I know. Guess what! I just took another HIV test. They have some test you can take and find out in twenty-minutes."

"How long ago did you take the test?" Curtis asked.

Daunte looked at the clock on the wall. "It's been about five minutes."

Curtis grabbed Daunte's hand. "Come on man let's go and get those results. I'll be here with you man." Curtis was just as nervous as Daunte but he knew he had to be strong for his friend. Twenty minutes later, the nurse walked into the waiting area and saw Daunte and Curtis talking to one of the guards. Curtis turned and saw the nurse and stopped her.

"Excuse me, Nurse. Daunte is here for his test results."

"Yea, I remember, let me get the doctor for you." The nurse disappeared through the pulled curtains. A few minutes later the nurse walked out with the doctor.

The Doctor looked at Daunte. "Why don't you come into my office so we can talk?"

Daunte and Curtis started to follow the doctor, but they wouldn't let Curtis go in. "You're going to have to wait out here," the nurse said. "Only one inmate at a time. That's the rule."

"Daunte, man, don't worry. I'll be here when you come out."

Daunte looked back and nodded his head before walking behind the pulled drapes.

"Daunte, have a seat," the doctor said, as he pointed to the chair. The doctor pulled the file off his desk that had Daunte's name on it. "Oh, here we go, right here."

"Daunte, your test results are negative."

"Negative?!"

"Yes, negative. But in six months you need to have this test again just to make sure."

"No problem DOC!" Daunte said, smiling from ear to ear.

"Good luck Daunte, and I'm glad to see you're getting out of here."

Daunte rushed out of the office without looking back. Standing and waiting, just like he said he would, was Curtis.

"So what's the deal?" Curtis asked.

"I'm fine man! I'm fine! I just have to get re-tested in about six more months!" They both embraced each other, one not wanting to let the other go. The embrace was not like that of two friends but more like that of two brothers who were very close. Curtis stepped back and looked at Daunte. "See, you need to listen to your buddy sometimes. I told you everything would be okay."

"Yeah, you did and yes, you were right!"

As they both headed back to their cell they noticed no guards were present. Out of no where, Carlton appears with two of his flunkies.

"So where you two bitches think you going?" Carlton asked, as he got into Daunte's face.

Curtis saw Daunte's fist balled. He knew Daunte would love to kick Carlton's ass before getting out. Curtis jumped in front of Daunte. Daunte tried pushing Curtis out the way but he refused to move. Curtis turned to try and persuade Daunte to back off. Curtis leaned into Daunte, causing them both to fall to the floor. Daunte tried to pull Curtis to his feet.

"Curtis! What's wrong? What are you doing?"

Daunte got his answer when he felt a shank sticking out of Curtis's back. The back of Curtis' shirt was blood stained. Daunte yelled for help, as he watched Carlton and his boys run away. From a distant, Daunte saw the security guard as Carlton and his boys ran by. By the guard's reaction, he could tell that the guard was probably on Carlton's payroll. Daunte felt hands on his back as the security guard from the infirmary ran up behind him. They both carried, an unconscious Curtis, to the infirmary. The nurses and doctor immediately came to Curtis' side. Daunte's heart dropped hearing the nurse say.

"He doesn't have a pulse! Doctor there's, no pulse!" Daunte tried to walk back to Curtis' side but the security guard grabbed him and escorted him back to his cell.

"We're about to go into lock down," the security guard said.

Daunte tried to resist but knew he couldn't. As he was unwillingly escorted back to his cell, the look on Curtis' face kept flashing in his head. The closer he got to his cell the angrier and angrier he got. The thought of losing his friend became overwhelming. Locking Daunte back in his cell, the officer turned back to look at him.

"I'll go back and check on your boy. I'll let you know how's he's doing."

"Thanks, man, I appreciate it," Daunte said.

"No sweat, man! Your boy Curtis helped me out about a year ago. We had a riot here in the prison. The guys in here got hold of my weapon and held me captive. If it wasn't for Curtis those guys would have killed me. So I owe him."

Daunte looked at the security guard as he walked away. He walked over to his bunk and sat down, impatiently waiting for news from the guard. Daunte sat on his bunk for what felt like hours. Daunte saw the guard approaching. He immediately walked up to the bars to find out what Curtis's prognosis was.

"How's Curtis? Is he okay?" Daunte spit out questions.

"Don't worry man. Curtis is going to be okay. Whatever they stabbed him with hit his belt, but he got about two or three stitches. He's going to be in the infirmary for a week or so, I think it's more for his protection. He did ask to see you. I'm going to work it out so you can work in the infirmary for the remainder of your stay. You should be starting tomorrow."

"Thanks, man, I appreciate it!"

"No problem. I need to get back to work."

Daunte walked back over to his bunk. 'Carlton needs to be stopped. I'll get his ass before I leave here!'

Chapter 45
Reese, Antonio & Keith

Antonio drove up to the gym and parked in his usual spot. Turning off the car, he caught a glimpse of Keith through his rear view mirror. 'Damn! I got to hear this niggah's mouth again!' Antonio thought, as he got out of the car and walked over to Keith's car.

"What's up bro?" Keith replied, as he opened the trunk of his car.

"It's all good man! Bout to go in here and get my workout on. You know pre-season will be coming up before you know it. So I definitely got to stay in shape!" Antonio stood there and watched Keith, as he rummaged through his trunk.

Keith grabbed his bag. The cloth that laid there caught onto the zipper of his bag as he pulled it out. Antonio noticed a can of paint pushed to the back end of the trunk. It was a silver can that looked like it had a few drops of pink paint running down the side of it. Keith immediately covered it back up.

"What, you got some painting to do?" Antonio asked, knowing that, was the same color paint that was put on Reese's car door.

"Oh, naw man. I've been meaning to take it back to the store it was the wrong color."

"Wrong color? Looks like it's been used, they may not take it back," Antonio said, as he reached inside the trunk.

Keith pushed his hand back and immediately closed the trunk. "Man, it's just a can of paint that's all! If they don't, I'll just toss it. But enough about that, let's go hit the weights," Keith suggested, as he walked toward the building.

"I wonder where Reese is. He must have come and gone or

he's running late."

Keith stopped in his tracks and looked at Antonio. "Why you still hanging with a dude like that?"

"What do you mean, like that?" Antonio asked.

"You know, him being gay and shit!"

"That don't bother me man. It's not like it's going to rub off on me, or something. Plus, man, if you're secure with your sexuality, it shouldn't bother you!"

"Reese my boy and all, but I just think it's wrong, man, two dudes lying up in bed together just ain't right," Keith said.

"Hmm. Well, what about two women, is that wrong?" Antonio asked.

Keith smiled, "Naw man that shit is sexy!"

"Oh yeah! But what's the difference, Keith?"

"It just is!"

"You a funny dude! That's the best answer you can give? I hear so many guys say the same thing and when you ask them the difference, you all come up with the same answer. So what does that tell you?"

"It doesn't tell me anything. That's just how it goes. Why we keep talking about this anyway. Do you need to tell me something bru?"

"Naw, man, I don't need to tell you nothing. All I know is Reese has always done right by me as a friend. He has always stood by me when I needed him. You know what's most important to me about people?" Antonio asked.

"No. But I'm quite sure you're about to tell me!" Keith said, as he stood there with his arms crossed and gym bag over his shoulder.

"What's important to me is how people treat me. Maybe you should try that!" Antonio shook his head and walked away leaving Keith standing by himself.

Antonio hurried inside the gym. Walking into the locker room, he saw Reese changing clothes.

"I thought you bailed out on me!" Reese said, as he stuffed his bag in the locker.

"I didn't even know you were here. I didn't see your car

out front," Antonio replied.

"I got my boy's car today, mine is being repainted. I should have it back in a couple of days."

"Good. Cause you definitely don't want to be driving around with no pink door." They both laughed. As mad as it made Reese that someone would do that to him, he had learned to ignore it.

"What's so funny guys?" Keith asked, as he walked in.

"Oh man, we were just talking about Keith's car. Somebody painted his door pink!" Antonio said with sarcasm.

"Really, when did that happen? I hadn't heard anything about that!"

"As much as the niggahs talk around here, how could you not know?" Reese asked.

"Man, you know me. I don't ever really get into gossip and shit!" Keith replied.

"Yeah, gossip and shit!" Antonio snapped.

"Well, I'll catch you guys later," Keith said, as he walked away.

"What's up with you two?"

"Why you asked me that?" Antonio asked.

"I don't know, something seemed a little different in your interactions. You sound like you mad at him or something," Reese responded, as he put on his tennis shoes.

"You know Keith, sometimes he can get under your skin."

"Yeah, I know. I also noticed he doesn't talk to me as much anymore. You think maybe he's going through something?" Reese asked.

"Maybe. I'm going to go and get started so I can get out of here."

Chapter 46
Mia, Daunte & Curtis

Mia was excited about seeing Daunte. She actually arrived at the prison about ten minutes before her scheduled visit. As she sat in the car, she thought about the conversation she and Daunte had over the phone.

'What did Daunte need to talk to me about?' she thought to herself. Mia looked at her watch and saw that she had about five more minutes. Getting out of the car, she walked up to the door. "Hey Mia!" The security guard yelled to her. "You're here to see Daunte? I haven't seen you in a while!"

"I know, work has been crazy. My job has had me working on the weekends." What she didn't say was that she hadn't been here because Daunte didn't want to see her. Mia was determined not to leave without being told the whole story behind Daunte's actions.

Mia walked through the security alarm while the guard checked her pocket book. No matter how many times she had gone through this process, it never got easier. As Mia walked down the long hallway, the sound of the clanging cell doors and the sound her feet echoed, as she walked down the corridor. Walking in the door, Mia was surprised. There was Daunte, but he wasn't behind a glass window. Mia ran over and embraced him. She melted in his arms. She yearned for his strong hands to be all over her. They both sat down and Mia couldn't help but notice the peace and calmness that surrounded Daunte.

"Baby, why are you smiling so much? Are you that glad to see me? And why aren't you behind the glass window?" Mia asked, without giving Daunte a chance to answer.

"Can't I just be glad to see my baby girl?"

Blushing, she started to speak but Daunte interrupted. "I have a few things I need to tell you." Mia's smiled quickly vanished, not sure why Daunte, all of a sudden, looked so serious.

"I have good news and I have bad news," Daunte said. "Which would you like first?"

Mia immediately stood up and started to pace, trying to prepare herself for what her man was about to tell her. "Give me the bad news first," Mia said, as she sat down and took a deep breath.

Daunte sat quiet for a moment. Mia could see that whatever he was about to say was hurting him. Mia rubbed his hand. "Go ahead baby, it's okay. No matter what, you know I got your back."

Daunte took a deep breath before speaking. He looked Mia in the eyes. That sadness that Mia thought had left was back again. "The reason I had been so distant with you was because I was raped by one of the other prisoners".

Mia immediately let go of his hands, stunned at what he told her. It was almost like somebody scared her. "Oh my God, No Daunte!" she said, as she reached for his hand again, "How did they let this happen to you in here?"

Mia gently stroked his hand. She could see that this was hard for him. Mia had never seen him in so much pain. "Did they get the guy who did this to you?" Mia asked, as she reached over placing her hands under Daunte's chin.

"No, they didn't. Here in prison, you learn to deal and keep quiet."

"How could someone be so cruel?"

"Baby, there's more."

"More!! What more could there be?" Mia asked out of concern.

"Baby Girl, I had to take an HIV test."

"WHAT! DAUNTE NO!" The tears started to flow down Mia's face.

"It's ok Mia. It's okay. I took my first test and it came back negative. I just have to take another test in six months and if it's still negative, I'll be fine."

Daunte had to comfort Mia. She was beside herself.

"I'm sorry, Baby Girl… I'm sorry Baby Girl," Daunte said, as he confronted her. When she calmed down, he got up and walked away from the table.

Mia watched Daunte pace back and forth. At that moment, Mia realized that it wasn't about her and her feelings. It was about the man she loved and wanted to spend the rest of her life with.

Daunte walked back over to Mia. "Baby girl, I'll understand if you don't want to be with me anymore."

"Daunte, how can you say that to me? I mean, it's a lot to take in," Mia said, as she leaned back in her chair. "I know we're not married yet, but I'm here for better or for worse, Daunte."

"But what if I'm HIV Positive?" Daunte asked.

"And what if your not?" Mia replied. "We 'll deal with this when the time comes."

"They both sat quietly. One not knowing what to say to the other. They both knew how much they loved each other. As Mia looked at Daunte, she knew that he would do anything for her and she knew how much he loved her. But she wondered if he really knew that she loved him just as much.

"Baby," Mia said, as she raised up.

"Yeah!"

"I thought you said you had some good news!"

"I do."

"All this bad news. I can use some good news," Mia said, with a smile.

"I'm getting out of here! My boy Jay worked some things out for me and I'll be getting out of here by the end of this week or early next week!"

"That soon? Oh my goodness! Daunte, that is good news!"

"How did Jay do it? Does he know everything that's happened?"

"Yeah, he does, so I guess he figured he needed to get me out of here. But, Baby Girl, are you sure you want me to come home?"

"Fast, quick and in a hurry! You've been through so much

Baby! You took care of me for so long. So now, I need to take care of you," Mia said, as she leaned over and gave Daunte a kiss.

"Thank you, Baby Girl."

"For what Daunte?"

"For being you girl!. Just for being you!"

Chapter 47
Barbara & Tonya

As Tonya lay in bed, she could smell the coffee brewing and the strong scent of bacon being cooked in the kitchen. Getting out of bed, she headed straight to the shower in the spare bedroom. Tonya had not been back to the house since the incident with Larry. She had been staying with Barbara. As Tonya sat on the bed fully dressed, she still felt some guilt about what happened to Larry. No matter what he had done, he was a man that she once loved. Tonya also found it a little strange that Barbara had moved on like nothing had ever happen.

"Morning, Girl," Tonya said, as she walked in the kitchen.

"Hey T. I didn't wake you, did I?"

"No. The smell coming from this kitchen woke me. Girl, that food smells good!"

"Well, grab you some juice and sit down and I'll fix you a plate," Barbara said, as she grabbed a couple of plates. "So, what are you going to do about your place?"

"I can't stay there. I need to find me another place. Every time I walk into my bedroom, it reminds me of that night," Tonya said.

"You need to be strong. It's all over. We need to go on with our lives."

"Do you regret anything that's happened?" Tonya asked.

"No. I don't and you shouldn't either. Larry was crazy. That brutha would have ended up killing you. Always remember, only the strong survive."

"I'm scared Barbara. Do you think we can get away with it?"

"Get away with it? We already have! Unless Larry comes back from the grave and talks to the cops!" Barbara laughed at her own comments.

"Barbara, that sounds so cold."

"Tonya, you need to move on and forget about this. I know I don't want to go to jail. I know you don't either. So let's just forget about it and worry about our next move. We too deep in this shit now to be worried."

"You right."

"How are things with Antonio? Does he still think he's the baby's father?"

"Yeah, he does. What if he ask for a paternity test after the baby's born?"

"I never thought about that," Barbara said. "We'll have to cross that bridge when we get to it. Have you mentioned to him about you guys getting married?"

"Married!" Tonya spit out.

"Yeah married. Because once you married then nothing really matters. Maybe you should start throwing hints out there!"

"What kind of hints are you talking about?" Tonya asked, as she ate her bacon.

Barbara thought for a moment before speaking. "How bout you tell him you don't want your baby born without being married. Play that old school card."

"I guess I could do that."

Barbara walked over and turned on the television. Tonya and Barbara continued to talk, then silence, as the television caught their attention.

"Turn up the television!" Tonya said.

Barbara looked at Tonya and said, "That's Chuck!"

"It's him! When did he get out of jail?" Tonya asked.

"I don't know. I wonder if Carlton and Curtis got out too?"

"When was the last time you talked to any of them?"

Barbara thought before finally saying, "I stayed in contact with them the first year then things got kind of busy."

"Maybe we should call the prison and see." Tonya suggested.

"But what the hell is Chuck doing on TV and with a music video?"

"I didn't even know Chuck could sing! Did you Barbara?"

"I used to hear him sing here and there. I always thought he had a nice voice, but I never knew he was that good!"

"I'll call the prison today and see what I can find out!" Barbara said.

Both sat there and watched the little segment on Chuck. And they were really surprised when they found out he was on tour.

'Chuck is out of jail and a big time celebrity,' Barbara thought to herself.

Chapter 48
Curtis, Carlton & Daunte

Clang! Clang! The sounds of the cell doors closing and opening, woke Daunte up. Raising up, wiping the sleep out of his eyes, he walked over to the small square window with a screen. He could see that it was about to rain. The clouds covered the sky, not a sign of the sun. He quickly got dressed and laid back down on his bunk. He wanted to lay in bed all day.

"Get up out of that bunk and get out here for the morning count!" The officer spoke. Daunte fell in line with the rest of the inmates. Some stood in just their boxers and some fully dressed. After the count, Daunte went back in his cell and minutes later headed out to grab a bite to eat. After breakfast, he headed over to the infirmary to start his job. He was excited about seeing Curtis. As Daunte approached the infirmary, he saw Curtis and the Security Guard who had looked out for him. The guard handed Curtis a couple of items. One item appeared to be a bottle of lotion or something. The closer Daunte got, the more he could hear bits and pieces of their conversation. Whatever they were talking about, Daunte could tell it was something that they didn't want anyone to hear.

"After tonight man, we square. I don't owe you anything else," Daunte heard the guard say.

"Right, man, we'll be all square. By the way, thanks for getting my boy set up in here," Curtis said.

"'Sup, fellows?" Daunte asked, as he walked up.

"I have to get to my rounds. Catch you guys later," the security guard said, as he walked away.

"What's that all about, Curtis?"

"What's what about, Daunte?"

"It looked like you guys were planning something when I walked up, what's going on tonight?" Daunte asked.

"Nothing that concerns you," Curtis said, changing the subject. "How does it feel to be a short timer?"

"Curt man, I can't wait to say good bye to this place. I met with my girl the other day and I told her everything."

"Everything, D?"

"Everything!"

"So how did she take it?"

"Well, I know she's scared. But she said she's with me for better or worse."

"Bru, you have a good woman there."

"Yeah, I know and my foolish pride almost caused me to lose her."

"Men and our foolish pride." Curtis shook his head. "Well, you better get busy before these knuckle head guards come in and catch you not working."

"You right. Don't want to get fired on the first day," Daunte said, as he chuckled.

Daunte walked away and stayed busy the remainder of the day. He looked up at the government issued clock on the wall. Another ten minutes and his day was over. Since he had finished his work, he figured he'd kill a few minutes with Curtis. Walking in that direction, he saw the familiar security guard once again.

"They work you hard today man?" The officer asked

"Naw, it was a light day. I'm just about to get out of here. I figured I would stop by and see Curt before I left."

"A'ight man. I just got here. My day is just starting. I feel like I just left," the officer said, as he headed out on his rounds.

Daunte spent the last fifteen minutes or so chatting with Curtis in the infirmary.

"I better get out of here and get something to eat. I'll see you tomorrow, Curt."

"A'ight D," Curtis said, as he pulled the covers over his head to sleep.

A few hours had passed and Curtis woke to see the guard standing over him.

"We need to do this now, while the other guard is on patrol," the officer said.

Curtis gingerly got out of bed.

"You sure you can do this? You moving kinda of slow," the officer said.

"Don't worry, I'm a soldier. This niggah got to pay. I can deal with pain. Plus, if I don't do this now, no telling when I'll get another chance," Curtis continued. "No one would even suspect me."

Both the officer and Curtis headed down the hall to Carlton's cell, where he lay asleep. The officer stopped just short of Carlton's cell, making sure no one was around.

"I'll be right here. Just make this quick. Cause guards are going to be all over this place," the officer said.

"No problem. I'll make it quick."

Curtis walked over to Carlton's cell and looked in and watched him sleep. Curtis pulled out his bottle and started squirting it in the cell.

"Hey Bitch! Wake up!" Curtis said, just above a whisper.

Carlton jumped and looked in the direction of the voice. "Niggah what the fuck are you doing in front of my cell?"

"I owe you something and it's time I give it to you. You thought you could do what you did to my boy and stab me in my back! You're a coward! I'm going to show you what happens to cowards," Curtis said, as he continued to squirt the liquid in Carlton's face and all in his cell.

"What the fuck is that you squirting in here?" Calton asked, as he rushed to the front of the cell trying to grab Curtis.

Curtis stepped back. "I learned a few things while I worked in the license plate shop. I thought all this time all T-Eleven did was remove those stickers off the license plates, but come to find out when you put a match to it, it burns uncontrollably. Not even water alone will put it out," Curtis said, as he pulled a book of matches out of his hospital gown pocket. Striking the match, Curtis threw it inside the cell. Carlton backed up toward the wall. He grabbed the bedspread off the bunk and threw it on the fire, trying to put it out. Carlton's screams for help started to echo throughout the jail. Curtis hurried out of the area and back into the infirmary. The further he walked away, the louder Carlton's shouts for help became.

Carlton frantically tried to put out the fire, but nothing was working. The fire caught to the sleeve of his shirt. As Carlton grabbed his arm to put the fire out on his sleeve, he could hear the security guards rushing to open the cell. He could hear the officer asking, "Where are the fire extinguishers?" Curtis had planned everything carefully. He had the guard remove the extinguishers off the wall and put it into the other room.

"Get me out of here! Help me please!" Carlton shouted.

Finally, a guard came in with a couple of the extinguishers. Handing one of the extinguishers to another guard, they continued to try and dowse the flames. More guards came in with blankets, trying to put out the fire. The flames had died down just enough for a couple of the guards to jump over. Carlton laid there unconscious from the smoke. One guard grabbed his feet and the other held onto his shoulders. The guards were able to get Carlton out but not before his face and arms were burned.

One of the guards tried doing CPR. Carlton wasn't breathing. They continued for what seem like an eternity. Finally, Carlton started to cough. His coughs turned to screams, as he started to feel the pain from the burns. Some guards continued to try and fight the fire while others emptied the other cells. The guards rushed Carlton to the infirmary. Curtis watched, as they wheeled him on the gurney.

"What's going on?" Curtis asked, as though he was surprised, but he was still mad as hell when he saw that Carlton was still alive.

Curtis could hear Carlton's screams over the alarm system that sounded throughout the prison. As Curtis looked through the large window inside the emergency room, he cursed the nurse when she pulled the curtains shut. He could no longer see inside.

Daunte, as well as other prisoners, stood at the front of their cells in the other dorm trying to figure out what was going on. Daunte heard one of the prisoners ask the guard what was happening. "There was a small fire. We got it under control now and an inmate got burned. That's all we know."

Daunte remembered what he'd heard earlier and put the pieces together.

Chapter 49
Antonio, Keith & Reese

Antonio and Reese finished up their workout. As they walked into the locker room, Antonio saw Keith standing at Reese's locker. Antiono quickly backed up, knocking Reese backwards.

"What's wrong man?" Reese asked, as he noticed Antonio peeping inside the locker room. Antonio pointed to Keith. Keith was standing by Reese's locker. He and Reese watched him as he threw something in the locker and hurried away.

"You in a rush?" Reese yelled out to Keith as he walked away.

"What's up Reese & Ant? I didn't know you guys were here."

"Apparently," Reese said, as he walked to his locker.

When Reese opened his locker there sat a stack of gay porno magazines. "Black Inches."

"What's this shit you put in my locker Keith?" Reese asked.

"Ahh man, don't be so sensitive Reese. It was just a joke."

"A Joke! A Joke!" Reese shouted. "Antonio do you find this funny?"

"Naw, I don't get that joke Reese. So Keith what's the punch line?" Antonio asked. "All this time it was you. Wasn't it Keith?"

"Antonio, what do you mean it was him?" Reese asked.

"The other day, when Keith and I were talking, I saw a can of paint in his car and he tried to cover it up. I wanted to make sure I had all my facts straight before I came to you Reese. But looks like Keith just got caught and confirmed everything."

Reese was keeping his cool. "Keith, man, I thought we were boys. How could you do this to me?" Reese asked.

Antonio was shocked at how well Reese was maintaining his composure. He just knew Reese was going to flip out, after all the drama he had endured over the pass few months. Reese stood quiet for a moment and then he spoke.

"Keith, man I could kick your ass right here and now with no effort on my part, but what would that prove? That would only make us both look like fools," Reese continued. "Yeah, I am a gay man," Reese said, as he noticed other players coming in. "A gay man!" Pointing to himself. "I was your biggest supporter helping you get on this team. How do you thank me man? You thanked me by doing the shit that you did. I have no respect for you because you're a coward. The problem with you man is, you're not secure with your sexuality. Cause if you were, then what I do off the field wouldn't even matter to you! Antonio has been the only person that has treated me with respect."

"Reese, let's get out of here," Antonio said.

"Just a minute, bruh!" Reese said. "You guys are so busy worrying about what I do in the bedroom that you overlooked how good I am on the field. Or, how much I supported each and every one of you guys. I carried this team on my back. As I said, a while back, I'm here to stay and if you guys don't like it maybe you should try and get traded. Keith, I hope I'm not around to see when you experience the consequences of your actions. It will catch up with you. You call me a punk. I think you're the punk. You should have been man enough to say how you felt in my face bru. Not sneaking around like some little, what you call it, BITCH! I'm out of here! Reese started to walk away. Stopping in his tracks, he looked at Keith. "I'll be sending you the bill for my car." Reese walked out, never looking back, Antonio close behind.

"Reese, you okay man?"

"Man, you know, for the first time, I'm okay and I'm going to be fine!"

"Bru, I thought you would explode! How did you maintain your composer?

Reese smiled. "That was the easy part. I thought about this

story the coach told me and the one thing he asked me not to do."

"What did he ask you not to do?" Antonio asked.

"He asked me not to quit or give up." Reese looked up and smiled.

"Now I understand," Antonio said

"What is it that you understand man?"

"I understand why black, gay men, or gay men period, keep their lifestyles private. It's brutha's like that ass hole Keith and his buddies that make it hard to come out."

"Yeah, man! Sounds like you understand!"

Chapter 50
Daunte, Curtis & Mia

Its been a week since the fire and the injury to Carlton. The lockdown was finally over. Daunte was excited, this was his last day in this hell hole of a prison. Daunte, as well as the other inmates had gotten restless. So it was a welcome sight to see the guards coming by and letting everyone out and things getting somewhat back to normal. Daunte headed to the infirmary to work his last day, and to see Curtis. Daunte was going to miss Curtis. Curtis had helped him through so much.

"Sup," Curtis said, as he saw Daunte headed over towards him.

"Hey man, you feeling better?"

"I'm much better. At least, better than you guys. That lockdown is a bitch, man, ain't it?" Curtis asked.

"So what happened?"

"What do you mean? What happened?" Curtis asked.

"The rumor is Carlton got hurt really bad."

"Yeah, I heard the same thing. He was transferred to some hospital burn unit near by. He received burns to his arms and I think to his face, as well as, smoke inhalation."

"I wonder how that happened?" Daunte asked.

"Not sure man. I hear Carlton had pissed off a lot of people here. There's some investigation going on. So I think when he gets better they're going to transfer him to some other prison for his protection."

Daunte and Curtis both knew the real truth. They both knew it was best to talk about it as little as possible. You never knew who might be listening. In prison, everyone knew not to talk about anything directly.

"So you getting out of here tomorrow?" Curtis asked.

"Yeah, man! My girl is picking me up!"

"Daunte man, I don't ever want to see you in this place again. When you get out of here, don't ever look back or think about this place."

"Curt, man, I'll be back. My boy, Jay, has his friend looking into your case to see what they can do."

Curtis smiled. "I appreciate that man, but I don't think I will be getting out of here. The only way I'll leave out of here, will be in a box."

Daunte didn't want to hear that, but he knew Curtis was probably right. He knew but he still had to try.

"Daunte, you've been a good friend. I've never met anyone like you in my life. You know what's crazy D? In that short period of time I fell in love with the one thing I hated the most."

Daunte knew what Curtis was trying to say. "I know man, I'm sorry but…"

Curtis interrupted him. "I love you man but I wish you and your girl the best." Curtis turned and looked away. Daunte stood there and fought to hold his emotions, he felt he was leaving behind a good friend and he really felt sorry for Curtis, especially since he knew Curtis was probably right about everything he had said.

"I'll be in touch Curtis."

"Sure you will, man." One thing Curtis had learned from the other prisoners, once a person leaves, they're gone. He hoped this would be different and that Duante would keep in touch, but he had to be realistic.

"Thanks for everything, Curt," Daunte said, as he reached out his hand.

"It was a pleasure. Now, get out of here so I can get some sleep!"

Daunte walked toward the door, turned and raised his fist. "Be strong and keep your head up.

Curtis smiled and nodded and watched Daunte walk out. Easing under the covers, Curtis looked at the bars in the room, as well as, the dingy grey walls with the dirty posters that looked like they'd been there for years.

'How did I allow myself to fall in love with a straight brutha? Am I becoming the very thing I once hated?' Curtis thought to himself.

$$* \quad * \quad *$$

Early the next morning, Daunte walked out to the lobby where he saw Mia waiting for him with a big smile on her face. He smiled, as he saw his woman standing there in a tight fitting, blue dress that showed all her curves. Daunte saw he wasn't the only one caught by her beauty.

"Excuse me sir! Excuse me sir!" Daunte angrily said, trying to get the officer's attention.
"I need to check out please."

Throwing the brown folder with markings on the counter. "Check and make sure all your belongings are in the folder and sign here," the officer said.

Mia walked over to Daunte, gently massaged his back and grabbed his hand. Daunte looked up, smiled at her, and signed his release papers. Throwing the pen on the counter. "Let's get out of here baby girl," Daunte said, as he gave the officer an angry stare.

"Six months, you'll be back. Guys like you always come back," the officer said.

"No. You're wrong this time, Sir! My man will not be back! You can bet yo life on that!" Mia spit out, as she rolled her eyes.

"Forget him, Baby Girl. Let's get outta of here!"

Daunte took one last look at the front of the facility, turned and smiled at Mia, as they walked through the gates of freedom and got in her car. After a few minutes in the car, the drive home got quiet until Mia finally spoke up. "You okay baby?"

"I'm cool. Why you ask?"

"Because you're so quiet. You should be jumping up and down being out of that crazy place!"

Daunte looked out the window and then looked down.

"You know, I had so many dreams about the day I would be leaving that place and riding home with you. Then I would wake up and be laying there, right in my bunk. I'm just trying to let it sink in." Daunte was also missing Curtis, and wondered if he would be okay.

Mia placed her hand on Daunte's leg while he spoke.

"Baby, a lot has happened behind those walls. I was only in for a short time, but it felt like it had been years. Now I got to focus on trying to get my life back on track. I got to find a job. I'm scared Baby!" Daunte said.

"Baby, we'll get through this. I got your back," Mia said, stroking his hand.

Daunte smiled. "I know you do, and you always have." Daunte looked at the monitor on his ankle. "Even though I'm out, I still feel as though I'm a prisoner."

Mia glanced at his ankle and then back on the road. They both sat quiet the rest of the way home. As they pulled up to the apartment complex, Daunte leaned over, making sure his pants were covering the GPS Monitor on his ankle. Mia leaned back, she could see that he felt a little embarrassed. Mia leaned over gently and turned Daunte's face towards her and planted a tender kiss on his lips.

"What was that for, Baby Girl?"

"I just wanted you to know that I'm with you. We'll get through this together, I promise you that. So let's go inside and get you all cleaned up. For once, I'm going to take care of you."

Chapter 51
Barbara & Keith

Barbara sat looking at her watch. 'Keith is fifteen minutes late,' she thought. Reaching in her purse for her cell phone, she started to dial his number when she saw him walk through the door.

"You were supposed to be here fifteen minutes ago!" Barbara snapped.

"Whatever. You better be glad I showed up. What is so important you need to talk to me about?" Keith asked, as he sat down. "I got things to do."

Snapping her neck and rolling her eyes. "You know what? I don't have time for your stink ass attitude. So I'm going to say what I got to say."

"So what is it?"

"Well, I just want you to know, that I'm pregnant and you the daddy."

Keith stood up, knocking back his chair. "You goddam hoochie! What the hell you mean!? I'm the daddy?"

"What about that nigga that popped up at your crib that day I was there?" Keith asked.

"I'm not pregnant by no gay guy. Are you crazy Keith?"

"Oh, so you're trying to say you weren't sleeping with that niggah?"

"No, I wasn't. He ain't into women. Hell, he wanted you?" Barbara knew there was a chance that Wil could be her baby daddy, but she wanted what Tonya was about to get.

Keith sat there shaking his head. "If you think I'm just going to go by what you say, you one dumb ass woman. I ain't like Antonio. I know how you and your girl roll."

"You remember that night you came by after we went to dinner. It must have been that night."

Keith thought back to that night and smiled, as he remembered what actually happened. She had been too drunk to remember anything, but he remembered it all too well.   Barbara stood up, "You know what, I'll see you in court. 'Cause you are going to take care of me and my baby whether you want to or not!"

"You do what you got to do. I ain't nobody's daddy. I'm too smart to let some hoochie like you trap me into becoming a daddy. So you bring it on. I can't believe you wasted my time with some bull shit like this. I'm out of here," Keith said, as he turned and left Barbara standing there.

Barbara followed Keith out to the parking lot. "You think you can dismiss me like that, brutha? I don't think so. I guess you don't know what kind of woman you dealing with. You can best believe, I always get what I want!"

By this time, part of Keith's body was inside the car and the other side of his body was out with his foot on the concrete ground. "I suggest you go back inside and get out my face, before I do something I will regret."

Barbara walked up to Keith and mushed him in the face. "Nigga, what you gonna do?"

"Don't put your hand in my face like that again! Keith shouted.

"Oh, I'm scared. What you gonna to do if I do? You don't scare me."

"You dumb bitch. Get away from my car," Keith said, as he pushed his door trying to get out of his car.

As Keith tried to get out the car, Barbara pushed the door trying to close it, the door slammed on Keith's leg. Keith yelled out in pain. Barbara knew she had fucked up and started to walk away quickly. Keith stood up and headed in her direction but couldn't walk any further. The pain in his leg was too intense.

Keith yelled out to her. "Bitch you ain't seen the last of me. You better pray like hell that my leg is ok," he said, as he limped back to his car. Barbara turned and saw that he was headed back to his car and stuck up her middle finger, turned, and walked away. Keith sat in his car fuming and massaging his leg.

Chapter 52
Antonio, Tonya, Barbara

Antonio drove up in front of Barbara's house to pick up Tonya. Picking up his cell, phone he called Tonya.

"I'm out front," he said, as he watched a car pull up behind him. He saw that it was Barbara and she appeared to be upset. He chuckled, as he watched her cussing to her self and slamming her car door. She walked right pass Tonya and kept going.

'Hmm, someone must have pissed her off,' he thought to himself.

Tonya walked up to the car and got in, keeping her eyes on Barbara. "Somebody must have pissed my girl off. She walked right on by without even speaking to me," Tonya said.

"They must have. Did you want to go and check on her?"

Tonya thought for a minute, "No. I'll just talk with her when I get back. She'll be okay."

"You sure?"

"Yeah, I'm sure," Tonya said, as she sat wondering what was going on with her girl.

Antonio pulled up in front of the Doctor's office. Tonya had an appointment, and Antonio wanted to be involved, as much as possible. This day was particularly special because Antonio was looking forward to hearing the baby's heartbeat for the first time. After parking the car, the two made their way to the doctor's office. The young nurse took Tonya back to the examining room as soon as she checked in at the desk. Antonio watched the two walk away, as he took a seat.

'This baby has got to be mine. But what if it isn't? I love this baby already and it hasn't even been born yet.' His mind was consumed with conflicting thoughts. Fifteen minutes later, the nurse reappeared. "Are you Antonio? Please come with me."

Antonio got up and walked in the examining room. He smiled, as he saw Tonya on the table with her stomach exposed. The doctor began to push buttons on the equipment. Antonio got chills when he heard the sound of a little heart beat. It was overwhelming.

Tonya watched Antonio as he sat there smiling. Her attention suddenly became drawn to the doctor as he appeared to be distracted.

"Doctor, is there something wrong with my baby?" Tonya asked nervously.

"Just relax Tonya," the doctor said. He looked up at the nurse. "I need you to bring in the sonar gram equipment."

Antonio was starting to get nervous, "Doc is there something wrong?"

"Everything is fine," the doctor said, as he watched the nurse wheel in the sona gram equipment.

The doctor immediately put on his gloves and rubbed the gel onto Tonya's stomach. Antonio knew something was wrong, as Tonya squeezed his hand.   The doctor put on his glasses and looked closer at the picture on the monitor.

"Just what I thought. How did I miss that?" The doctor asked.

"Oh my God, doctor. Is there something wrong with my baby?"

"I'm sorry I didn't mean to scare you. But both babies are fine."

Antonio wasn't sure what the doctor meant. Tonya spoke up. "What do you mean babies? Are you saying what I think you're saying?"

"That's exactly what I am saying," the doctor said with a smile.

Antonio was confused. "Can somebody fill me in please?"

Tonya looked at Antonio and smiled, "We're having twins!"

Antonio almost fainted. "Twins! Twins! We're having

twins? His worry was replaced with joy and happiness.

"Do twins run in either one of your families?" The doctor asked.

"They don't run in my family," Antonio said, shaking his head.

Tonya looked at the doctor. "I'm not sure doctor. I was adopted. I was never able to find my biological parents."

Antonio was surprised at what Tonya had just said.

* * *

The drive home was quiet. Antonio finally spoke. "How about we go get some lunch? I'm starving."

"Sounds good to me, I'm hungry too." Tonya said.

"It must have been hard?" Antonio asked.

"What must have been hard?"

"Not knowing who your biological parents are."

"It's gotten easier to deal with. I do wonder sometimes if I have a brother or sister out there looking for me? After my adopted parents were killed, I was moved from foster home to foster home."

"I can't even imagine how that would feel."

"Some days when I walk down the street I wonder if the person that I passed could be my brother or sister."

"So you could actually meet someone, go on a date, and it could be your brother and neither of you know it." Antonio said.

"It's possible. You don't have any sisters that you never met do you?" Tonya asked with a slight chuckle.

"No, I think we're okay in that department. We don't have to worry about that. Twins…Twins! Who would have thought twins?" Antonio asked.

"You think you're surprised. I'm speechless!" Tonya said, as she looked down and rubbed her belly.

"I wonder if it's two boys or two girls? Shoot, I really don't care, as long as they are healthy," Antonio said with a smile.

Tonya beamed, as she watched Antonio's excitement about

becoming a father. 'These babies have got to be his,' she thought to herself.

Antonio and Tonya pulled up in front of the restaurant and headed inside. The waitress came over and sat down two glasses of water.

"Would you like to order drinks now or do you need more time?" She asked, as she pushed her glasses up on her nose.

"I'll have a gin and tonic," Antonio said.

"I'll have a glass of juice."

Tonya sat back, looked around, not used to being in such a fancy restaurant. She sat quietly thinking. 'What will I do if the babies aren't Antonio's? It would be a struggle taking care of one child and now we're talking about two,' she thought.

"You're kind of quiet over there."

"I'm still trying to get over the fact that I am carrying twins."

"Marry me," Antonio said.

"What did you just say?"

"I said, marry me," Antonio repeated himself.

Tonya smiled. "Antonio, this is all so sudden!" She didn't want to appear too anxious. Tonya felt warm inside. She was about to get everything she'd ever wanted and everything she worked so hard to get. She thought about everything that had happened in the past months. Tonya realized that she had actually fallen in love with Antonio.

"Hello in there!" Antonio said, breaking her train of thought. "Yes or No works for me, preferably yes!" He said laughing.

"Are you sure this is what you want, Antonio?" Tonya couldn't believe those words were coming out of her mouth. "We don't have to rush into things."

"I just want to do the right thing by you and my kids."

"You can do that without marriage you know," Tonya said.

"Are you trying to let me down easy? Is this your way of saying no?" Antonio felt he had to ask.

"No, I would marry you today, if I could." Tonya realized that the money was not as important as it used to be. For the first time in her life she felt something more powerful than money. Tonya was in love.

"Oh I get it?" Antonio said. "I need to get a ring."

"A ring would seal the deal." Tonya laughed.

"Well, here comes the waitress to take our orders. How about we order and eat, and afterwards I'll drop you at the house. Then I'll go and find that perfect ring."

"So you don't want me to help?" Tonya asked.

"No, I want to do it myself. To me, it makes it more special. I want it to be a surprise."

"Okay then. I love you Antonio," Tonya was stunned at her words.

Antonio looked Tonya in her face and could see that she really meant what she'd just said. "I love you too, Tonya," Antonio said, with a smile on his face. "Now eat your lunch. Our boys or girls have to be hungry!" They both laughed. After finishing up lunch and dropping her off, Antonio headed out to find the perfect ring. Deep down he felt that the kids were his and he would no longer question it.

Tonya walked inside the house only to find Barbara sitting at the dining room table pouting.

"Girl, I saw you earlier. You looked mad as hell. What happened?" Tonya asked.

"I found out I was pregnant and went to tell your friend's boy he was the father and he talked to me like I was some crazy ole fool off the street."

"Is he the father of your baby?"

"Of course he is. He's the only guy I slept with over the past few months." Barbara replied.

"What about that guy you met?"

"What guy?"

"The guy you told me about. I think his name is Wil."

"Naw, he ain't my baby daddy?" Barbara said, as she sat at the table glaring at the television.

"Are you sure, Barbara?"

"What's with all the questions Tonya? I said that Keith's the father and that's that."

Tonya could see that Barbara was getting irritated by all the questions. Tonya felt it was best not to tell Barbara about the proposal and the fact that she was pregnant with twins.

"Well, I think I'm going to go and lay down for a while," Tonya said.

"Yeah, why don't you go do that?" Barbara said, rolling her eyes.

Barbara picked up the phone to dial directory assistance to find out what the number was to the prison. The deep voice on the other end asked, "May I help you?"

"Yes. Sir I wanted to check and see if Carlton Williams and Curtis Johnson were still inmates at your facility."

"Sure ma'am let me check. Can you hold on for a minute?" The officer asked.

"Yes sir, I can," Barbara said, as she noticed her nails needed a fill in.

"Ma'am we do have both those names on our roster."

"Thank you sir. Can you tell me what days they can have visitors?" Barbara thought, as she reminisced about the past. That deadly day that Curtis and Carlton killed James.

"Visiting hours are from 9:00 a.m. until 5:00 p.m."

"I appreciate your help sir. Thanks again. Good bye." Barbara sat there looking at the calendar that hung on the wall. 'What day should I go up to visit?'

Chapter 53
Jay, Chuck, Carlton & Curtis

A few months had gone by and Chuck was finishing up his tour. Daunte and Mia had been trying to get on track with their relationship. Reese was having a great season, on track to be the number one Rusher in the NFL. Tonya was starting to waddle around because of all the weight she had picked up from carrying twins. Seven months pregnant, and about to go into her eight, month. Her belly was huge! She looked as though she could give birth at any moment.

Ricky and Jay's relationship strong as ever, and both happy that they hadn't heard any more from "Wil the psycho."

Curtis, back in his cell, hadn't heard from Daunte since he had gotten out three months ago. Carlton was transferred to another prison. The warden felt Carlton's life was in danger and he needed to be in a place where he could heal from the severe burns he'd received. Barbara was about three months pregnant and was still trying to get Keith to believe that the baby she was carrying was his. Keith was put on the injured and reserved list. Not being able to play ball, he was depressed. Barbara had done more damage than he thought she had.

Antonio was looking for a new house for him and Tonya. They planned to get married before the children were born. Antonio didn't want his children to come into this world without his last name.

Jay walked inside the apartment building. Looking around, he thought about how long it had been since he had been standing in front of this particular apartment complex. He walked up to the door and knocked.

"Who is it?" The voice from the other side said.

"It's me, Jay. Open the door, man!"

The door opened and the two embraced. "Welcome home, Daunte!" Jay said.

"Thanks Jay, man, I really appreciate what you and your boy did for me," Daunte said, as he embraced Jay once again.

"I would have been by sooner but I wanted to give you some time to adjust." Jay noticed the big gray bracelet that was on Daunte's ankle, as he sat down in the chair across from him.

Daunte caught a glimpse of Jay looking at his ankle. Unconsciously, Daunte crossed his feet trying to hide the gadget. Jay realized what Daunte was doing and knew he was probably embarrassed.

"I'm sorry man. I didn't mean to stare," Jay said.

"It's okay."

"Anyway, how are things going with you and Mia?"

"We're dealing. She's great! She's stuck by me."

"I'm not surprised," Jay said, with a slight smile on his face.

"You're not?"

"No, I'm not. Because when you really love someone, like she loves you, ain't no mountain too high to climb," Jay said, as he thought about him and Ricky.

"So how are things going with you and yours?"

"Ricky and I are doing great! Thanks for asking."

"I have to thank your boy in person for helping me out. I owe him and you?"

"Naw, you don't owe him or me anything, Daunte. Friends help friends. That's what I did for you. I would do that for all of my friends."

Jay became more serious, as looked to make sure Mia wasn't around to hear his next question.

"On a serious note man, are you really doing ok? What about…"

"What about what? Are you asking me about my HIV results Jay?" Daunte asked, as he too checked to make sure Mia had not come into the room.

"Another few months, if I my results are negative, then I will be fine. Mia has been great. We haven't had sex yet. My mind is still kind of fucked up. I just can't take that chance. I want to make sure everything is okay. If I infected her, I couldn't live with that. Mia says she understands."

"Have you thought about what you will do if the results come back positive?" Jay asked.

"No, I haven't. I can't think about that right now. I will deal with that when the time comes."

"I understand man."

"Jay, has Ricky started looking into my boy's case yet?"

"He put in a request for the file. So, as soon as he takes a look at it, he will let us know."

"You know, while I was locked up, he had my back. He really looked out for me. I just feel I need to do something."

"I'll talk to Ricky again. He practices family law, not criminal. But I'm sure he can get some one to look into it."

"What was his name again?" Jay asked.

"Curtis Robinson."

"Curtis Robinson...Curtis Robinson. Why does that name sound familiar?" Jay asked trying to figure out where he'd heard that name before.

"Who knows? But he is a good guy, and a good friend. I appreciate anything that you or your boy can do. Once you find out, let me know. I want to go and visit him."

Daunte and Jay both looked at the door as it opened. Mia appeared from the bedroom.

"Hi Jay." Mia said, as she walked over and gave him a hug. "Thank you so much for everything."

"No problem. I'm glad I was able to help."

"We both thank you so much Jay. Did you ask him Daunte."

"Ask me what? About helping his boy out?"

"No, Jay," Mia said.

"Ask me what then. You guys can ask me anything, you know that."

"Daunte, now is as good time as any. Ask him!"

Daunte walked over and grabbed Mia's hand. Daunte took a deep breath. "Jay, I wanted to know if you would be my best man in our wedding?"

"Is that what this is all about? I would be honored to be your best man. Hell, I would have been mad as hell if you had asked anybody else, unless, it was family of course."

Mia smiled. "Jay, you are family."

"Thanks, Mia," Jay smiled. "So, when is the big day?"

"I'd marry this man today. I don't know what this man is waiting for," Mia said cutting her eyes at Daunte. But deep down she knew he wanted to find out what his test results were first. So she decided to just let it slide for now.

"Well, I got to get home. I have to meet Ricky. We're going out to catch a movie."

"Tell Ricky I said Hello." Mia said.

"I sure will," Jay said, as he walked out and headed home.

Chapter 54
Reese, Antonio, Ricky & Jay

Reese walked in the bar and quickly spotted Antonio sitting at a table in the back of the bar drinking a beer. Reese walked over to the bar and leaned over to the Bartender.

"Yo man, can you send a pitcher of beer over to that table?" Reese asked. pointing at the table. "You can put it on my tab."

"Sure." The Bartender said, as he nodded at Reese.

"Hey man, have you been waiting long?" Reese asked.

"No. I got here about ten minutes ago."

"Cool. I just ordered a pitcher of beer. The way you sounded on the phone, I figured you could use it."

"Oh it's nothing like that man. I kind of need to tell you something."

"I'm all ears man, what's up."

Antonio took a sip of his beer before speaking. "You remember the girl we talked about?"

"I remember. She's the one who says she's pregnant, right?"

"Yeah. Well, I decided to marry her. Reese she's having twins."

"Wow, man! She's having twins?!" Reese leaned back. "So you going to be okay if you're are not the father?"

"I'm not sure about anything. But I do know that I have fallen for this girl and I'm already connected to those babies. Man, when I heard their little heartbeats, it did something to me. I proposed to her!"

"Congratulations, man! I wish you the best!" Reese said, reaching over and patting him on the shoulder.

"Reese, what do I do if the babies aren't mine?"

"I don't know bru. This is a sticky situation. What would make you think that the babies aren't yours? I hope it doesn't have anything to do with what Keith said."

"Keith got that info right from her girl!"

"I wouldn't be surprise if Keith made everything up," Reese said.

"Speaking of Keith, can you believe how Keith hurt his leg?" Antonio laughed.

"I heard. I knew one day that one of those women was going to catch up with him."

"Man, not one of those women. It was Tonya's girlfriend!"

"You mean it was your girl's best friend?" Reese asked.

"Yea, he pissed her off. My girl says her friend is pregnant by him, and he told her she was crazy or something. I only got bits and pieces of the story."

"Well Ant, if you aren't there biological father, just remember this, man, when they come into this world, they didn't ask for all this craziness. If you're going to be there for them, they will come to depend on you. Any man can make a baby, but it takes a real man to be a father. But whatever you decide, man, you know your boy is here to support you."

*   *   *

"Beep, Beep, Beep, Beep." Ricky reached to turn off the alarm clock. He noticed Jay was still asleep, as usual. 'How he sleeps through the sound of the alarm clock, I just don't know,' he thought. He nudged Jay. "Baby it's time to get up."

"Already? I feel like I just got to sleep," Jay said, as he stretched.

"I feel the same way. I'll let you sleep a little while longer and I'll wake you when I get out the shower," Ricky offered.

"Thanks, Babe."

Ricky finished his shower and then he woke Jay up. He got dressed while Jay was in the shower and headed downstairs to fix them some coffee. Every morning before the two left out to work, they would sit down and drink a cup of coffee together. Ricky poured the coffee in the cups. Jay appeared dressed and ready.

"Good morning. Man, that shower felt good this morning," Jay said, as he walked over and gave Ricky a quick peck on the lips.

"Good morning to you too, sir!" Ricky said, as he sat down at the table.

Jay grabbed the cream out the refrigerator and sat across from Ricky. "So do you have a busy day scheduled?" Jay asked.

"This morning, I'll be in court, but the afternoon is pretty free. What about you?" Ricky asked.

"I have meetings throughout the day."

"Well why don't you call me, maybe I'll come and take you to lunch," Ricky offered.

"Okay, sounds good. Speaking of work, I was wondering if you had a chance to look at that guys file."

"The file should be on my desk within the next couple of days. I'll look at it and have one of my colleagues look at it, as well. If there's a loop hole or anything to help get this brother out of prison we will find it." Ricky looked down at his watch "Babe, I got to get out of here. I have to be in court first thing this morning."

Ricky walked over and gave Jay a passionate kiss. "You have a good day, man," Ricky said, as he grabbed his brief case and shot Jay a wink.

Chapter 55
Barbara, Tonya & Antonio

It was late in the afternoon on a Saturday. The sky was cloudy. The dark clouds slowly glided across the sky, at any minute they would release the rain. You could smell it in the air. The sounds of thunder vibrated. As Tonya drove up to the house, she noticed a police car out front. Her heart dropped. 'Could they have found out about what happened with Larry?' She asked herself. Minutes later Barbara came out escorted by a male and female officer. They had Barbara handcuffed. You could hear her fussing at the officers. "It was an accident! It was an accident!"

Tonya got nervous and pulled off. "I can't go to jail. I can't go to jail," she kept saying to herself. "What about my babies. I will not let my babies be born in prison." Tonya drove around for hours trying to figure out what she was going to do. Tonya grabbed her ringing cell phone and looked at the caller ID. Houston Police Department appeared across the caller ID. Tonya ignored the call and immediately dialed Antonio. After a few rings Antonio answered. As Tonya spoke, he could hear the fear in her voice.

"Antonio, I need to talk to you! I need to tell you something! I need for you to take care of my babies!" Tonya said, as she rolled up her window to keep dry from the rain that was starting to fall.

You could hear Antonio's voice booming through the phone. "Tonya, what's wrong?! What's wrong?! Where are you?! I'll come and get you!"

Tonya pulled over and parked. The rain was coming down so hard, she couldn't see. "Antonio, you have to promise me! Promise me you'll take care of my babies!"

"Tonya, listen to me! Tonya, listen!" He yelled through the phone.

"Antonio, I don't want my babies to grow up like I did, going from foster home to foster home! Please don't let them separate my babies! Promise me you will take care of my babies! Promise me!"

Antonio continued to try and calm her down. "Okay, I promise! I promise you! We will take care of the babies! I won't let anything happened to them! I swear on my life! Now, tell me where you are! I'll come get you!"

Tonya calmed herself enough to tell Antonio the entire story about Larry. She figured it would come out anyway.

"I'm sorry, Antonio, I'm so sorry! I didn't mean to hurt anybody! I didn't know I was going to fall in love with you! Please don't hate me! Please don't hate me!" Tonya said through sniffles.

"Tonya, why are you telling me all this now?"

Tonya started to cry hysterically. "I'm sorry, Antonio! I'm so sorry!" On my way home, I drove up to the house and the police were taking Barbara away in cuffs! I got a call but I didn't answer cause I know they're coming after me next! I need to make sure my babies are going to be okay! Please take care of our babies!"

"Don't worry, let me call my attorney! We'll come and meet you and we'll go with you to turn yourself in. I promise I won't turn my back on you. I'll do everything I can to help you out. So just tell me where you are!"

"I'm going back to the house."

"Okay, I'll meet you there. Don't worry, everything will be fine!"

She hung up the phone and pushed it inside her pants pocket. Looking down, she rubbed her stomach. "Don't worry my babies. Daddy's going to take good care of you. Mommy will be going away for a while. But mommy loves you. Always remember, Mommy loves you," she said, as the tears started to fall again.

As Tonya started the car and pulled off, she was immediately blinded by the heavy rain and didn't see the headlights of the oncoming car. She screamed as the airbags released in her face. Having been too distracted to remember her seatbelt, Tonya's body was thrown around inside the car like a rag doll. After what seemed like hours, the car finally came to an abrupt stop.

Tonya had been knocked unconscious. Later, she woke up to unfamiliar voices. "Check her vitals!" She heard someone say, "Her pressure is up!" Tonya realized that she was inside an ambulance. "Please save my babies! Please save my babies!" She just kept repeating that phrase.

"Don't worry ma'am, everything is going to be okay. We just need you to relax so we can take care of you and your babies," the paramedic said.

"Is there anyone we can call?" The paramedic asked.

"Can you call my fiancé? His name is Antonio. Tell him to remember his promise. Please tell him to remember his promise."

Tonya passed out again. "Ma'am, what's the number?" He asked, as he looked down and saw she had passed out again. The ringing of Tonya's phone, caught the attention of the paramedic. He found the phone stuffed down in her front pocket. Looking at the phone, he saw that Antonio had called. He hit the call button to call Antonio.

"Antonio, this is Allan, I'm a paramedic. Your fiancé has been in a car accident and we're taking her to the hospital."

"Is this a joke?" Antonio asked.

"No sir, but you should meet us at the hospital."

"Can I talk to her?" Antonio asked.

"That won't be possible, she's unconscious! I have to go," the paramedic said, hanging up the phone without even saying goodbye.

Antonio grabbed his keys and dashed out the door. 'Oh God, I can't lose her and the babies.' Within minutes, Antonio was at the hospital and he rushed in through the Emergency entrance.

Running up to the desk, he startled the nurse. "I just got a call that they were bringing my girlfriend here! She is pregnant and was in a car accident!"

"Yes sir, they did. She went into premature labor."

"Premature labor? But she's only 8 months ma'am!"

"Sir, if you would have a seat, the doctor will be out shortly."

Antonio paced the floor, back and forth, back and forth. Finally pulling out his cell phone, he dialed Reese. The voice mail came on and he left him a message. "Reese man, I need your help! Tonya was in a bad accident! I'm at the hospital now, and she's gone into premature labor! I was wondering if you could come by?"

Hanging up the phone, Antonio sat down for a while, then got back up and started to pace again. Walking over to the counter, he interrupted the nurse. "Excuse me ma'am. I was wondering if you've heard anything yet, it's been about forty minutes."

"Let me see what I can find out for you sir," the nurse said, walking away quickly.

Antonio waited fifteen more minutes and impatiently headed back up to the nurse's station. He heard someone call his name. He turned, it was Reese and Mike. Reese walked over with Mike close behind.

"Antonio man, I got your message! What happened?"

"All I know is Tonya was in an accident and she went into labor and she's in surgery!" Antonio was so emotional he never really noticed Mike standing along side Reese.

"Reese, man, this is a nightmare!"

"Excuse me gentleman," the nurse said, as she walked up. "The doctor will be right out."

Just as the nurse walked away, the doctor appeared. "Gentleman how about we go and sit down over here."

Antonio sat down along with Reese and Mike. The doctor sat directly across from them. The doctor looked over his charts. You have a beautiful baby boy and baby girl. The boy is about 4 pounds, 5 ounces and your daughter is about 4 pounds 2 ounces. A little small but they appear to be very healthy.

Antonio grinned from ear to ear. "When can I see them? When can I see Tonya?"

The doctor lowered his head. Sir, we had to do a Cesarean birth. During surgery, your girlfriend went into shock. I'm sorry to say sir, but she died on the table."

Antonio's head dropped, he was stunned into silence.

The doctor stood up and patted Antonio on the shoulder. "I am really sorry son, we did all we could to save her," he said, before walking away.

Allan, the paramedic, walked over to Antonio after the doctor walked away.

"Excuse me," I'm sorry to interrupt, and I'm sorry to hear about your fiancé. When we were bringing her here in the ambulance, she asked me tell you something."

Antonio looked up with his big, sad, watery eyes. "What was that?" He asked.

"She wanted me to tell you to remember your promise."

"My promise?" Antonio remembered the conversation he'd had with Tonya before the accident, the promise that he had made about the two new lives that had just entered the world."

The nurse walked over and asked Antonio if he wanted to see the babies. Reese and Mike sat back down and told Antonio they would be waiting when he came back from seeing his babies. Antonio followed her to the Newborn Intensive Care Unit. As he peered in the window, the nurse pointed to the two babies who were sleeping. They had tubes all over them. Barely breathing, they looked as if they were fighting for air. Antonio wiped the tears that rolled down his cheeks and smiled. "Rest my babies, Daddy's here and he's going to take care of you."

Chapter 56
Barbara & Antonio

It had been a week since Tonya's death. Antonio was preparing for her funeral. He decided to stop by the hospital and see the babies, before going to the service. Taking off his jacket, the nurse helped him put on the white gown and mask. The babies were still weak, and their immune systems were not that strong. So he wasn't able to hold them just yet. Antonio sat in the chair that they had placed between the two incubators. Quietly, he sat, and just watched. The baby girl started to stretch. Antonio had fallen in love with these two new lives that were now going to depend on him. "Hey Baby girl. Hey Baby girl. Daddy's here, I'm going to name you Tonya after your mother. She would love that. Your brother's name will be Tony after me and your mom. Your mother loved you guys so much and she's in heaven watching over all three of us." Antonio stood up. "Daddy has to go and put mommy to rest, but I'll be back."

Antonio made it to the service, but not many people were there. 'Tonya didn't have a lot friends,' he thought. A few minutes later a woman appeared, dressed in all black. He thought it might be Barbara, since he could see the woman was pregnant. The hat she wore had a small veil which covered her face. As the lady got closer, Antonio realized it actually was Barbara. She made her way over to Antonio, putting the tissue that she used to wipe her tears back in her purse.

Antonio wasn't sure how he should feel towards her. In some ways he blamed Barbara for all that Tonya had done. Tonya had made bad choices in life but they were influenced somewhat by Barbara. Antonio remembered the story about Larry that Tonya had told him right before she died. Barbara walked over to Antonio. "How are my God babies doing?" Barbara asked.

"Your God babies? My children will have nothing to do with you!" I blame you for this," Antonio said. "Shouldn't you in be jail now?"

"No, I shouldn't. Your boy dropped the charges," she said.

"Dropped the charges? What are you talking about?" He asked.

"Your boy Keith had me arrested. Can you believe he had me charged with assault on him?"

"I thought you…Tonya thought…"

"You and Tonya thought what?" Barbara asked.

Antonio got quiet for a second. "It doesn't matter at this point. All I know is I don't want you around my kids. If you ever come around them, just know that Tonya told me the real story about what happened that night at the house with Larry. I should turn your ass in. I advise you to not make me change my mind," Antonio continued. "What goes around comes around and yours is right around the corner. I need to get out of here and go back to the hospital and check on my kids."

Barbara stood there and watched Antonio walk away. As he disappeared through the doors, Barbara sat on the bench and stared at the coffin that was now closed.

"Don't worry Tonya, I won't be chased away that easily. I'll keep an eye on your babies. It's going to take more than some punk like him to keep me away. Love you girl." Barbara sat for a while, her thoughts interrupted by the workers who came to pick up Tonya's body. Antonio had found out where Tonya's adopted parents were buried and bought a plot right next to them to bury Tonya. He also found out that, ironically, they were both killed in a car accident. Deep down, he felt Tonya would have wanted to be buried with them, since they were they only parents she ever knew.

Chapter 57
Antonio, Reese & Keith

It was the Sunday before Thanksgiving. The team headed into the locker room. The guys were happy because they'd just beaten their division rivals and took the first place spot in the division. The coach walked in a half an hour later, stood on the bench and whistled loudly for the team's attention.

The coach looked at his team and then spoke. "I just want to say that you guys played like champs today. I'm proud of each and everyone of you," the coach said, as he held the football in his hand. "Today, the game ball goes to Antonio. You played like a true champ today." The coach tossed the ball over to him.

"Speech! Speech!" Some of the guys yelled out.

Antonio stepped on the bench next to the coach. "Thanks coach. I appreciate this. This has been a rough year for me. But I would like to give this ball to the real champion of this team." Antonio looked around the room and saw Reese standing over near his locker.

"Coach, I'd like to give this ball to a guy who understands what it means to help your teammate on the field and off. This person has overcome adversity and has carried this team on his back regardless of whatever was going on. To me, that signifies a true champion. I only made one play today that helped us to win this important game. But this guy has gotten us where we are today. We've all learned a little something from this guy. He played a hell of a game today. That 60 yard run he just did took us into first place. So Reese, I give this ball to you! My Friend! My Teammate!" Antonio tossed the ball over to Reese. All Reese could do was smile. The guys who had once treated him as an outcast now started to chant his name. All you could hear throughout the locker room was, "REESE! REESE! REESE!" Followed by claps and the guys banging of the lockers.

After fifteen minutes of celebrating, Antonio noticed that most of the guys had started to leave.

"What's up partner?" Antonio asked, as he walked up behind Reese.

"Hey, man, I appreciate everything you said. That truly meant a lot."

Antonio smiled when he saw the pictures of his twins on Reese's locker door. Reese was happy that Antonio had made him the God father of his children.

"How are my God children?" Reese asked.

Antonio started to speak but then stopped when he saw Keith walking over on his crutches.

"Niggah, what do you want?" Antonio asked.

Reese turned and immediately ignored him.

"Why you guys trippin?" Keith asked.

Antonio started to speak but Reese stopped him. "Keith, I've always had your back and I thought you had mine. The one thing I thought I could always count on was my teammates."

"Reese, do you think you're innocent in all this? Here it is, you're a fairy and you couldn't even tell your boy," Keith said.

"Who, I sleep with and what I do behind closed doors, in my own home, has nothing to do with you! It didn't then and it doesn't now!"

"What ever! You two niggahs deserve each other!" Keith said.

"Looks like you got what you deserved," Reese said, as he looked at Keith's leg in a cast. "Karma's a bitch and it appears you've met!"

"Hey, man, let's get out of here! I need to swing by the hospital to check on my kids, " Antonio said, throwing his gym bag over his shoulder and headed toward the door.

Chapter 58
Mike, Reese & Demetrious

It was a cool day with a slight breeze. Brown and orange leaves moved with the wind. 'Man, that is such a beautiful sight,' Demetrious thought, as he looked out the window.

So deep in thought, he never heard Tariff coming down the stairs. Tariff walked up behind him, massaged his shoulder and slowly moved his arms around Demetrious' waist.

"It's good to be home. I thought Chuck's tour would never end," Tariff said.

They both stood there, continuing to look out the window. "Baby, can you believe it's almost another year coming to an end?" Tariff asked, as he leaned his head back onto Demetrious' chest.

"I know. Time has gone by so fast. Last year Chuck was stabbed. I was in that wheel chair. Mike lost his mom. Then this year Reese had to deal with those ass holes about his sexuality. It's been a rough couple of year's babe," Demetrious said.

"Yeah, but a lot of good has come too. We still have all our friends. We're all closer than ever before. Chuck's career is doing well. Jay finally found someone he loves and we're all happy. Look at us. We're doing fine. So, some good did come out of all this madness," Tariff said.

"Yeah, look at us! I have so much to be thankful for and what better day than Thanksgiving Day? Happy Thanksgiving baby!"

"Happy Thanksgiving to you too, Tariff!" They shared a kiss.

"Well, we better get dressed. I'm so glad that we decided to have dinner at Mike and Reese's place this year. Being on tour and everything, it would have been too much to do it here," Tariff said.

* * *

"Damn, baby you got the house smelling good!" Reese said, as he walked over and gave Mike a kiss.

"Happy Thanksgiving!" Mike said.

"Happy Thanksgiving to you too, Baby Boy. So what do you need me to do?"

"Can you start on your famous Macaroni and Cheese?" Mike asked.

"Sure I can," Reese said with a big smile on his face. "What time will the guys be here?"

"Around 7:00 p.m," Mike said.

"What's your boy doing today?"

"Who you mean Antonio?" Reese asked.

"Yeah."

"I'm not sure."

"Why don't you call him and see. Nobody should be alone on the holidays."

Reese walked over and kissed Mike on the cheek. "See that's why I love you, Baby Boy. You're so thoughtful."

"Yeah, I am, aren't I?" Mike asked. They both broke out laughing.

Reese walked over and grabbed the cordless phone and dialed Antonio's number. After a few rings Antonio picked up.

"Sup, man. Happy Thanksgiving!" Reese said.

"Happy Thanksgiving to you too, man!"

"So, did you find a nanny yet for the kids?"

"My family will be here sometime today to celebrate the holidays with me. They're gonna stay awhile and help me get ready to bring the babies home. My sister's here and she's downstairs cooking. She's thinking about staying a couple of month until I find a nanny"

"A'ight man. We were just calling to check up on you and invite you over for dinner, but it looks like you got plans. So I'll holler at you later."

Chapter 59
Curtis, Daunte & Mia

Curtis sat in his cell reading a black history book he picked up from the prison library. He always said you can lock a brutha up but you can't lock up his mind. He didn't want to be one of those dumb asses in prison.

"Yo Curtis!" One of the inmates called him.

Curtis turned to see it was his boy Nate. But everyone called him Fats because he was little bit over weight. Every time you saw Fats, he was eating. He took Carlton's place in the mail room after he was transferred out.

"Hey, Fats man! What's up?" Curtis asked, as he closed his book.

Fats reached inside his shirt and handed Curtis a letter. "This letter came for you yesterday. I know you guys aren't sup-posed to get mail today but I figured you might want to see this one," Fats said, as Curtis reached for the letter.

Curtis was puzzled. "Who's the letter from?"

"I remember you talked about your boy Daunte a lot, so I figured you might want it right away."

"Good looking out man!" Curtis said, as slapped Fat's a five dollar bill. Curtis watched as Fats walked away. He scooted in the corner of his bunk and smiled as he saw that the letter was indeed from Daunte. Ripping open the letter, a picture fell out. It was a picture of Mia and Daunte. Turning the picture over, he read the writing. *Thank you for looking out and protecting him. Love Mia.* Curtis felt warm inside and he smiled. For once in his life, he had done something meaningful. Getting up off his cot, Curtis took the picture and taped it on his mirror. He then sat in his chair and pulled out the letter from Daunte.

> *Sup Curtis:*
>
> *I told you I wouldn't forget, you, my brutha. How can you forget someone who saved your life? I've always been a believer that God looks out for babies and fools. I believe God put you in my life to look out for this fool. If it wasn't for you, man, I don't know what would have happened to me in there.*
>
> *I talked to my boy and he's having his friend look into your case. I don't know if anything can or will come out of it, but I at least wanted to try and help someone who helped me. I always hear that people don't change but there is always an exception to the rule. Mia and I both thank you and expect a visit from us real soon.*
>
> *Hopefully, you still have my phone number, feel free to call us collect, it would be good to hear from you.*
>
> > *Be Safe,*
> > *Daunte*

Curtis got up and walked over to the window and just stared out. 'So this is how it feels when people really care about you,' he thought.

*   *   *

Mia wanted this day to be special. A year ago today, Daunte had asked Mia to marry him. He was finally starting to smile again. In a few more months he would be able to take that prison monitor off his ankle. Daunte sat in the living room watching some football, drinking his beer. Mia was talking on her cell phone while she was cooking dinner. As he looked over at Mia, he smiled. It seemed things were starting to get back to normal. Mia caught him, as he stared at her, and threw him a kiss and went back to her conversation. Daunte's attention was drawn to the ringing phone.

"Happy Thanksgiving!" The voice said from the other end.

"Happy Thanksgiving to you too, Jay! How are things with you?"

"Everything is good man! I'm leaving here in a bit to go over to my boyz house for dinner."

"That's good. Mia's in the kitchen cooking now. She got it smelling all good up in here," Daunte said, as he looked at her and smiled.

"Oh yeah, man, one of Ricky's colleagues is looking into your buddy's case."

"Thanks, man. Tell your boy I appreciate his help!"

"No problem! Make sure you watch our Cowboys play today."

"Man, you know it! Don't let your boy hear you talk about the Cowboys?"

"Come on Daunte, he knows I support his team. But I still love my boys!"

"Yeah right!" Daunte said, as he chuckled. "I'll chat with you later Jay."

"A'ight man. Tell Mia I said hello and Happy Holidays!"

Daunte hung up the phone, sat it down on the coffee table and went back to watching TV and drinking his beer. Just as he sat down, the phone rang again. Daunte was now a little irritated. He didn't like being interrupted while watching his football. His irritation faded, once he heard the operator say that he had a collect call from the prison he once lived in.

"Yes, operator, I will accept the charges."

"Sup Daunte," Curtis shouted in the phone.

"Hey, Curtis, how are you? It's good to hear from you!"

"I'm hanging man! All is good! I got your letter today!"

"Today? How you get it today? Today's a holiday!"

"Come on Daunte, you know I have connections. Since Carlton left, I now have a connection in the mail room. One of the guys, his name is Fats, hooked me up!"

"You sound great D."

"I'm good man. My baby's in the kitchen cooking our dinner now."

"So, that must mean things are getting back to normal for you two."

"Yeah, man, its great! Everything is great!"

"Daunte, I appreciate you having someone look into my case. But I can tell you right now, ain't no help for me. I've accepted that man."

"Think positive, Curt."

"I can't afford to D. If I was to get my hopes up and nothing comes out of it, that would be emotionally draining."

"I understand Curtis, but I just wanted to try and do something for you," Daunte said.

"Actually D, you can do something for me."

"Sure man, anything. What is it?"

"Don't come back to this place. Help out our young black brothers. Man, I'm seeing too many of them coming up in here. You bruthas on the outside have to step up and show them another way.

"I got you Curtis. I will man!"

"Well, D, I got to go now. They're actually serving us a turkey dinner or something here for the holiday."

"A'ight Curt man! Keep your head up and be strong!"

"No doubt, D. Talk to you soon!"

Daunte hung up the phone and just sat still for a second and thought about his conversation with Curtis. Daunte went into the kitchen. Mia was finally off the phone.

"You want another beer baby?"

"Yeah, but I'll get it. Do you need me to do anything?" Daunte asked.

"No, you go and watch your football. I got everything under control."

"Thanks, baby." Daunte said, as he kissed her on the cheek and headed back into the living room to watch his game.

Chapter 60
Deception, Lies & Truth
(The Secret's Out)

It was Friday morning, the day after Thanksgiving. Barbara sat in the hospital, waiting for the nurse to come out to get her. She got the creeps seeing all the people wrapped up in bandages. She watched the security guard, as he walked down the hall next to the gurney with someone laying on it. When she looked down she could see that part of that person's arm was burnt. She sat and sat but was starting to wonder what she would find when she saw Carlton.

"Excuse me ma'am," the skinny nurse said. "Follow me please."

Throwing her hair back and clutching her purse, she followed close behind. Walking to the room, she noticed the security guard sitting outside the door reading the paper. As she got to the door, the guard stood up and called for a female guard.

"Give us one minute ma'am. All visitors have to be checked before going into visit the prisoners," the guard said in his smooth silky voice.

"Sure. By all means sir, go ahead and feel me up," Barbara said, as she raised her arms.

'Yeah right,' the security guard thought, as he waived at the female guard.

The closer the female guard got, Barbara thought, 'Damn she looks like a man.'

As the guard finished checking her for contraband, Barbara rolled her eyes. "I hope you got your jollies off!" Barbara walked away sticking up her middle finger. "Bitch," she said under her breath, before going through the door. As she walked in, she no-

ticed the curtain pulled around the bed. The room was real quiet.
Walking around the curtain, she saw a man with his face completely covered in gauze, as well as, one hand and half of the other
arm.

"Carlton, is that you?"

Carlton turned and saw Barbara. "Look what the damn
wind blew in. Barbara is that really you?" He said in a whisper.

"Yes, it's me. Oh, Carlton, are you okay?" Barbara asked,
as she grabbed a chair and pulled it beside his bed.

"Looks like you put on some pounds, Barbara."

"Boy, that's cause I'm pregnant!" Barbara was trying hard
not to show the pity she felt for him.

Carlton's voice was muffled.

"Did you bring Tonya with you?" Carlton asked.

Barbara wasn't sure if she should tell him what happen.
"She's fine, she couldn't make it today. But let's talk about you.
What happened to you?"

"Curtis happened!"

"What do you mean Curtis happened? Is he hurt? What's
going on?" Barbara asked, not giving him a chance to answer.

"I mean Curtis did this to me! He tried to kill me!"

"Kill you! What do you mean kill you?" Barbara asked.

"He tried to burn me alive! He may have thought he got
the best of me but it ain't over!"

"What did you do to him, Carlton? Curtis would never do
something like this to you. You guys were like Peanut Butter and
Jelly."

"Your boy Curtis is gay," Carlton spit out, knowing damn
well he was lying.

"Say it ain't so. Damn, is everybody gay?"

"What do you mean Barbara?"

"Nothing." Barbara said, as she thought about Wil.
"Changing the subject, I see Chuck got out of jail and can you believe he's a big time celebrity?"

"Where did you see that snitch?" Carlton asked, getting
agitated.

"He was on television and he even has a CD out."

"CD, you mean like a music CD?" Carlton asked.

"Yeah, who'd have thought?"

"So, who did you trap with that baby? If I know you, who-ever the daddy is got to be some big time ball player or some vic-tim with some money."

Barbara laughed. "He's a professional football player. But he doesn't want to admit he's the father and you know your girl ain't having that."

"I know you ain't. I need you to do me a favor."

"Sure, what's up?" Barbara asked. "What you need?"

"I need you to go and see Curtis and pass a message onto him for me and see if you can find that bitch-ass Chuck. If it weren't for him, I wouldn't be here now!"

"Sure, I can do that, but what you gonna do Carlton? Look around you in the hospital?" Carlton struggled to lift his head looked around the room. He motioned for Barbara to come closer.

"Once I'm better, I got a way outta of here."

Carlton nodded his head to confirm what he'd just told her. Barbara stood up and looked down at Carlton.

"I'll be back in a week or two and I'll let you know what I find out." Barbara threw Carlton a kiss. "Now, you get better."

"Don't worry, I will. I got scores to settle."

Barbara gently touched his hand. "Me too Carlton, I might need your help."

"Barbara, you do this for me and I'll owe you."

"I'll be in touch, Carlton," Barbara said, as she headed out the door.

*　*　*

Wil had been arrested and convicted for driving under the influence of a controlled substance and vehicular manslaughter. Wil sat at the table and listened as his attorney pleaded his case before sentencing. As his attorney finished his closing remarks, Wil turned and looked back at the woman with tears streaming down her face.

"I'm sorry." Wil mouthed.

"William Achy, please stand," the judge said. "You have been found guilty of driving under the influence and vehicular manslaughter. Do you have anything to say before sentencing?"

Wil looked back at his mother and then back at the judge. "Judge, all I can say is that I am truly sorry for the woman and her family. She pulled out in front of me. It was raining and I tried to stop, Judge. I tried to stop!"

The judge sat quietly but became distracted for a second when he glanced over at the gentleman who had just walked in and took a seat. "Mr. Achy, not only were you driving on a suspended license, but once again you are in this court room for your third offense of driving under the influence. Your carelessness has cost a woman her life. A death that has seriously affected other people."

The judge heard the sniffles of the woman who sat directly behind Wil. "With that being said, I am sentencing you to fifteen years in jail with no possibility of parole, young man. I hope you take that time to think about your actions and the consequences that have come from them." The judge raised the mallet in his hand and banged it down. "This court is adjourned."

Wil stood up and the officer handcuffed him and escorted him through the door. Wil's mother's cries echoed through the courtroom, as he was lead out the door. All she could think about were the judge's last words. She was so overwhelmed that she began to feel faint, as she was about to exit the court room. Antonio stood up and caught her.

"Are you okay, Ma'am?"

"My son. My son," she managed to say in between her tears.

"Why don't you have a seat?" Antonio led her to a bench.

"Thank you so much young man."

After Ms. Achy regained her composure, she opened her purse and pulled out some tissue to wipe away her tears. With a strained voice she whispered, "She was my daughter. How can I tell my son that the woman he killed was his twin sister? "Wil always felt a part of him was missing. I wanted to tell him about his sister but I knew he would hate me for it."

"Why are you telling me this story?" Antonio asked.

"Last year I wanted, no, I needed to find out where my child was and explain to her why I did what I did. I hired a private detective to find her. A few days before she was killed, the detective came to me and gave me some pictures of her and of you."

"Why did you give your daughter up?"

"I didn't know I was pregnant with twins. I couldn't take care of two babies. It was easier to get her adopted than my son. The family wanted a girl," Ms. Achy continued. "I kept in touch with them, even when they moved to Dallas. Later, both the adoptive parents were killed in a car accident. I tried frantically to find my daughter, but I couldn't. I couldn't! I had heard she was in foster care." Ms. Achy became even more emotional, as she told her story.

Antonio looked around and noticed that they were the only two left in the court -room. "I can't believe you're here now. Tonya told me about you and she wanted to find you. We were going to be married before the babies were born," he volunteered.

"Babies?" Ms. Achy said.

"Yeah, she was pregnant with twins."

"Those poor babies!" Ms. Achy's heart became even heavier.

"I'm sorry, what was your name, Ma'am."

"Ms. Achy. My name is Ms. Achy."

"Well, Ms. Achy the babies are fine and they are with me."

"Oh my lord! My grandbabies are okay? Praise God! Praise God! Ms. Achy said, as she raised her hands in the air.

"Tonya and Tony are what I named them, after me and their mother."

Ms. Achy's tears of sorrow turned to tears of joy. "Can I see them?"

Antonio sat quiet for a second. He knew that his children had to depend on him to make smart decisions. He needed to check out her story before even allowing this stranger to come into their lives. He reached in his pocket, pulled out a pen and piece of paper and wrote down his contact information.

"Here's my number ma'am. I have to go but give me a call in a couple of days and we can work something out."

"Thank you! Thank you so much!" She said, putting the number in her purse.

"You can call me Antonio." Antonio walked out the court-room and hurried to his car. He decided to make a quick call to his lawyer. Once his lawyer answered, Antonio gave him a run down of everything that had occurred since he met Tonya. It was impor-tant to him to find out if this woman was really Tonya's mother. Hanging up the phone, he grabbed the envelope that sat on the seat. Houston Memorial Hospital was typed on the envelope. Antonio knew it was the results of the paternity test for the kids. Staring at the envelope, he became distracted by the light that caught the heart shaped pendant that hung on his rearview mirror. Reaching for it, he opened it to see the picture of his two babies. He couldn't help but smile, as he made his decision. Reaching down for the en-velope, he ripped it into shreds. No matter what, deep down those kids were his and no one would take them away.

*   *   *

Ricky walked into his office and was greeted by Ms. Tyson. "Hi Ricky, this file came in for you."

"Thanks Lisa. Please hold all my calls," he said, as he headed inside his office, closing the door behind him. Pulling the envelope from the file, three pictures fell to the floor. He looked at the first picture. It had Carlton Lewis typed on the back. The sec-ond picture had Curtis Morgan typed on the back. 'Oh, this must be the guy Jay's talking about,' he thought to himself.

Ricky's heart started to beat fast, as he looked at the third and final picture. He could not believe the mug shot that stared back at him. "Oh my God, what is a picture of Chuck doing here?"

Ricky grabbed his jacket and cell phone and headed out the door. "Lisa, I'm gone for the day. You can contact me on my blackberry. Something has come up."

"Is everything okay Ricky?"

She got no answer. Jumping into his car, he made it home in record time. Pulling into the driveway and throwing the car in park, Ricky hurried into the house.

"Jay! Jay! Where are you babe?"

"What's with all the hollering? I'm right here." he said, as he emerged from the kitchen.

"We need to talk Jay!"

"A'ight man. Must be important, because you home early."

"It is important and I think you need to sit down on this one."

"What has Wil done now?" Jay asked.

"Naw, baby, I wish it was that simple, but this is definitely not about Wil," Ricky said, as he pulled the folder out of his brief case and threw it on the table.

"What is this Ricky?" Jay asked, as he reached for the folder. "This is the case I was looking into for you, Jay. This is your boy's case."

"I don't get it. I don't understand. Why is Chuck's picture a part of this file?" Jay asked.

Ricky took the file from Jay and started to read it closely. "Jay, what was Tariff's lover's name again?"

"James, James Thompson."

Ricky dropped the filed, as the realization of what he had in his hands hit him like a ton of bricks. "Jay this looks like the file of your boy's killing and from what I'm reading. Chuck turned states evidence against these other two guys Curtis and Carlton.

"You mean to fucking tell me Chuck shot James?"

"Well, it looks as though this guy Curtis was the one that shot him."

"Chuck was there, so that makes him just as guilty, as far as I'm concerned." Jay said.

"Jay, you need to get the whole story."

"I've heard enough! I need to call the guys!"

"Jay, we need to think about this first."

"Ricky, what is there to think about?"

Jay sat for a moment. His thoughts were racing a mile a minute. It finally hit him that Daunte's friend had something to do with the killing. "Dammit! I knew when I was talking to Daunte that the name Curtis Morgan sounded familiar. Shit!"

Jay grabbed his keys and headed out the door.

"Jay! Where are you going?"

"I got a run to make. Call the guys. I'll be back."

Ricky stood there and watched Jay rush through the door. Ricky slowly picked up the pictures that were now on the floor. He picked up the sheet that had Chuck's name on it. It was his testimony about what happened the day of the shooting.

Chuck Williams
Testimony

I was hanging with a couple of Friends of mines name Carlton and Curtis and some females. We saw this guy cleaning his Acura. One of the girls mentioned that the guy was gay. The guy Carlton, thought we should follow the guy and take his car.

When dude finished cleaning his car, we followed close behind. Then the guy stopped at a stop light. Curtis and Carlton hopped out the car and I got into the driver's seat. Curtis pulled a gun out and told the guy to get out of his car.

When dude got out the car, he had his hands raised and told Curtis that he didn't want any trouble.

Then the guys cell phone rung and without thinking, he reached for it and Curtis shot him. I could see it was an accident on Curtis' part, I guess he got nervous. Then Carlton grabbed Curtis and we took off leaving the guy on the ground. We all just knew he was dead.

I dreamed about that incident for days. That guy had a family, that guy had friends. I felt bad. So, that's why I turned myself in.

I know it's not cool to snitch, but what we did was wrong.

Ricky finished reading the document. He held the pictures in his hands and looked at the door. Ricky thought back to the night that Jay made the comment about the guys needing each other more than ever. 'Will their friendship be able to survive this mayhem?' Ricky thought, "The shit is about to hit the fan."

What to look for in the Sequel:

Now that Tonya is dead, Antonio is raising the kids, not wanting to know the results of the paternity test. Will Ms. Achy be a part of the kids lives?

Barbara's pregnant. What will she do when she finds out that Wil, who is now in prison, is the father of her baby? Will she still try to push her hand to get Keith to take care of her and her unborn child?

When Wil finds out that the woman he accidently killed was his sister that he never knew about, will he forgive his mother?

Chuck and Tyrell are now back in town. Chuck was responsible for the death of James, Tariff's first love. Tariff has forgiven him, but what will happen when Jay, Mike and Reese find out the secret that only Tariff, Demetrious and Tariff know?

What are Carlton and Barbara's plan for Curtis and Chuck?

How will Ricky and Jay handle the news about Chuck and will it tear the group apart?

Also By Dwayne Vernon

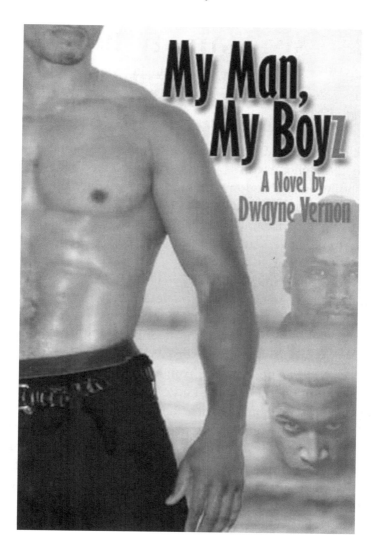

My Man My Boyz
Excerpt

Unconsciously, James reached for the cell phone. Just as he grabbed the phone, Curtis nervously pulled the trigger, firing a deadly shot to James' abdomen. For a second, James thought he'd been punched, but when he touched his stomach he felt the sticky warmth of his blood. James was shot. He struggled to stand, but collapsed to the pavement. Shock and fear began to choke him and everything began to turn white.

"Shit! Shit! Shit! Shit! Why that niggah have to move, huh? Why he have to move?" Curtis yelled hysterically, knocking himself in the head with his hand. Chuck sat in the car, petrified, his head buried in the spokes of the steering wheel. He kept repeating to himself, "What did we do? What did we do?"

"Man, come on, let's go! You done killed dude we gotta get the fuck outta here! Come on niggah, let's go!" Carlton said, pulling Curtis away from the scene and into the waiting getaway car. "Move niggah!" Carlton snapped, pushing a catatonic Chuck out of the driver's seat. With Curtis' head spinning a mile a minute and Chuck whispering prayers to himself, the three drove off, hoping that the horror of the last five minutes was nothing more than a terrible nightmare.

James heard his cell phone ring for the second time. He momentarily blocked out the sleepy sensation that was overtaking him. He struggled to pull himself up on one elbow to answer the familiar ring.

"Baby, where are you, you should have been here over 10 minutes ago," Tariff said chuckling with mock annoyance.

My Man My Boyz Excerpt

James heard the words in his head and struggled to make them leave his mouth. Finally, he faintly heard himself say, "A couple of blocks away near Elm Avenue, I've been shot!"

Tariff felt the shot of adrenaline and panic hit him. Before the words had completely settled in his brain, he yelled, "I'm on my way baby, hold on, don't hang up!" Tariff sprinted up the street toward where James lay dying. His pace didn't affect his dread-drenched words of support to his soul mate. He didn't want to lose the sound of James' voice. When Tariff reached James, his body dangled between the car door and the ground. He desperately looked around to see one of the neighbors coming around the corner. Tariff yelled for her to call 911 as he slammed his own cell phone to the ground and ran to James' side. Tariff slid down next to James and put his upper body in his lap as he waited for help to come.

"I'm sorry to spoil our anniversary, baby," James uttered with short breaths, his eyes almost completely closed.

The sound of James apologizing shattered Tariff's heart. "You didn't spoil anything baby. We're goin' to have plenty more to celebrate," Tariff said, tears streaming down his cheeks. James could feel the life force slipping out of his wounded body. James suddenly started to see a warm soft light, and the sound of Tariff's voice grew muffled and faint. He fought to look at Tariff, but his vision became blurry and all he could think about was whatever was waiting for him on the other side.

"Listen, Tariff," James dribbled out, "I want you to know that I have always loved you and I always will. Baby…" James paused before continuing, "if I don't make it I want you to know I will still be with you. As he felt his heart drumming to a slower beat, he finally said, "But I want you to love again, okay?"

Tariff shook his head from side to side in disagreement, not wanting to hear what James was saying to him. "Don't talk like that James, just hold on for a little longer. It's going to be alright. You're not going anywhere." Realizing that time was rushing by, Tariff looked up frantically, eyes darting from corner to corner, wishing to see flashing lights and hear siren sounds of hope, but there were none. The cool and eerie silence told the story.

My Man My Boyz Excerpt

As Tariff looked back down at James, he had closed his eyes. They would never open again. Rocking James in his arms, Tariff cried and kissed James' lips.

Excerpt from A Private Affair
by Mike Warren

I pulled up in front of Thomas' door at seven o'clock sharp. When I got out of the car, I began to get nervous as I walked up to the door. Something about tonight didn't feel right. But despite my feelings, I tried to psych myself up as I rang the doorbell. Besides, I couldn't wait to see Thomas. I was anxious to tell him how proud I was that he hadn't caused a scene earlier. After waiting for what seemed like eternity, Thomas finally opened the door, wearing a small towel around his waist.

"Come in, Sean. I hope you weren't waiting too long. I just got out the shower."

I couldn't help but stare at his body, which glistened from the water that still clung to his skin. "No, I didn't have to wait long," I responded, knowing that was yet another lie. *Boy, I'm on a roll today.*

I walked in and sat down on the couch, like I was really on

A Private Affair Excerpt

date. This time there was no smell of weed in the air, or no fat ass Harrison to look at. He closed the door and walked into the living room behind me. Once he got closer to me, he snatched the towel off and threw himself on top of me. I instantly got hard as I inhaled the sweet scent of his Armani cologne. Even though I wanted to fuck him right there on the carpet, we needed to talk.

"Can we just talk for a minute?" I asked, slightly pushing him away.

"Do we have to do it now?" he asked, grabbing my dick.

"Yes, right now. I need to know what you want from me."

He looked at me with frustration. "Right at this moment, I want you to fuck me," he said.

"Naw, man, seriously what do you want from me?" By the look in his eyes, I knew he was wondering where all this Oprah shit was coming from.

"I want a lot of things from you. Like your friendship, your hot passionate sex and anything else you're willing to give. I like you because we're both in the same boat. I want someone that I can be intimate with, without having to explain why I gotta go home. You would understand that. And I don't think you're looking for someone who's a threat to your marriage, because I know I'm not. I'm married, and I wanna stay married, but I'm a niggah that likes to get his urges satisfied. So maybe I should ask you the same question, what do you want from me?"

I tried to digest everything he said before answering. "I don't know. I was hoping to find that out, that's why I'm here. And how did you know I was married?"

"Cameron told me, like he probably told you I was married as well."

"Yeah, he did. So answer this, how can you be gay and married at the same time?" I asked.

He looked at me with a cold stare. "I don't consider myself as gay," he snapped.

"Well, what do you call fuckin' another man?" I snapped back.

"I don't like the term gay. I consider myself bi-sexual, and apparently so are you!"

A Private Affair Excerpt

I held my head down and thought for a few seconds. "To be honest, I don't know what I am. But what I do know is that I didn't enjoy sex with another man, until I met you."

"Oh, so it's my fault that you're gay now?" he taunted.

"I don't know, maybe."

"No, Mr. Matthews, that doesn't mean I made you gay. It means that it was in you all along. I guess I was just the only nig-gah to bring it out. I seem to have that affect on people."

"Definitely," I said, reaching for his hand.

After we talked for over an hour, I wasn't sure if Thomas still wanted to have sex, but I did. I finally knew what he wanted from me, therefore I wasn't nervous about the unknown as I had been in the past. I couldn't wait to touch him, smell him, and feel the warmth of his body against mine. I wanted him so bad, and I could feel the pre-cum trickling down my pants. He must've read my mind, because at that moment, he moved closer toward me and began sucking on my earlobes. It was amazing how his slightest touch could send me into another world. Not even Venus had ever made me feel this way. I've always been the aggressor when it came to having sex, but in this case, I found myself enjoying the passive role. Thomas was definitely in charge, and knew what he wanted and how to get it.

To find out more about Mike Warren or to purchase
A Private Affair
visit
www.lifechangingbooks.net

COMING JUNE '09
A Sweet Swagger
The Sequel to A Private Affair

PICK UP YOUR COPY TODAY!!

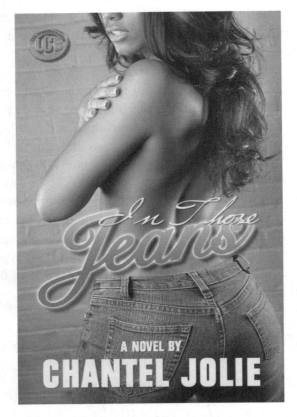